CONFLUENCE

Other Books by
Nyri A. Bakkalian

Grey Dawn: A Tale of Abolition and Union

CONFLUENCE

A Person-Shaped Story

自流人形範

Nyri A. Bakkalian

BALANCE OF SEVEN

Dallas

For information, contact:
Balance of Seven, www.balanceofseven.com
Publisher: dyfreeman@balanceofseven.com
Managing Editor: tntinker@balanceofseven.com

Cover Design by Eben Schumacher Art
ebenschumacherart.artstation.com

Editing by D. Ynes Freeman
dyfreeman@balanceofseven.com

Formatting and Proofreading by TNT Editing
www.theodorentinker.com/TNTEditing

Proofreading by Amanda Mills Woodlee

Publisher's Cataloging-in-Publication Data

Names: Bakkalian, Nyri A.
Title: Confluence : a person-shaped story / Nyri A. Bakkalian.
Description: Dallas, TX : Balance of Seven, 2022. | Series: Confluence; book 1. | Includes 12 b&w illustrations and 1 b&w photo. | Summary: Searching for new wholeness and purpose, an Armenian American combat veteran remakes herself as a cybernetic being called a combat doll. Living in Japan, she and her wife embrace their roles as Wielder and blade to fight for justice for disadvantaged dolls who are preyed upon by a callous world.
Identifiers: LCCN 2022949308 | ISBN 9781947012417 (pbk.) | ISBN 9781947012424 (ebook) | ISBN 9781947012431 (itch.io ebook)
Subjects: LCSH: Isawa, Iekage, ?-1221 – Fiction. | Cyborgs – Fiction. | Lesbians – Fiction. | Transgender women – Fiction. | Veterans – Fiction. | Japan – Fiction. | LCGFT: Cyberpunk fiction. | BISAC: FICTION / Romance / LGBTQ+ / Transgender. | FICTION / Science Fiction / Cyberpunk. | FICTION / Science Fiction / Military.
Classification: LCC PS3602.A35 C66 2022 (print) | PS3602.A35 (ebook) | DDC 813 B35-- dc23
LC record available at https://lccn.loc.gov/2022949308

26 25 24 23 22   1 2 3 4 5

To Mihara Ryōkichi (1897–1982),
whose love of Miyagi, its stories, and its
dolls inspired my own.

Trusting my horse to know the way, I ride home.
En route at people's houses:
"How far til Sendai?"
Each time, it is far indeed.
Spring rain dampens my sleeves; the sun's already
    begun to set.
And are they blooming yet:
the flowers that wait back home?

—Date Masamune (1567–1636), "Masamune-
    kyō Shikashū"

Contents

A Word of Caution ix

Acknowledgments xi

Map of Miyagi Prefecture xiii

Prologue: Mount Hiyori 1

One: Rain Drive 10

Two: Mount Jōbon 17

Three: The Visitor 28

Four: Mist on the Bay 35

Five: The Armorer 44

Six: The Mothers' Oath 52

Seven: An Invitation 64

Eight: Steward of the North 69

Nine: Tsutsujigaoka 78

Ten: Flower of Words 85

Eleven: Directions 92

Twelve: Takasago Pines 97

Thirteen: Even the Proud 104

Contents

Fourteen: Echoes the Impermanence   112

Fifteen: Child of Exile   121

Sixteen: Bury Your Heart   130

Seventeen: Polaris Unbowed   141

Eighteen: Loyal from the Start   155

Nineteen: Sowing the Wind   169

Twenty: Loyal She Remains   184

Twenty-One: One Heart Together   191

Twenty-Two: Path of the Straw Thief   203

Epilogue: A River of Stars   216

Historical Essay: North Star Forever   223

Illustrations   237

Glossary   249

References   251

Works Cited   257

About the Author   259

A Word of Caution

This story has elements that may be difficult reading for some people.

As a trauma survivor myself, I understand the importance of taking this sort of thing into consideration. This is the first time I've written so directly about such difficult things, so it seems fitting to offer a word of caution for you, the reader. *Please heed it.*

- This story involves transhuman topics and themes, which I aim to convey in a positive light, as a means of self-expression and reclamation of agency. Some might find it difficult reading, nonetheless.
- This story features protagonists who have a power-exchange dynamic—usually abbreviated in fiction as D/s—that ranges far beyond the one brief bit of sexual intimacy that appears in the story and extends into their everyday, mundane shared life. This dynamic, in which River is the blade and Kasu is the Wielder, is chosen freely, embraced gladly, and maintained through constant communication and effort by two people eager to continually earn each other's trust and who prize and respect each other's agency. Some might find it difficult reading, nonetheless.
- This story involves intergenerational trauma of the sort that I've lived with for years, as a member of the Armenian diaspora, three generations after the genocide

of 1915. This is a daily challenge for me in real life. Some might find it difficult reading.

- Finally, and most notably, this story features a measure of corporate malfeasance, kidnapping, and physical and psychological abuse, all of which are all too real in the everyday world. They appear because of the conflict at the center of the plot, which our protagonists strive to solve, to set things right and help others who are in need. I have endeavored to be measured and not gratuitous in my depiction of these things, because they are all too real and gratuitousness in general does not appeal to me as a writer or as a reader. It is better to be deft and measured rather than excessive when it comes to difficult topics like these. These most prominently and directly feature starting at chapter thirteen, and they continue to the end of the book.

I hope very much that people and people-adjacent beings reading this book heed my word of caution.

Please be good to yourselves.

—NAB

Acknowledgments

This book began as a series of short stories in which I screamed into the void and tried to figure out how to put myself back together in the face of homesickness, exhaustion, and layers of trauma. It was the result of my having found, and resonated with, something called Empty Spaces. This is a loose collective of writers and artists, many of them queer folk and trauma survivors, who write with a shared, loose constellation of themes and motifs, often with the goal of reclaiming agency and finding healing.

This screaming into the void quickly grew a plot and a cast, and before I knew it, I had more than fifty thousand words written and wasn't sure what to do with them. Through a chain of events that I'm frankly still stunned at, in a time frame that has me gobsmacked, they've become the book you now hold in your hands. As with any book, I couldn't have done it alone. Be it through a traditional press or self-publishing, we authors need people to save our sorry asses and help us hone our writing into something better, sharper, and more presentable than its raw form of screaming into the void.

So, thank you to Kerry Lazarus, Gracie Jane Gollinger, Sevag Bakalian, Lily and Alex Tackett, F. Zoe Blackheart, Vera Lycaon-Blackheart, Sarah Kendall, Grace Dordevic, ENN-15, Alison 065, E. P. Beaumont, and Emily Thornley for your friendship, encouragement, love, coffee, and advice.

Thank you to Eric Muirhead, J. P. Der Boghossian, and Ani Hopkins for your encouragement and the inspiration of your own writing, which led to my creating this, my first-ever story with a queer Armenian protagonist.

Particular thanks are also due to Claude Berube, a fellow historian-novelist, for saying the words that I needed to hear about breaking through the dreaded Second Novel Syndrome.

Thank you to Ynes Freeman and Leo Otherland for your guidance and support on the publishing and editorial side. Thank you to Eben Schumacher for the cover of my dreams.

Thank you also to my patrons at www.patreon.com/riversidewings, whose support allows me to be an independent scholar, novelist, artist, streamer, and all around delightful queer nuisance.

Now, swiftly and with style and without further ado, let's get to it!

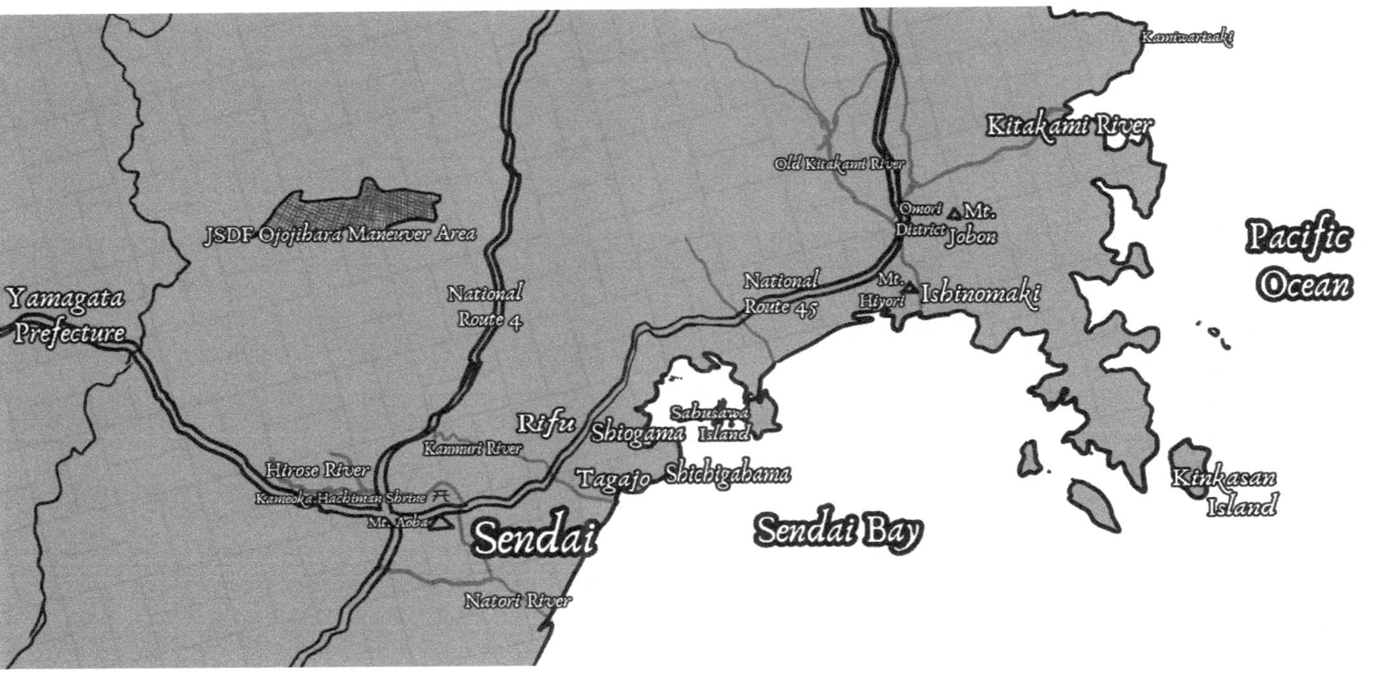

Pacific Ocean
Kinkasan Island
Kamiwarisaki
Kitakami River
Omori District
Mt. Jobon
Old Kitakami River
Mt. Ishinomaki
Hiyori
National Route 45
Sendai Bay
Sabusawa Island
Shiogama
Shichigahama
Rifu
Tagajo
Kanmuri River
National Route 4
Sendai
JSDF Ojojibara Maneuver Area
Kameoka Hachiman Shrine
Mt. Aoba
Hirose River
Natori River
Yamagata Prefecture

PROLOGUE

Mount Hiyori

Ishinomaki, Miyagi Prefecture
April 24, 2011

River Victoria Eginian sat atop an upturned crate, canned coffee in hand, cane resting beside her. For the moment, her sketching had been set aside. There was plenty yet to be done in the recovery of Ishinomaki and northern Japan. Even if she was only on its sidelines, her own small part in Santaku Group's contribution—as an artist working in tandem with the photographers—would be ongoing, as the recovery itself was ongoing.

Still, she felt powerless—useless, in the face of everything. All she could do was bear witness.

From her vantage point atop Mount Hiyori, at the JGSDF command post under Kashima-Miko Shrine's stone torii, the city's ruins lay at River's feet in an ashen swath. She was still new here, still learning her way around, but River had heard so much about it from her wife that some things about her environs she recognized, however faintly, in the tsunami's wake.

She ran a hand through her brown hair tinged with fading blue dye and sniffed curiously at the salt air coming off the bay.

"Ap mə mokhir, hayreni dun," River murmured, recalling the words of an Armenian poet of a century prior lamenting their lost home after the slaughters at the turn of the century. ‹*A handful of ash, O ancestral home.*›

The shape of the terrain was the same, mostly. Sendai Bay still filled much of the horizon on this side of the Ojika Peninsula. But in the middle distance, all River recognized, at a glance, was the Kitakami's southern estuary and the barely cleared lines of the highway. Everything else was unrecognizable—a terrible desolation.

Yet in the debris field, the woman spotted periodic motion—and the beginnings of new hope.

Squads of combat dolls—both transhuman dolls and their all-synth counterparts—maneuvered through the ruins in power armor freshly painted in SDF Type 3 camo. They sifted through the debris, clearing away containers, ruined cars, and shattered rebar—followed closely on foot by human soldiers of the Japanese and American militaries, who did the finer work of searching and clearing with hand tools.

River sighed. There could not have been anyone out there—anyone still alive in the ruins—not after more than a month.

She and her wife had still been in greater Seattle on March 11, when the tsunami came.

Some of their friends and colleagues knew that Santaku came from somewhere north of Tokyo, certainly, but this was the first time that the place names they knew well were on everyone's lips.

It was, in a word, overwhelming.

Once, it had seemed that nobody cared about the Tohoku region, the section of northern Honshu that had been so badly scarred by the triple earthquake-tsunami-nuclear disaster. Now, places like Sendai and Sōma-Nakamura, Natori and Ninohe, Ōtsuchi and Rikuzentakata were household names, and for the most terrible reason.

For three days, all either of them could do was try their best to muddle through their usual day-to-day routine and follow the news as best as possible.

One thing was clear from the start: Across the Tohoku region, the impact of this disaster was calamitous. Burning, flooded plains—where once had stood ports and roads and seaside homes and fields. Fallen eaves and forests.

Somehow, Kasu was deeply, frighteningly calm in the face of it all.

That was the land that had borne Isawa Kasu. For more than a thousand years, her ancestors had been warrior-scholars, and for more than eight centuries of that millennium, since the time of Isawa Iekage, Steward of the North, they had lived on and around Sendai Bay. Santaku Group, the Isawa family's holding company, was one of the preeminent forces in local business, and thanks to its contract work for the SDF, it had no small measure of political clout. Kasu's father had raised her to be his successor, heir apparent to both the family headship and the position of CEO, but she had thrown that arrangement off kilter by dint of being queer and unwilling to hide any longer. Handing headship and chairpersonship to her younger brother, she left Japan to head Santaku's North American operations in the Pacific Northwest. That was where she met River, who had just received her first set of Santaku-made prostheses amid her recovery from combat wounds.

River began as a friend from work. Kasu was overseeing Santaku USA's pilot program, a contract job providing prostheses for the US Department of Veterans Affairs. River was part of the first set of patients receiving them.

They became partners in short order and made a life together.

But even after the tsunami had passed and the world became still, the dam broke for Kasu.

On March 15, they were driving home to Bellevue from shopping in downtown Seattle. Their usual lively banter was still subdued. The stereo, synced up to Kasu's phone, played through her music at random, a steadying way to fill silence born of shock—of all they knew, lost.

River noticed the steady onomatopoetic cadence— once meant to help sailors keep time—of the last verse of "Saitara-bushi."

> Ishinomaki sāyō
> sono na mo takai
> ā korekore!
> Hiyoriyama to e
> *‹In Ishinomaki,*
> *even its name is lofty:*
> *Mount Hiyori.›*

Kasu gasped and rapidly recovered from the beginning of a swerve.

"Hey—"

Kasu made a sound, a choked moan of distress, pulling into the parking lot of the nearest business sharply enough that River reached for the overhead grip handle. The cars that had followed behind them honked as they sped past the Subaru, its caution lights suddenly on.

They sat frozen for a long moment—River with her hand on the grip handle, Kasu clinging to the steering wheel.

"Hey," River finally murmured. "Hey, you okay, darling? Talk to me?"

At last, the dam broke. Kasu buried her face in her hands, shoulders trembling as she wept, long and desperate and inconsolable.

River undid her seatbelt. As best she could across the center console, she pulled her sobbing wife into her arms.

After a conference call with headquarters in Ishinomaki, they decided that night to depart at once so Kasu could lead Santaku's efforts on the ground in tandem with the military's Operation Tomodachi, to help Ishinomaki and the rest of Tohoku dig out.

A month later, on Mount Hiyori—still lofty of name— River watched those recovery efforts. It was galling to just talk and watch and draw, even on scene rather than an ocean away. Witnessing the dolls at work stirred something within her.

River had gotten to know some of the dolls who were on recovery detail in the shoreside plain below—in particular, Aneha C-306, the tall, powerfully built doll who supervised the Santaku facility on Sabusawa Island together with her short, sprightly, curly-haired second-in-command and armorer colleague, A-065. Aneha, who had been in the SDF as a human, had brought her detail and their armor up to

Ishinomaki within days of the tsunami; they had worked tirelessly since then. Every day, River watched them in admiration, with stirrings of something she could not quite articulate yet.

She turned to glance at the rough four-post SDF field tent nearby. Kasu took questions from international press that came to tour the command post and get briefed. Kasu was one of the civilian leaders of this effort, alongside the military and local government officials, and had the best command of English, so she and a young enlisted public affairs specialist from the SDF handled international briefings.

River contemplated the view, the power-armored dolls doing their work in the distance, her frustration, the ache in her back and knees, everything—and she once again felt that growing sense of something strange. It took her a long time to find the word for it, but one day, at last, it dawned on her.

Envy.

The word was envy.

Once, when she was in the army, before the battle that had injured her enough to end her career, she might have at least been one of the Americans following the power-suited dolls in the plain below, the ones sent up from Camp Zama and seconded from Camp Humphreys. Now, things were different: her body was more fragile, and all she could do was watch—watch and contemplate this feeling of envy.

She wanted to be alongside them, clearing the broken city after what nature's fury had wrought upon her wife's hometown. She wanted to have the cybernetics to manage joints that could handle that kind of strain, interfacing that would allow her to wear that kind of exosuit.

She wanted to be a doll.

Ningyō, the Japanese word for doll, was written in two characters: "person" and "shape." River could not unmake her scars, but she could put them back together into something new—not quite what she had been before but close enough—something person shaped.

A new whole.

She wanted to have the wholeness to be of use. To serve, yes, but to have the strength to heft broken concrete and shattered rebar, to help save lives and protect them.

To protect what remained.

To be in that vanguard of renewal.

To be whole again.

She was envious, yes—and now, she was going to do something about it.

She pounded the last of her coffee, skipped a few pages in her sketchbook, and began to draft a message.

From: River V. Eginian
To: Isawa Kagekiyo, Director, Santaku Group
Date: May 13, 2011
Subject: Petition for Doll Conversion

Dear Director Isawa:

I will not mince words today and instead get right to the point: I write you to petition for combat doll conversion under Santaku Group's auspices.

I make this request freely and of my own volition, for reasons that I list below.

The circumstances of my military career's end are a

matter of record, as are the difficulties I've faced in acclimating to civilian life as a result. You know the details well, but to put it simply, I am, in a word, broken.

While some of my injuries have healed and transition has saved my life, in other respects, the path ahead of me remains an uphill battle. Even if I have mind and body in some measure of alignment, the world is too loud and too fast and too much for me far too often.

I know that I have a community to rely on here in Ishinomaki. Starting from your sister, Dr. Isawa, I have begun to build a home and a new family by choice here. I cherish it. I know I do not need to be of use, but I want to be of use, and all too often, I feel like I am simply a burden.

I feel too broken, too tired, too preoccupied with holding the different pieces of myself together to be of use to anyone here in Ishinomaki. I want to change this.

Since the days of the Bakumatsu era nearly 160 years ago, Santaku Group has been in the business of building and caring for dolls, on and off the battlefield.

In learning what I have of Kasu's work and needs, I know she travels much, is often in some measure of danger, and is in need of a personal weapon. I want to be that personal weapon and ensure her safety. My brokenness needs to be rehoned, forged anew into a new wholeness. I am convinced that combat doll conversion is the answer.

I know that this is not an easy process. I know that the matter does not simply end at the other side of conversion. But in talking to the dolls who work here, and others throughout the prefecture, I know this is a path I must take.

If I spent the rest of my days simply a burned-out husk of a mostly human being, I don't know that it would be an especially meaningful existence, even if it were comfortable and nothing were expected of me beyond being myself.

Director, you must understand that service is in my blood. It is my soul. Even before I picked up a weapon, it was my calling. It suffuses all of me. Service in devotion to my spouse, as her weapon, is how I will continue to rise to that calling.

I am humbled to report that after lengthy discussion, Kasu has not only given me her support and voiced her willingness to become my Wielder but has also expressed interested in a shooter-spotter type interlink. I enclose her own message and modding proposal as an attachment.

Ultimately, I simply wish to be whole and of some use to the woman I love and the city that has so graciously welcomed me as one of its own. But I can only do all of this, Director, with something to hold all my broken pieces together, inside and out.

I am like a vessel broken that waits to be remade, fragments joined in gold. That gold joining—that *kintsugi*—is to be found in doll conversion.

Finally, in discussion with Kasu, we have chosen an alphanumeric designation.

As far as we are concerned, from this day forward, I am River Victoria M59A1.

Respectfully yours,

RVE

Enclosed: physiopsychological profile and interlink concept

ONE

Rain Drive

Sendai, Miyagi Prefecture
Eleven years later

The Wielder and her blade doll rode in tense silence, east on Japan National Route 45 under darkening skies and a steady rain. The sun had slipped under the distant line of the Ōu Mountains behind them, leaving only a dark purple glow lingering through a break in the clouds. Ordinarily, one of them might have waxed poetic about the view, but today, they were preoccupied with other terrible matters.

They were used to making waves, be it as trans women, as lesbians, or as spouses in an international marriage. Then one of them had become a combat doll, and there was some understandable shock in the community when people who recognized them once again started seeing them together. There was a person-shaped being who looked a lot like that battle-scarred American they had known but different somehow. Yet when they saw the two of them carrying themselves with a new sense of pride, as one heart together, many of them began to understand.

But even a life together spent making waves was no guarantee of success.

That evening, it was a long way home to Ishinomaki, on the far side of the bay, and longer in the rain, but there was nothing to do except put the car in gear and get moving. Yet when the two of them had come back to the car after the disaster that was supposed to have been a business meeting in the Ichibanchō Night Market, River M59A1 had taken the driver's seat, but her Wielder had asked to switch spots.

River knew that look. Kasu was angry—the kind where driving could, with time, bring new emotional equilibrium.

Dolls often spoke of the aspiration of serene clarity of purpose and presence in the moment—capital-S Stillness. There was Stillness in a silent drive, but to River, the current drive was not still. The air felt heavy with all that was unsaid after their visit to the night market.

Yet River could not blame Kasu. River was upset too.

Half an hour into the drive, they were passing the Rifu-Shiogama interchange, with Matsushima Bay to the right, beyond the trees.

"So. At the risk of gross understatement, that was . . . eventful," the doll tentatively offered, fidgeting with the fishtail of her denim-blue mane. "Wasn't it, ma'am?"

The Wielder's gaze, still fixed on the road, was like fire. If she heard, she showed no sign of it.

For a time, the traffic crawled. Through the window and rain, River met eyes with the human driver of a nearby vehicle as it slowly passed. The driver's eyes momentarily widened with recognition of the combat doll in the Subaru's passenger seat. Inasmuch as she took pains to cultivate balance, she did not blame the human driver for their shock. As a combat doll, River *was* a weapon, after all.

From some angles, River easily passed as human, but her ocular augmentations made her status as a combat doll clear. When she wore her hair up, her nape-mounted diagnostic ports were a tell. Those particularly familiar with local heraldry might recognize her by affiliation. Whether on her overcoat or as a patch on her working uniform, the doll wore her Wielder's crest, a doubled cherry flower over a trio of straight-edged blades fanning from its center.

The doll sighed, shook her head, and let her mind wander, eyes flitting over the different HUD markers that flowed through her field of vision as they hurried east.

"Useless," Kasu suddenly spat. "I'm fucking *useless!*"

The doll closed her eyes, doing her best to ride the current of sadness and anger flowing over their wireless neural interlink.

"At least we tried, Kasu-*sama*. That's better than not having bothered at all."

"Didn't do us much good, did it?"

There, Kasu paused, caught her breath. Over the interlink, the fire subtly ebbed as she glanced at River. In the car's dim interior, the tiny dots on her cheek that were her sensory upgrades dimly glinted.

"I'm sorry, doll. I'm sorry. I'm just . . . this problem isn't going away, and smug little price-gouging shits like Masuya Heisuke aren't helping matters at all."

Masuya Heisuke was one of the most well-known merchants of the Ichibanchō Night Market, a human specializing in used components for dolls in need. He stocked Santaku, Arai, Iwasaki, and Agatsuma parts, as well as parts from some foreign makers.

That was not all. His was also one of the few places to find parts from defunct makers. Satomi and Yahagi parts, yes, but also Nogami.

Therein lay the problem.

Nogami had been a builder and converter, primarily of combat dolls entering government service outside the military, but market forces had caused its closure, and the government had hurried to divest itself of any responsibility for legacy care. As a result, parts were rare and, with every passing year, getting rarer.

Yet somehow, Masuya had a semiregular supply flow, and every time there was a new stock, the price climbed just a little more—and the dolls most in need bled for every yen. He was in a seemingly unbeatable position, enriched by the desperate need of dolls who had no other choice, and he damn well knew it. Kasu had taken it upon herself to force his hand—to make change by jumping in headfirst and negotiating.

Masuya had received Kasu and River in person that night. All smiles and platitudes and courtesy, decked out in his shop's crested overcoat.

"Korewa korewa Santaku no okata-sama. Wazawaza no goraiten, makoto ni arigatai." ⟨*Well, well, O Lady of Santaku. Thank you for coming all the way to our shop.*⟩

For her part, as the emissary of a powerful force in the region's business world, Kasu had given it her best. She had appealed to his compassion, to his sense of community. To underscore her point, she told the story of a friend with a Nogami chassis.

Yui ゆ-633 had pursued combat doll conversion upon seeking a career in the security arm of the Foreign Ministry. The Nogami crisis had left her unable to continue in her career, so she and her human spouse, Tomoka, had moved to Sendai and retooled for a new career in baking. Cost of living in Sendai was relatively low compared to Tokyo, and the doll community in the Tohoku region was significantly more organized and independent than anywhere else in Japan. For all their success with setting up Kakuzen Bakery—just a couple of blocks away from the night market, off Jōzenji Avenue—it was contingent on the availability of Nogami parts.

Even that had not moved Masuya's heart. He had shaken his head and chided Kasu as though she were an uppity schoolgirl.

"Uchi wa tada jimoto no ningyō buhin uriba desu. Hodokoshi ni wa hodo ga aru to omoimasu." ‹Our business is just vendor of doll parts. I deign to venture there is a limit to charity.›

They were in Matsushima, traffic slowing on the approach to the Naruse bridge, when that moment flashed through River's mind's eye.

I deign to venture there is a limit to charity.

It had set something off in River's Wielder. Kasu's eyes had come aflame. Her body instantly, visibly tensed. Over the interlink, the inferno of her rage, a torrent of fire and indignation, screamed without words, *I'm going to fucking kill you myself, you little shit!*

"Hodokoshi da to?" She had leaped to her feet and roared across his desk. "Komatta ningyō o sukuu koto koso shōbai no ichibu dake de naku; *warera no sekimu dearimasu!*" ‹Charity, you say? Helping dolls in need isn't just part of our business; it is our duty!›

"Maa, maa, ochitsuke, Santaku no okata-sama. Chotto migurushii to omowanai kashira." ‹Now, now, calm down, O Lady of Santaku. Is this not a tad unseemly?›

That smile. He had not moved an inch from that relaxed posture, leaning back in his chair.

He knew he had won.

Kasu had managed to smooth things over. She had offered perfunctory apologies, and once again, they were exchanging pleasantries. They were all smiles for the rest of the meeting, which passed without any meaningful result.

It was galling.

His parting words, however, had made River bristle.

"Wakatta ka na, Isawa-hakase. Masuhei koso Nogami ja." *‹Do you understand, Dr. Isawa? Masuya Heisuke is Nogami.›*

Rage had flashed across all of River then, neurons and circuits, flesh and nanofiber. Yui was trying her damnedest to make life work, first screwed over by the government and again by this petty *tyrant*. This man had not just refused to help her; he had talked down to River's Wielder too, as if she were some high-strung child. River had spent a moment imagining how her hand would feel around his throat.

When she had become a doll, she and Kasu had sworn an oath to each other in turn.

Here and now, before you and my gods, I swear service in battle, in the home, and in bed. Here and now, I swear to be your sword, your comfort, your right hand, the instrument of your will—

Kasu's fingers had tugged subtly at her sleeve, pulling her back to equilibrium. Their pledge to each other was not a one-way street.

They were crossing the Naruse bridge into Higashimatsushima, trying to gather themselves in the rain on the way home.

"Can I put on some music, ma'am? The silence is getting to me."

"Mm? Oh. Sure."

River called up an ambient rock playlist, then flopped back into her seat, burying her face in her hands. She needed to think. She needed to help find a way through. Cutting through obstacles was not just for the battlefield, after all.

"We have ten Nogami-type dolls who work for Santaku Group," the doll remarked. "We've met a couple dozen more, personally, per my recollection. How many would you estimate are here in Miyagi?"

"At least a couple thousand in the prefecture, I'd guess," Kasu murmured. "More across the entirety of Tohoku. We can check on government stats from the last census, if you want a particular number. What do you have in mind, River?"

"The group can afford the cost of sourcing parts for dolls on staff," River observed. "But the bottom line is, some doll parts are interchangeable as is, others are inter-changeable with some modding, and others have to be proprietary. And Nogami doesn't exist anymore."

"What are you suggesting?"

"Ahead of the next board meeting, propose getting into the aftermarket parts business for Nogami dolls. There is a community in place that's badly in need, to the point that they're going to Masuya with little other alternative."

Kasu glanced sidelong at her. "It's going to take a lot of doing, doll. You don't just spin that up overnight."

"We can start small, see if we can find any volunteers internally who would be willing to help with prototyping and field-testing aftermarket parts."

There was a long silence. The Wielder flexed her fingers around the steering wheel as she contemplated the suggestion.

"Let's do it. I want to help these dolls," Kasu declared. "I want to ruin Masuya, but above all, I want to help these dolls. Yui and everyone else like her. It's about time someone stepped up."

River nodded. "Ganbarou." *⟨Let's do our best.⟩*

"Nda'. Kepparisu." *⟨Yup, let's give 'er our all.⟩*

TWO

Mount Jōbon

The morning after that rainy drive home from Sendai, Ishinomaki was cool and slightly overcast. Through the kitchen window, over the tiled eaves and squat offices of the Santaku complex, River saw the fog drift over the forests of Mount Jōbon and drift south toward Sendai Bay.

Kasu's family had lived here since the early seventeenth century, when this valley was their quasi-independent landholding. Today, it was still a little rustic, but only in appearance. The Santaku Headquarters' central compound still bore the air of an old samurai estate, with its gatehouse, tiled eaves, and white plaster outer wall, but it comingled with newer buildings of hybrid architectural styles that housed the offices and operations of the 160-year-old industrial concern. It even still bore its name from that long-gone age: a wooden plaque over the lintel of the gatehouse proclaimed it as the *Kaiseikan*, the Hall of Progress.

The rustic appearance fooled some international visitors who ordinarily did not range too far north of Tokyo, and it amused River to no end how their presuppositions limited their understanding of what should have otherwise been perfectly plain.

Why on earth would the headquarters of one of Japan's most powerful conglomerates be nestled among agricultural fields—and this far away from Tokyo? they would ask.

Because the Isawa clan has never forgotten its roots and its debt to the land and people, River would tell them.

Inasmuch as it was true, it was far from the entire truth. She would smile to herself at how much the clueless visitor failed to notice. The headquarters sat on strategically advantageous terrain that used to be a castle, with easy access to two big navigable rivers and their adjoining channels. It was a ten-minute drive from the nearest interchange of National Route 45. And it sat in the shadow of Mount Jōbon, home to one of the JASDF's series of coastal ARSR installations that monitored the trans-Pacific air routes entering that part of Japanese territory.

Despite all this, River had always loved how peaceful life was here in Ōmori. It was the perfect little corner of Ishinomaki to live in, and as busy as work got here at Santaku Headquarters, just being here had a steadying influence. It had been the perfect backdrop for her earliest days of dollhood too. Even for a human, it was so very still in the little community that sat along the roads at the foot of Mount Jōbon.

Some of the main roads, especially those that carried traffic out toward National Route 45, did get a bit busy from time to time. Out just a little way from that, either into the fields or up into the woods, it was different. One would never know there was anything but peace and quiet here.

She had gone for walks on these roads right after her conversion, hand in hand with Kasu. She had spent them learning the terrain and relearning her relationship with the woman who was now her Wielder just as much as she spent them relearning a body both familiar and new, as much servo and nanofiber as sinew and bone. The walks had been short at first, for her body had needed time to acclimate. With time and her gathering strength, the walks had ranged farther. Now, the doll knew the terrain as well as she knew her body and the Wielder who earned her loyalty and service over and over.

River drew strength from this place. She drew comfort from it. It had become part of her, in all the years since then.

River belonged at her lady's side, but Kasu was a daughter of this part of Japan. In all that this region and this prefecture had to boast, this place was special.

This was home.

Slowly, River's breath settled as she moved about the kitchen, readying the usual morning coffee for two. The mist. The forests. The eaves and antennae and utility poles against the gentle blue-gray sky. It was grounding after the previous night's negotiation-turned-tense-standoff.

Fresh, hand-ground coffee and a hint of cardamom and cinnamon in the *macchinetta*. Two mugs, whiskey ice cube in each. The *click-click* of the induction range coming on. The hum of the fridge. The rising burble and hiss of the *macchinetta*. The rhythms were comforting. This, too, was Stillness.

An alert ping, a flash in the corner of her HUD. *Message from Yui.* With a flick of the eyes and a carefully placed finger and thumb, River called up the message.

> <yui.φ633>: Looks like it's going to be a busy day over here today. Let's do our best!
> <yui.φ633>: We're going to be selling the first batch of tahini bread from your recipe.

A picture, translucent in River's field of vision, showed a view from the counter at Kakuzen of a handful of tables and windows that looked out on the sidewalks of Jōzenji Avenue shaded by zelkova trees.

With a subtle dance of the fingertips, River tapped out a reply.

<river-m59a1>: Good luck today. Try not to stay on your feet all day, all right? Rest is important.

After a moment, Yui responded.

<yui.め633>: Hamono-san koso! ‹*You too, Miss Blade!*›

The *macchinetta*'s bubbling rose to a crescendo, and River dismissed the projection. At last, the coffee was ready, two mugs' worth. Black, no sugar, as usual. It was tradition.

With mugs in hand, River strode confidently across the house, from the kitchen and through the quiet living room to where Kasu sat on the veranda, leaning against a pillar. The Wielder was in leggings and loosely buttoned flannel, sleeves rolled up to her elbows, handwriting some notes in pen on the pages of a paper journal.

"Sounds like Yui's selling the first batch of tahini bread this morning." River sat down beside Kasu, legs folded, dipping her head as she set down the mugs carefully on the well-polished floorboards. "Nice to see my mother's recipe getting put to good use in a place she wouldn't have ever dreamed. Soshite, ohayō, okata-sama. Kōhī wa dekita no yo." ‹*And good morning, ma'am. Coffee's ready.*›

Kasu set down her pen and journal and carefully leaned in to plant a kiss on River's forehead. "Areyaa, aina haigu ni. Gokurō, gokurō. Ohayō degansu, kokesu yo." ‹*Oh my, and so quickly too! Well done, well done. G'mornin', doll o' mine.*›

It was in the little quiet moments like this that the sight of her Wielder took River's breath away. None of the polished, put-together, take-charge-and-kick-ass power couple that the rest of the world saw of Wielder and doll together. Here, with both comfortable and unguarded and the rest of the world temporarily at bay, the sight of her Wielder made the doll's heart flutter.

The curve of her chin. The laugh lines framing her mouth. The little specks of the sensory augment nodes glinting on her cheeks. The subtle tinge of gray in her hair. Her scent. The gentle curve of her belly and the little birthmarks at the small of her back. The strength of her thighs and arms.

Her anchor. Her rock. The root of her Purpose.

They caffeinated in the birdsong-punctuated morning stillness together, as the mist drifted down from Mount Jōbon into the garden and among the ranks of greenhouses. For the moment, the world's storm was at bay.

"So, how's Yui doing?" Kasu asked quietly. "Baking aside."

"Sounded all right so far. Told her to take it easy, but you know how she is."

"Just like you, bad at listening to your own body?" Kasu chided with a smirk. "Rui wa tomo o yobu." ⟨*Birds of a feather.*⟩

"Ooh, ouch." The doll chuckled sheepishly. "But more importantly, Kasu-*sama*, how are *you* feeling? After the unpleasantness in the capital last night."

"You're changing the subject, but all the same . . ."

The Wielder sighed, pinched the bridge of her nose, and rubbed tired eyes. "Aiyaaa. Lots to do, sure, but right now it feels like a bad dream."

They had fallen into bed dead tired upon arriving home

the night before. Even if they had hashed out the beginnings of a plan of action, they were physically and emotionally spent after going toe-to-toe with Masuya at the Ichibanchō Night Market. River herself had barely managed to plug into her diagnostic cabling before passing into standby and sleeping curled up against Kasu for what must have been nearly ten hours.

"Bad dream feels like the right descriptor, Kasu-*sama*." River nodded, taking another sip of coffee as she rearranged her legs and straightened her back to ease the tension. "But I guess if it's anything, it's a lucid dream, now, isn't it? We can take charge here. We've got options at hand. We've got tools to fight with. And we're going to kick ass, just like we always do."

The Wielder allowed herself a tired smile. "Wielder and blade, one heart together, onward to victory."

"Isshin dōtai." River raised her mug in reply. "Iza, senshō e." ⟨*One heart together. Onward to victory.*⟩

Kasu set down her mug and sat back against the veranda pillar. "That said, I don't know about any fighting today, though." She sighed. "The problem will still be there when we come back to it, and there's not much we can make happen right this second. Today, I think I just want to have a quiet day with my beloved blade doll and think about gentle and mundane things. 'Tending the sharpness by softness' and all. Maybe we can do some baking and pastry-making together—that is, if you're feeling up to it too, doll."

"Yeah?"

The Wielder grinned. "Yes, visiting Kakuzen and Hinoki lately has me in mind of buns and ovens, y'know."

The blade doll sputtered midsip, coughing and giggling all at once. "K-Kasu-*sama*! Hidoi!" ⟨*So mean!*⟩

After over a decade and a half together, they were starting to talk through feelings about having children of their own. Even if the conversation was on-again, off-again, it was happening and was generating plenty of jokes along the way between them.

"Oh, darling, you're so cute when you blush." Kasu grinned, wagging a finger as she tipped back her mug. "So, do you think we've got the fixings for *yatsuhashi* and matcha *kasutera*? I'm craving stuff from my grad school days—those pastries we used to snag during trips to Kyoto. And not just for us either; the staff at the head office might enjoy a homemade pick-me-up."

River called up a roster on her HUD and swept through with a flick of an index finger. "Huh. According to the kitchen manifest, we do, though we should probably hit up Ebisuya downtown soon. Looks like we're running low on some essentials, like daikon, brown rice, and potato flour."

"Mm. I could do with another drive later today, River. How about you? No pressure, low vis, just you and me on an errand run. Besides, I know that place is a little rough on the senses, so I figure two sets of hands and eyes will be better than one."

The doll smiled. "Of course. You have but to command me, love."

Two mugs' worth of coffee finished. The morning light growing around Mount Jōbon. A new day underway.

"Let's get some breakfast and then see about some baking, then," Kasu suggested. "Yes, today I think I want just a quiet day with my beloved blade doll, tending the home fires."

They kissed, long and slow and satisfyingly deep.

"Shōchi," River murmured happily. *⟨By your command.⟩*

The midday light was bright on the bustle of Makiyama Avenue, where downtown Ishinomaki's humans and dolls hurried about their days. Ishinomaki was not nearly as busy as Sendai, and compared to the prefectural capital, it felt a little silly to call this a *downtown*. Regardless, it was the nearest thing and with a charm all its own. After everything, it was good to call this home.

Adjusting her sunglasses and then tugging smartly at her jacket, Kasu paused to feel the sun on her cheeks. She and River had parked in one of the municipal lots near Ishinomaki Station. The walk to Ebisuya would do them both good.

Even a decade after her return to Ishinomaki, being here was a little bittersweet for Kasu. Of course, her family history was deeply intertwined with Miyagi in general and this side of Sendai Bay in particular—and the same went for her own past. She had attended school here in Ishinomaki through junior high. Even if those years following her mother's death had been spent under her father's domineering thumb, she had always been curious about these streets, rivers, and hills, wanting to know them for herself.

Her father had sent her farther and farther away—first to a private high school in Sendai, then to higher education in Tokyo and Nagoya—but the farther she went, the more tightly she clung to the memory of the land that bore her. Her family's illustrious history seemed intangible and abstract compared to standing in Naruko Gorge, hiking Mount Kurikoma or the boulders on Kinkasan, running her hands over Sendai Castle's stones, drinking sake fresh out of the vat in Shiogama, or listening to old folktales from some of the elder humans and dolls in Shiroishi or Ōsaki.

When her father died, Kasu at last took the opportunity to transition so she could be herself. It had come at the price of handing over family headship and Santaku Group directorship to her brother—and leaving Japan for a time. But even during her time in Seattle, she had never forgotten her roots.

Now, it had been more than a decade since she had been back. She was older, grayer, but all the more eager to make the most of being there for good. Even if work kept her on the road at least some of the time, at the end of the day or the trip, it was to Ishinomaki she would return.

And she would return with River at her side. They had become lovers, partners, and now they were Wielder and blade. After the difficult lives they had had, both appreciated days this mundane. Things were still often busy and eventful for Wielder and blade alike, but they treasured time spent at home in Ishinomaki all the more. It was simple and mundane, a point of calm in a life all too often busy.

Combat-specialized dolls like River evoked a curious combination of responses in both humans and noncombatant dolls alike. Sometimes, it was a gut-level wariness, even fear. Yet around Ishinomaki, many humans—especially the elderly— just as often found the blade doll adorable.

"Areyaa, menkoi kokesu da!" *Oh my, what a purdy doll!*

It always made the doll blush. And given the low-level interplay of their emotions and senses over their interlink, Kasu herself would blush just a bit.

Kasu had been the one to ask for their interlink during River's conversion. It better harmonized their ability to move and fight together, if needed. And as she had told

River, *It will keep me humble so I don't forget this dynamic is a two-way street.*

"Tsuita wa yo," the doll announced. ⟨*We're here.*⟩

Ebisuya, the supermarket on the ground floor of one of the newer towers in central Ishinomaki, was a business almost as old as the Wielder's own. However, it had opted for the contemporary aesthetics of its much younger competitors from Tokyo whose branches now ranged up here.

The blade paused before she entered. This was ritual, but it was born of scars from her life as a human and sensory processing issues that her dollhood had, over time, begun to iron out. The lights in a business like this tended to "scream" if River didn't at least engage visual attenuation.

"Attenuation up," she murmured. "This, too, is service."

"Good." Kasu nodded, gently patting her on the shoulder. "I was going to remind you. You ready?"

"Ready as ever."

"Ndaraba, igube." ⟨*Well then, let's mosey on.*⟩

It was second nature after all these years, but it had taken effort from both of them and would continue to do so. By steadfast effort, by showing up daily, by mutual patience and respect—and with the further aid of cybernetics—they were becoming "one heart, together," as the old ballads said of wise lords and their devoted retainers.

They strode confidently into the supermarket, passing into a sea of obnoxiously peppy jingles and digital displays.

"Okay, run me down the list. Let's be sure we have everything accounted for before we get started."

River's eyes shifted, fingertip tracing a little circle in midair as she consulted the shopping list. "Okay, we have coffee beans, dark, whole form. *Watari-no-sato* brown rice, one standard two-and-a-quarter-kilo bag. Baking mochi, two boxes' worth. A few boxes of instant curry—the actually spicy kind this time. Jar of peanut butter. One bundle of daikon, one box lotus root, one bag potato flour, one root burdock, one box shiitake, one box *sasa kamaboko*, matcha chocolate, two large jars dill pickles, one pouch *takuan*, two cans of red bean paste, a box of *taiyaki* ice cream, and a bag of *shokupan*. Are we missing anything, ma'am?"

"No, I think that's all. Let me snag a cart, and we can begin."

The doll grinned, dipping her head in acknowledgment. "To battle, then, by your command."

Kasu chuckled. "I think a successful grocery run will be quite enough."

Even amid other worries and tensions in life, the simple, mundane joy of being in Ebisuya on a quiet day was quite enough. It was an anchor and a reaffirmation of the ties that, after everything, would bring them home.

THREE

The Visitor

The next morning, River was crouched beside one of the low lights that lined the garden walk, replacing a burned-out compact fluorescent. Kasu had hurried out early that morning, on business elsewhere in the complex, and River's services were—for the moment—unnecessary. The doll enjoyed a cool, clear Ishinomaki morning, tending to little things that needed her attention around the house.

Then came the call.

"Gomen kudasai!" *‹Please excuse me!›*

"Hai. Ah, Tokiwa-san, irasshai!" River rose to greet her unexpected guest. *‹Yes. Ah, Tokiwa-san, welcome!›*

Tokiwa リ-602, one of the dolls that ran the front desk here at the head office, bowed in greeting. River bowed back. "Nan no yōji deshō?" *‹What can I do for you?›*

The doll momentarily fidgeted with the hem of her surcoat. "Isawa-hakase ni chotto kowai kyaku ga otozuretandesuga." *‹There's a slightly scary visitor here for Dr. Isawa.›*

River cocked her head, brushing the dirt from her hands against her thighs.

"Chotto kowai kyaku? Kore wa shitari. Kasu-sama wa

dōryō no Nogami-gata ningyōtachi to no sōdan ni dekaketa bakkari nanoni." ⟨*A slightly scary visitor? Well now. And just when Kasu-sama has gone to consult with our Nogami-type colleagues too.*⟩

It was significant that Tokiwa would use that word: *scary*. It seemed that yesterday's calm had not lasted.

Nervousness was not the thing to surrender to. Not here, not now.

"Kano ningyō wa kakyū no yōji da to," Tokiwa replied. ⟨*That doll says it's an urgent matter.*⟩

River was not sure what it could be, but it needed tending, and she was her Wielder's right hand. She gestured over the narrow hedge toward the main hall's high, tiled eaves.

"Mm. Jaa. Kaigishitsu ni annai shitekure. Soshite tō ningyō wa atte yarō to tsutaetekure." ⟨*Hm. Well then. Take them to a conference room and inform them that this doll will meet them.*⟩

They parted ways, and the blade doll hurriedly washed up and changed into a fresh uniform. Kasu would not be back for another hour at least, and it was best to settle this sooner rather than later, if River could. De-escalation was the name of the game, even off the battlefield.

In the conference room, standing with hands folded behind its back and a long vulpine tail curled around its legs, a tall, formidable doll looked out a window over the rock garden beyond. The doll seemed as solid as a mountain, the *kintsugi* stripes in its chassis telling the story of a long, eventful life. River did not recognize its make or specialization at a glance. This may or may not have been a combat doll, but it certainly looked like it had been to hell and back.

The blade doll knocked on the door, then made her entry with a bow.

"Omatase itashimashita. Aruji no rusuchū wa taihen

gomeiwaku o kaketeorimasu. Isawa-hakase ni tsutau ha-mono ningyō, River M59A1 to mōshimasu. Yōkoso San-taku Gurūpu honbu e." *‹My apologies for keeping you waiting. Forgive us for the trouble of your having come while my Wielder is indisposed. I am River M59A1, a blade doll serving Dr. Isawa. Welcome to Santaku Group Headquarters.›*

The doll turned slowly to meet River, bowing in return.

"Hajimemashite. Tō ningyō wa Z33R0 to mōshimasu. Zee de ii. Yoroshiku tanomu." *‹Pleased to meet you. This doll is called Z33R0. You may call it Zee. Please regard it well.›*

"Kochira koso," River replied. *‹Likewise.›*

It peered down at River for a moment with intense gold eyes, its vulpine ears subtly flitting. Then it clasped its hands behind its back again.

"This one will come directly to the point," it said in English. "It's come to the attention of this one's employers that that one's Wielder is preparing for war against the doll-parts merchant Masuya Heisuke."

River's jaw dropped. Had there been a security breach?

"How did you know that?"

Zee chuckled softly. "It is this one's business to be aware of things. Especially matters like these."

As best she could, River collected herself. She folded her arms, circling the doll slowly, until she had closed the distance between them. Her head tilted in curiosity.

"If you know that much, then you likely also know we are exercising diligence and caution in our endeavor to—"

The vulpine doll shook its head. "That one misunder-stands. Masuya Heisuke is not a simple peon. He is . . . a *nue*. And he's just one part of a web."

"Wh—a *nue*?"

"Mm. A fearsome being indeed." It nodded. "That one's Wielder and her illustrious house have military power and political connections, and we respect that. But this one's Witch sends a message for that one's Wielder: You aren't going to end this by squashing Masuya like an insect, or by yanking the earth out from under him. You're coming at this with a hammer. What you need is the discretion to know which way to throw a dagger. If you aren't cautious, people will get caught in the cross fire."

A *nue*, River knew well from Japanese folklore, was a chimera: shifting and unpredictable and powerful.

In any other scenario, River might have bristled at such words. However, this was clearly not someone who had come simply to cast aspersions. There was more to this doll and its employers' motives. Zee had mentioned its Witch; River gathered that this was someone whose relationship with Zee was akin to Kasu's relationship with River.

"Well then," River queried gently, "what do you propose?"

The vulpine doll smirked and again glanced at the garden—lingering, seeming to weigh its words.

"This one is curious. What manner of stimulant do that one and her Wielder prefer?"

"Coffee," River answered without hesitation. "Black. No sugar."

"Espresso, French press, canned, or something else entirely?"

"My top two choices are stovetop double espresso or Arabic coffee out of an *ibrik*. Failing that, canned, especially while on the go, but most coffee is good coffee."

The vulpine doll nodded approvingly. "Impressive . . . very impressive."

"Why does that one wish to know about caffeine?"

"Because this one wishes to be properly prepared to receive that one and her Wielder as guests," the visitor replied courteously. "And this one's Witch has taught it that one's choice of coffee says a lot about them."

River was genuinely impressed. She dipped her head in respect. "This one's human ancestors often said the same. That one's Witch is wise."

"Indeed, she is."

"So," River queried, "if this one understands correctly, that one's Witch desires . . . an alliance?"

"Patience, please." Zee shook its head and gestured in reassurance with a powerful, similarly *kintsugi*-webbed palm. "This one's Witch simply desires a meeting with the great lady of the illustrious Isawa house and to receive honored guests with due courtesy. What comes of it is a matter for that one and her Wielder to decide."

River dipped her head in respect. "That is . . . eminently fair."

"This one thought that one might feel that way."

For a moment, River caught a hint of a smile, sharp and likewise vulpine.

The visitor bowed again. "That was all. This one will take its leave now. An invitation will arrive from Keyaki Solutions, a company based in Sendai. Be watchful for it. This one looks forward to coffee with that one and her Wielder."

Message received, River thought, bowing in return.

"Our respects to that one's Witch," the blade doll said. "We look forward to a good meeting and to enjoying your hospitality. But where will we be hearing from you?"

"Hm. Don't worry about that too much. We'll be in touch, and that one and her Wielder will know it. But in the meantime, this one is very impressed. Perhaps our discussions may be fruitful yet."

River escorted Zee to the gate. An electric sports car, windows subtly tinted, waited for it.

"Until next time, River M59A1."

"Abayo." River waved. *⟨So long.⟩*

The door clicked shut. The car rolled away, soon vanishing in the direction of the roads leading to National Route 45.

River turned the visitor's words over in her thoughts as she lingered in the shadow of the gatehouse's eaves.

What you need is the discretion to know which way to throw a dagger.

"Oh, Kasu-*sama*," the doll sighed, heading back into the safety of the facility walls. "This just keeps getting more interesting, doesn't it?"

An alert pinged to one side of her HUD. *Message from Kasu*-sama.

A turn of the head, a flick of the fingers, and a text message box snapped into view to one side of River's HUD.

<k.isawa>: Are you okay? I felt that, whatever it was.

River paused, collected herself. Yes, her Wielder would be feeling her tension over the interlink, especially at a time like this. With a subtle dance of her fingertips along the keypad projection, she composed a reply.

<river-m59a1>: Yeah, you had an urgent visitor. I handled it, but it's a long story.
<river-m59a1>: It looks like we've got some people's attention after the other day.
<k.isawa>: Hang tight. I'm coming.
<river-m59a1>: No, don't worry, it's already gone. I just saw it off.

<river-m59a1>: But we'll be hearing from it again.
<river-m59a1>: I'll explain when you're home.
<k.isawa>: An ally, then?
<river-m59a1>: Don't know yet. But that's what I'm hoping, ma'am.

After a pause came one further message.

<k.isawa>: Not that I regret any of this, but what have we gotten ourselves into?

River smiled wistfully.

<river-m59a1>: Doing good for this place as best we can, same as we always do.
<river-m59a1>: I'm with you all the way.

FOUR

Mist on the Bay

They rose before dawn, while the fog still lay thick. With their gear packed the night before and the traffic mostly clear, their departure was quick. They drove out of Ishinomaki mostly in silence, westbound down National Route 45, as the light gradually grew around them. Breakfast, taken in the car, was peanut butter croissants and coffee in their well-worn travel mugs.

Seat reclined just a bit for the sake of her back, Kasu watched the terrain zip past in the growing predawn light as she ate and went through the day's itinerary in her head. There was a lot to do today, and none of it had to do with the new Nogami project.

The roads were traffic-free and clear most of the way, only slowing in Higashimatsushima, north of the SDF base and the bridge over the Naruse. There was an accident in the opposite lane, and drivers on their side were slowing as they passed.

"C'mon," River muttered at the traffic. "Freaking make up your minds already! Stop gawking, ya damn rubber-neckers."

Briefly, River scanned the sky in a broad arc but caught no sign of air traffic either inbound or outbound.

"On the other hand, it looks like the SDF is having a quiet morning. Shame. Those F-2s always cut a pretty silhouette against the sky this early in the day."

Soon, they were rolling over the causeway that crossed the Naruse just above its confluence with the Yoshida.

"River's lookin' pretty today too," the doll observed, eyes flitting between the road and the Naruse far below.

"Ndabe." Kasu smirked, glancing sidelong at River from the left-hand seat. "Menkoi kokesu da." ⟨*Ayup. She's a purdy doll, she is.*⟩

The blade doll blushed. "Ma'am!"

"You set yourself up for that one, darling." The Wielder chuckled, waggling a finger.

"Yeah, fair enough." River laughed sheepishly. "Guess I did."

The day promised to be full. The work on the big SDF project—the Shirakami rifle—was entering a new phase, and the first shipment of production-model Shirakami units had just arrived for testing. Before Kasu began a new project—especially one so personal—the rest of her work needed to continue.

In the back of Kasu's head, the hum of ambient anxiety grew. Would it be enough? Would she manage? Would it all blow up in her face? Sighing, she closed her eyes and basked in the morning sun. There was not much distance left before they reached their destination, and once they did, she would be in motion for the rest of the day.

Merging into traffic, they turned off the highway over the Naruse exit and off to points south on Prefectural Route 60. Below small hills that caught the rising daylight, agricultural fields and small houses lined the riverbank.

At last, they arrived at the commuter lot in Tōna Beach as the sun rose.

On the bay, the mist still hung thick over the pine-clad islands that gave Matsushima Bay its name, shrouding the bay clear out to Shichigahama and the Shiogama side beyond. After locking the car and rounding up their gear, they paused for a moment in the growing dawn to look out over the bay in silence together.

Poets had written about this place as far back as the eighth century, when it was on the edge of the world for the cultured aristocrats in Kyoto. Nearly a millennium later, on his sojourn in the north, Matsuo Basho, known for popularizing the modern haiku, was so moved by the sight of the bay as to have been rendered speechless.

Anchoring the bay's mouth, their morning destination rose above the fog like a rocky curl of fire: Sabusawa Island.

"Never gets old." River sighed, hefting her Wielder's day bag. "This is home. This is a part of me. And I fucking love that we get to work here, ma'am."

"I'm just glad I get to see it through your eyes, doll." The Wielder smiled, trying her best to straighten up and steady herself. "I always took it for granted, the way anyone does if they grow up somewhere. You keep reminding me that it isn't just the humans and dolls I'm working for. It's the places we share too."

"All worth fighting for."

"Mm. Speaking of." Kasu tilted her head toward the ferry pier. "Hondemazu, abain?" *‹Shall we get going, then?›*

"Yeah, let's be off."

There were only a few passengers on the morning ferry—the first of the day between Tōna Beach and Sabusawa Island—and the doll and Wielder had plenty of room for their gear near the boat's bow.

The lines were cast, the engine rumbled to life, and the ferry headed southwest toward the Urato Islands.

In the lingering mist's comforting embrace, Kasu's mind wandered to the events of the last few days.

After her initial conversations with the Nogami-type dolls on staff, Kasu had sent the initial proposal for the Nogami project to her brothers, who held two of the most powerful seats on the Santaku Group board. They tended to give her broad latitude, but their support would be invaluable for this kind of effort. Besides, if she was to use company resources, she needed to have this on the record, one way or the other. How she was going to make it work was something she had yet to figure out, but it was a risk she needed to take.

She had not told them about the visit from Zee.

She knew she was going to catch hell for leaping into this single-handed. It was how she had always done things, from school to her transition to her marriage to becoming River's Wielder. But some things needed doing, and there was nothing quite as infuriating as the habit all too many people in her life had of throwing their hands up and abdicating responsibility, saying the three words she despised above all.

Shikata ga nai. ⟨That's just the way it is.⟩

This view and this ride never got old for River. It was not every day that she worked on the island, though she was there often, and she had come to treasure the experience.

Through the dim mist, her HUD marked off nearby marine traffic—mostly small fishing boats coming in from a night out on Sendai Bay beyond the islands—heading in the opposite direction. Their day was just wrapping up, even as River and Kasu's was only beginning.

The doll felt her Wielder's fingers reach for her own and squeeze. The doll squeezed back. Over the interlink, the ambient current of Kasu's emotions washed over the back of River's mind—anxiety and frustration, yes, but also determination.

The determination would make the difference.

The ferry rounded the rocky cape that was Sabusawa Island's northern tip. The channel between Sabusawa Island and Nono Island was narrow enough that the ferry had to slow to mind traffic in both directions. The high bridge spanning the channel glimmered in the morning light.

"Kokoro no junbi wa ii?" River asked. *‹You ready for this?›*

"Ready as ever." The Wielder nodded, straightening up in her seat. "It'll be good to get the stress out with some time on the range."

The rumble of the ferry's motor throttled back as the pilot maneuvered for rendezvous with the Sabusawa pier.

Once, 160 years ago, this had been a port and military base. The Date clan, onetime rulers of this region when it was the Sendai Domain, had had a transshipment port here, along with a coast artillery bastion and shipyard. The pier was a remnant of that shipyard, modernized and grown over the decades. The old military base had survived and grown as a research facility in the hands of a determined Date vassal from Ishinomaki—named Isawa Jinsai—and his cadre of students, who had gone into private business after the Boshin War and the early Meiji era ended the Sendai Domain.

Four generations later, River was the wife and right hand of that determined man's descendant, ambling along sleepy dockside streets and up the slow, steady slope to the tree line. Among rocks lining the roadside to the facility, stray cats sunned themselves in the growing morning light.

Closer to the hilltop, astride the footpath, River caught sight of the facility's sign. In Japanese and English, it read: *Santaku Dynamics Urato Research Center: Forge of Victory.* Beside the name was emblazoned the facility's crest, a straight-edged sword superimposed on Sabusawa Island's outline, which curled around it like a flame.

The facility was still relatively quiet at that early hour. After dropping off their gear at the head office, the duo's first destination was the armory.

"Hey, 065!" River waved to the curly-haired doll sitting behind one of the workstation displays.

A-065 rose, tugged at its shirt, and came to greet them. "Good morning! Aneha's out at the moment—on the range getting things set up—but we've been expecting both of you. Just a moment; I'll get the new arrivals."

A-065, from whom River always learned a great deal about how to better steward her weapons and gear, was the Urato facility's chief armorer, working under the command of Aneha C-306, who ran the facility overall. It led the way to a workbench where a freshly delivered crate sat. A-065 keyed in the access code, opening the lid with a click, and gestured with a flourish.

"These are the first five production Shirakami rifles, delivered late last night and ready for field-testing."

Gingerly, with both hands and a measure of reverence she showed any newly forged weapon, Kasu lifted one of the rifles.

"Nagakatta naa." *⟨Such a long time coming.⟩*

River fixed her Wielder with a knowing, slightly mischievous grin. "Congratulations on the new arrival, ma'am."

Kasu momentarily sputtered, then bit her lip, mindful of the precious—and dangerous—cargo. While preparing for the production-model Shirakami's arrival, her conversations with River about children had continued apace.

"Yeah, yeah."

"If you two are ready," A-065 offered after a moment of confusion, "I can snag some ammunition and help you gear up, and we can head for the range. Sound good?"

"I'm ready to go; how 'bout you, ma'am?"

Kasu nodded, handing the rifle back to A-065.

"Nda'. Igube." *⟨Yup. Let's get a-movin'.⟩*

Route step under the pines. Distantly, the cry of seabirds. The rhythm of breaths, just barely held, as they walked up the forested path.

The Urato facility's maneuver range was small compared to others Kasu had visited in the line of work, but the terrain was interesting—lots of elevation changes and variety packed into a small space. The air was just warm enough, and only the barest hint of breeze rustled the trees.

The Shirakami rifle, loaded and slung on its two-point sling, felt good in her hands. It was a light weapon, almost elegant, built for use by humans or dolls operating without power armor. Still, the presence of her most reliable weapon was an even greater comfort.

Beside her, River hefted her own Shirakami, scanning left and right as she kept close to Kasu. There was no idle talk, just motion and breath and vigilance. Over the interlink, like a steady current, the confluence of their sense impressions coursed and swirled—two streams flowing together, strengthening each other's situational awareness.

"You are the Wielder, and I am the blade," River murmured. "We are unstoppable, one heart together."

"Isshin dōtai," Kasu echoed. ⟨*One heart together.*⟩

Dirt underfoot. Pine needles. A gentle rise.

River suddenly halted.

"You smell that?" the doll murmured, reaching out for her Wielder, gently tugging until both were in a half crouch.

"What am I smelling?"

River's hand was already flicking off the Shirakami's safety, and Kasu followed suit.

"I'm smelling the heat coming off the target quads' joints."

The current of River's sense impressions hit home, and the Wielder understood. She didn't *always* understand, but if there was one thing she trusted, it was their connection— with or without the help of cybernetics.

"You have incredible timing." Kasu chuckled, slightly raising her weapon.

"Together," River urged. "Back up nice and slow."

One step, another. Scanning left, then right, weapons at the low ready, back down the hill.

In breath. Out breath. In breath.

The Wielder felt her doll wheel, her rifle rising. There had been a time, early in their bond, when surrendering to the link had scared her. However, they had been working at it for years, and the link was now a river she knew well. She let it carry her.

Breaths and senses flowing together, feet pounding familiar earth. Weapons at the ready. By the time the Wielder's conscious train of thought caught up, they were at the bottom of the rise, sheltering behind a boulder. Deftly, River popped up to take potshots at the one quadrupedal robot she had seen bounding after them, its coaxial gun firing. Even if they were blanks, the danger was real enough—and the new weapon needed this.

The ebbing current of her blade's adrenaline and keen, sharp Purpose was heady. The Wielder could not help but laugh as she reloaded her own weapon, turning to scan in the opposite direction of the blade's firing arc.

"Ma'am, we can't stay here; we've gotta move, and there's—"

"A third one on the way. I see it; I see it!"

Heartbeat and heartbeat. Sharpness guiding sharpness.

"You good to run, ma'am?" River called.

"Always!"

The Wielder's anxiety—tempered by the blade's adrenaline rush. The smell of dirt flying under the feet of the target drones.

Run, pause to fire. Run, pause to fire.

Hands grasping, tugging, urging on.

"You still with me, ma'am?"

"Oou!" *‹You know it!›*

By the time the exercise had ended, they were out of practice rounds and had been overrun—but only after removing two of the three target quads from action.

Their clothes mud stained, hair disheveled, the duo strode off the range and back to the hangar side by side.

They had been bested, but they would learn, and they would return. Even if they had not won, the Shirakami itself had performed well.

For now, on the dirt path back to the Urato facility's main hangar, they walked proudly, hand in hand, hearts and circuitry beating as one.

"Hey, ma'am?"

"Nandabe?" *‹Yeah?›*

River chuckled. "You have incredible timing."

FIVE

The Armorer

*T*hat afternoon, Kasu was on a lengthy video conference about the Shirakami project, delivering her initial impressions after the first field test. The call with the head office in Ishinomaki and the SDF acquisitions liaison at Ichigaya in Tokyo ran long, and River's own debrief was not until later that day. Once the rifles had been signed back into the armory, River and A-065 wandered down the hill from the Urato facility to the harbor. The morning spent at the range putting the production-model Shirakami into its first bit of action had been full; it was good to step away and briefly decompress in the salt air among the humans, transhumans, and cats that plied the harbor's streets.

The harbor's one convenience store, Koboshiya, did a brisk business between the local fishers and the Urato facility staff. Bigger than an average country store but just smaller than one of its city analogues, its decor had not been significantly updated since the late Showa era, yet it still managed to satisfy the needs of its clientele.

After securing the makings of a light lunch, A-065 and River found a spot behind Koboshiya on the embankment overlooking the road that led to the pier. They were not on the water but close enough that their view of the little harbor and the boats riding at anchor was almost unobstructed. The bay was calm.

River arched her back, stretching with a yawn. A cat brushed past the two dolls, yawned too, and settled on the embankment nearby, flopping to bare a fluffy belly.

It meowed. River meowed back.

"So, how've ya been, M59?" A-065 popped the top of an energy drink and took a sip. "Other than the Shirakami project, I mean. Been a while since we got to just sit down."

River munched on salmon *onigiri*, legs crossed, cold can of coffee in easy reach.

"Well enough, I guess. Life and work have been okay. Kasu-*sama* and I have been doing some more baking lately. It's been nice, too, getting to Sendai a little more often and hanging out with some of the new doll friends we've met through mutual friends in and around Kokubun-chō."

A-065 pumped its fist. "Oh, sweet!"

"Yeah, we were just out there the other day on an emergency repair call." River shifted her posture, crossed her legs. "So, you know a bakery called Kakuzen, out on Jōzenji-dōri?"

A-065 shook its head. "Nah, haven't been on Jōzenji-dōri in a while; I'm usually out in Miyagino Ward at the big open-air market in Tsutsujigaoka district when I'm in the capital for shopping."

"Kakuzen's in one of the old buildings right on the avenue—older than most anything else around it; it's kind of wild! Anyway, Kasu-*sama* was doing some urgent repair for a new friend of ours, Yui あ-633, who oversees the bakery. Poor thing's conversion was done through a defunct company, so repair's a bitch."

"Dare I ask?" A-065 queried.

River frowned. "She's still running ex-MFA-assigned Nogami hardware."

The armorer visibly winced. "Bruhhhh, *fuuuck*."

"Yeah." River sighed. "Yeah, pretty much."

A-065 took another sip of its energy drink. "How'd it work out?"

"Well, we managed to get to her in time. She's already back to work, and a couple days more of going easy on herself will probably do the trick. I want to go back as soon as we can, though, and not just to hang out. I want to see what else we can do."

A-065 set its drink down and patted River on the shoulder. "Look, you've done good, and so has Dr. Isawa, but do me a favor, M59—friend to friend."

"Gladly."

"Think about the difference between suturing a wound and slapping a bandage on it. You and Dr. Isawa managed to intervene here, and you do a lot of good—pretty much constantly. But you can't save everyone, and the situation with dolls running legacy Nogami hardware has been a problem for years."

River gasped and bit her lip, nodding slowly in under-standing. "Yeah. Yeah, that's true. Until we got to know Yui, I hadn't been this aware, and I don't think Kasu-*sama* had been either. Mm. Still . . . for now, I'm glad we at least get to try."

"And you do pretty good, all things considered." The armorer nodded, devouring another of its own onigiri. "Nogami's got notoriously janky hardware, so if your friend out on Jōzenji-dōri's just needing some rest and is still on her feet, that's a good thing. But solving this problem is going to take more than that."

On the island, encountering a Nogami-modded doll was rare. Other than Santaku, most dolls tended to be Arai in make. There were more than a few Nogami dolls with which River and her Wielder had crossed paths around Miyagi, and even if River had known their situation was difficult, she had not been this keenly aware of it before. They had been betrayed by government bureaucracy and capitalist exigency.

"Yeah. Yeah, that's true. And we don't even know yet if we can get the company's support on this. Been a few days, and we still haven't heard back. Kasu-*sama* may have some pretty serious clout heading up one of the subsidiaries, but even that only goes so far."

The cat rose and padded over to A-065. The armorer doll scratched between its ears.

"Good." A-065 nodded. "Just so long as you keep that in mind."

The blade nodded slowly, trying to internalize her friend's words as she contemplated the fishing boats and ferry at anchor in the channel beyond the harbor.

Kasu's habit of leaping headfirst into new challenges was something that River had always found compelling about her, but it put her in danger. Even though River had pledged to be her Wielder's right hand, she could not help but worry for Kasu.

"Hey, 065?"

"Yeah, M59?"

"I wish it *were* simple to save everyone."

After war, after leaving her old home behind, after rejection and weathering bigotry and pain and death—after everything, River had lost count of the number of people she had seen vanish, die, or fade from her life and be as good as dead.

She wished she could have saved them all.

It was nagging at her, too, in light of all the conversations she and Kasu had been having about their desires and thoughts around motherhood. A combat doll—even one like River, who aspired to be a mom—with all her strength, all her cunning, all her transhuman ability, could not save everyone.

She would simply have to take her victories as they came and, in the meantime, do her best.

"Not to change the subject or anything, but do you think we can snag a few of the production-model Shirakami for internal use?" River queried. "Those felt so fucking satisfying on the range this morning. I kind of want one to mod and experiment with—see what else I can do with it as the program develops. The thing's got promise; I can tell you that right now."

"You and me both, M59." A-065 nodded. "Gonna be a little while before any of us can do anything like that, but let's see if I can't work some magic, huh?"

"Same as it ever was!"

The two dolls finished their meal at a leisurely pace, lingering on the wall in the company of the local felines.

At long last, they rose, wandered back up the streets to the Urato facility, and returned to their posts—A-065 to the armory, River to her Wielder's side.

Despite the world's best efforts to render it otherwise—each simply did their best.

That night, the dolls sat around the firepit under Sabusawa Island's tall trees. Beyond the swaying treetops, the stars stood in quiet vigil. The dolls were a stone's throw from the hangar, but the spot was secluded. Over the years, this had become a place where the dolls on staff came to unwind.

Aneha C-306 had been in service to the Santaku doll community as the range supervisor ever since she had gotten out of the SDF in the early two thousands. She had seen a lot of dolls pass through the Urato facility over the years—all kinds of specializations.

The Urato facility—officially named the Santaku Dynamics Urato Research Center—had begun its existence as a shipyard in the 1850s. Since the Isawa family took it over in the early 1870s, though, it had focused on research and development of all kinds.

Some of Santaku's land and waterborne vehicles were tested around here—boats and power armor and the like. New equipment was fielded here. Combat dolls, in particular, were put through their paces at the range here.

It was that Purpose—helping to build new craft and new tools and hone her doll comrades—that Aneha had taken as her own upon her conversion. Along the way, it had introduced her to more than a few memorable dolls—memorable for their idiosyncrasies or for being downright uncanny.

River M59A1, sitting across the fire from Aneha, was one of the memorable ones. She tentatively strummed a black lacquered *satsuma-biwa* with a triangular plectrum, then paused to twist a tuning peg on the soundboard.

"Hey, rookie, what'd you have in mind to play?" Aneha called her "rookie" even though River had been part of the team for a decade. It had grown into its own tradition.

"Huh?" The blade doll looked up from her instrument. "Oh. 'Fukuhara-ochi.'"

There were five of them around the fire that night, all combat dolls who worked on the island: Aneha, River, A-

065, Kitsuno み-113, and Eri あ-231, who ran the IT section. They poked at foil-wrapped sweet potatoes lying in the ash at the base of the flames.

Their shared domain might have included autonomous operation, decisive action, and at times, deadly force, but they, too, knew Stillness.

The stars. The waves. The swaying of the trees. The range after hours. Still. Peaceful. River was with them that night because Dr. Isawa was working late, via telepresence, in conjunction with colleagues in Tokyo.

A-065 looked up from its spot on a mat closer to the fire, where it tended the flames.

"Masaka, kore mo Heike-mono?" *‹Let me guess, this one's a Heike ballad too?›*

The blue-haired blade briefly fussed over another tuning peg. "Mm. Mata sonna mono o hiku kibun ni natta." *‹Yeah. Felt like playing something like that again.›*

Subtly, Aneha shifted her weight.

"Correct me if I'm wrong, rookie, but isn't that about the Heike having to abandon Fukuhara and make for the inland sea?"

The blade doll nodded slowly. "Yeah. Yeah, they don't win here." She grinned, gesturing with the plectrum in hand. "The bit near the end is a banger, though."

"Oh, yeah?" A-065 perked up.

The blade doll nodded. Taking *biwa* in hand, she launched into an up-tempo portion of the song. Her smoky contralto voice rose over the *biwa* notes.

"Kinō wa tōkan no fumoto ni kutsubami o narabete jūman yoki. Kyō wa saikai no nami ni tomozuna o toite shichisen yonin . . ." *‹Yesterday, they stood at Osaka Barrier, a hundred thousand horsemen strong. Today, they cast off mooring lines in the western sea, barely seven thousand.›* Her voice rose to a crescendo. "Unkai chinjin toshite! Seiten sude ni kurenan to su." *‹The cloudy sea was silent! Even the clear sky was growing dark.›*

With a flourish, she finished the excerpt, set down the plectrum, and immediately returned to fiddling with the tuning pegs.

"What, still not quite in tune?"

River nodded. "It sounds okay but doesn't quite feel right in my hands."

"That's what she said." A-065 snorted, shifting in place as it reached out to warm its hands by the fire.

After a while, Aneha chuckled. "Fushigi na kokeshi da na, Hamono-san wa." *‹You're a strange doll, Miss Blade, y'know that?›*

The blade laughed. "Ohome ni azukatte kōei desu, senpai." *‹You flatter me, senpai.›*

The dolls around the crackling firepit sat with the melody, the stars, the waves, the trees swaying.

Tomorrow, they would be back to work on the Shirakami project and the rest of the work that awaited the final phase ahead of handing the units over to the SDF and clearing the deck for the next challenge.

For now, *biwa* music and the night sky in good company were enough.

<h1 style="text-align:center">SIX</h1>

<h1 style="text-align:center">The Mothers' Oath</h1>

Even on the road, one of the things River loved more than any other was waking up with Kasu's arms around her, holding her tight even in sleep.

Between her Wielder's embrace and the charging and diagnostic cables secured to the ports at her nape, the doll was not going anywhere. Not that she would have wanted to. She was happy right where she was.

Several days after the firepit, they were in Shichigahama, just up the road from Sendai, on the west side of the bay. Santaku Group owned a little guesthouse there, on the slope of Tamonzan. Workers on long-distance business often overnighted there before continuing elsewhere. The Wielder and her doll had spent several days crisscrossing the region, both for the Shirakami project and to gather information for the nascent Nogami project. By the end, between their exhaustion and their plans for the next day, they had stopped in Shichigahama rather than continuing all the way home to Ishinomaki.

They had the place to themselves that morning. In the quiet, with the ocean audible beyond the window, the blade doll lingered in the warmth of her Wielder's arms, the softness of the pillows, and the soft hum of the power charging her circuits.

River called up the day's itinerary on her HUD, making annotations with her usual subtle motions—finger dancing in the air—before noting the weather forecasted for the day. *23°C and partly cloudy—perfectly comfortable.* Perfect weather for a visit to her home shrine.

There were no new messages yet. The latest chat log was with Yui the night before, while River had still been on the road.

<yui.ぬ633>: Had to let Tomoka take over the counter today. My right hand is complaining, and I don't want to push things too far. That tahini bread sold really well, though!

In her sleep, the Wielder squeezed the doll and mumbled. For a moment, River wondered if Kasu was waking, but there was nothing more. Through the interlink, the doll could feel the white noise of her Wielder still asleep.

That was a long day yesterday, wasn't it, ma'am? the doll thought with a tired smile. They had started in Ishinomaki and gone clear out to Hirosaki and back again. A long time in the car and out at various facilities. Now, there was time to catch their breath. Just a brief moment to linger. Today was a day off.

Her preparations complete, the doll nestled closer against her Wielder, steadying her breathing, syncing it. There was a long, comforting quietness of breath and warmth and the distant waves.

The Wielder shifted position, arm still draped around her doll, and she awoke with a gasp and a sigh.

"G'morning, ma'am," River murmured.

Kasu yawned, slumped back into bed, and gave the doll a squeeze.

"Ohayo gozarisu, kokesu yo." ⟨*G'mornin', doll o' mine.*⟩

"Sleep well?"

The Wielder yawned again. "Maa, tabun." ⟨*Eh, probably.*⟩

River turned, rearranging her cables as she rested her head inside the protective curve of Kasu's arm.

"Seriously, ma'am."

"I'm fine, darling. I'm fine. Dreams have been odd, is all." She paused, yawned again. "Mm. Although, I forgot to tell you yesterday, I heard back from my brothers about the Nogami project, just before we turned in last night."

River's eyes widened. "And?"

Kasu sighed, shook her head. "They heard about what happened at Masuya's office, and they're telling me that even if this is a crisis, unless I find a new business partner to balance things out for the sake of the company's reputation, they're not going to allow us to proceed. 'Shikata ga nai,' were Kagekiyo's words."

River frowned. *Shikata ga nai.* The all-too-ubiquitous *It can't be helped.* "Well, shit."

"Nda'." ⟨*Yup.*⟩

"We . . . we're not going to let this be the end of it, right? Yui and the others, they need something to change."

Kasu shook her head. "This isn't going to be the end. What do they say over in Fukushima? 'Naranu koto wa naranu.'"

"What must not be, must not be," River translated aloud. "Yeah."

"I need to think this over, try and find another way," Kasu said. "But we've got other things to do today, so for now, let's sleep in a bit more. What do you say?"

"This doll can hardly argue with your logic, ma'am." River chuckled, settling against her Wielder's chest. Sleep soon reclaimed them both.

After all, there was time.

After breakfast, they changed into their formal attire and drove up Route 45, through downtown Sendai, and over the Hirose to River's home shrine in the Kawauchi district.

Across the bridge over the little creek from the parking lot, River and Kasu stood under the broad branches of the ancient weeping cherry in full bloom. The cherry blossom wave had come late to Sendai that year. That morning, contemplating the sudden roadblock to their plans to intervene in the Nogami crisis, River was grateful for it.

The overcoat she wore, a black haori, bore the Isawa family crest in white. Cherry blossoms always caused River to reflect on her oath to her wife, on how humbling it was to bear her crest, and on the importance of softness and sharpness in balance.

It was all the more important now.

"Kind of wild to think that this tree's been here since before Date Tadamune set the shrine up in the 1640s," the doll murmured. "The firebombing in 1945 and the 2011 earthquake didn't kill it. And even now, it's still blooming."

The Wielder gestured at the wooden lattice that supported the tree along its many twisting, gnarled boughs.

"An old survivor, hanging on despite everything and still blossoming." Kasu grinned. "Sounds like a familiar story."

River blushed. "Yes, ma'am."

The doll tugged smartly at her overcoat, momentarily

fidgeting as she smoothed out her trouser pleats. This was not a casual call on her home shrine after all.

"Are you ready, ma'am?" she queried.

Dressed in her own kimono, her overcoat likewise bearing the family crest, Kasu nodded.

"After you, doll."

The midday sun was bright, but as they ascended old, mossy, weatherworn stone steps, the couple passed into the shadow of mighty zelkova and birch trees nearly a century old.

River smiled as she caught the distant sound of cicadas.

They were on the cusp of summer.

The stairs seemed to stretch on forever. Historically, there were 365 stone steps here, though time had worn them down to somewhere around 330. Even so, the thick forest and the hill's steep grade made the climb seem longer.

It was strangely fitting to make the long climb little by little, side by side. It would get them through the Nogami crisis and all the storms yet to come.

Eventually, they came to the *chōzuya*, the purification basin on the last landing before the hill's apex and the shrine's buildings. Wooden ladles sat in a row beside a waterspout sculpted like a dragon's head.

Hands and mouths cleansed, they washed and replaced the ladles.

"Hold my hand?" River asked.

"Of course."

Hand in hand, the couple passed under the upper torii.

Though a century old, the shrine hall had only been here since the 1960s, when postwar reconstruction took off.

Originally used elsewhere, it had replaced the previous shrine hall, which had burned in the firebombing of 1945.

Once, centuries ago, Kasu's ancestors had prayed here from time to time, as it was the tutelary shrine of their erstwhile overlords, the Date clan. The Date had once ruled this region as their fiefdom, one of the five most powerful in early modern Japan—a stark contrast to the small, modest shrine hall.

Today, it was River's home shrine, a place deeply sacred to her even before she became a doll. There were several prevailing interpretations of the kami enshrined here, but the one River favored—the one that had given her strength and comfort as a human and as a doll—was the mother in battle. The one to whom warriors of old prayed in the thick of battle, to land the impossible shot and make their way home.

Some humans River had known since her doll conversion were puzzled by the doll's spirituality. They would ask, sometimes her and sometimes her Wielder: Why did one who had been human but was remade into something Still and more machine than flesh pray? Was that not something only humans did?

River's answers varied.

Because it sustained me before and sustains me now.

Because it is fitting for one who is her Wielder's sword to maintain a relationship with the kami of battle.

Because it connects me with my local community and reminds me of what I'm fighting for.

Because even a weapon has a soul.

The wooden offering box. The shrine hall's doors—open but not to be entered. The long row of sacred bells above subtly fraying braided cord.

River squeezed Kasu's hand. Kasu squeezed back.

"Together now," the doll said.

Wielder and doll, one heart together, bowed before Hachiman-ōkami, kami of battle. Each gently tossed at the offertory box a handful of coin, which landed with a clatter and jangle.

The wash of their shared emotions over the interlink was a tangle: anxiety, anticipation, devotion, hope.

They remained hand in hand.

Together, they rang the center bell once, twice, three times.

Only then did they separate, though they kept close, to bow twice, clap twice.

"Himekami-*sama*," River said quietly, using one of the kami's epithets out of respect. "We're here together today to ask for your help.

"From the beginning, you have inspired me, helped me keep a keen eye, helped me hone myself. Helped me be a good woman, a good spouse, and a good blade in service. You have helped us both do the work we do—to heal and to protect.

"From the beginning," River continued, "you have been the mother in the battlefield to me. Guardian and nurturer and builder in one. We have a long way to go yet before we're even there, but help my Wielder and me be good mothers, when the time comes.

"In the meantime, help us keep a clear eye and steady hand in our duties to each other, this region, and its beings—organic and synthetic. Help us surmount the obstacles before us and find a way forward in helping our Nogami-type friends."

There was a pause. The spring wind rustled the zelkova branches as if in reply.

After a moment, the Wielder spoke. "Yoki tsuma,

soshite yoki aruji dearimasu you ni. Kore hodo no shinrai to chūsetsu ni fusawashii sonzai ni narimasu you ni. Yoki hahaoya ni narimasu you ni." ⟨*Help me be a good wife and good Wielder. Help me become someone worthy of this measure of trust and loyalty. Help me become a good mother.*⟩

Kasu paused, gathering her thoughts. The busyness of work, the roadblock imposed by her brothers, the expectations of everyone—family, community, colleagues. Her and River's future plans. How would she manage motherhood on top of everything else? The current of her anxiety rose.

The tide of River's thoughts washed over her own as the doll's hand reached for hers.

"Korekara mo nani ga attemo, tomo ni mae e susumemasu you ni." ⟨*Whatever happens next, grant that we may go onward together.*⟩

Wielder and doll, one heart together, bowed once more before Hachiman-ōkami, the mother in battle.

At the shrine office, they bought a few amulets to take home, plus a wooden votive plaque. This, too, was part of making this request of the gods.

River fished a brush pen out of the sleeve of her kimono and wrote out a brief entreaty.

"Yoki hahaoyatachi ni narimasu you ni." ⟨*Grant that we may become good mothers.*⟩

They each signed it in turn.

Kasu tied the plaque onto the racks that flanked the shrine hall, alongside many others from the shrine's recent visitors.

"Now we have the kami of battle watching our six," River remarked. "Medetashi, medetashi!" ⟨*Auspicious, auspicious!*⟩

There was still much to do. Still far to go. As they descended the long stone staircase, they did so hand in hand.

That evening, after their visit to the shrine in Sendai, River and Kasu returned to Shichigahama.

They were not needed back at the head office in Ishinomaki until the following afternoon, and after a day as momentous as this, it seemed the better part of wisdom to linger some more.

At the house on Tamonzan, they dropped off their purchases and gear and changed into everyday attire. Outside, the sun was already setting over the distant line of the Ōu Mountains, and on the Pacific horizon, there was a brilliant wash of color beneath a rank of puffy white clouds.

Hooded leather jacket draped over sundress-bared shoulders, River let her breath settle as she watched the horizon and drank in the moment. This coast, these forests, these streets and mountains—all of it was home, and all of it was entwined with who she was becoming.

This, too, was Stillness.

This, too, was a root of Purpose.

"River? Ah, there you are." Door locked behind her, Kasu hurried across the short drive to where River stood basking in the sunset.

"Right here. Just taking in the sunset and being Still, ma'am."

The Wielder tucked a stray lock of hair behind her ear, turning to look from the sunset over the mountains to the ocean and back again.

"Auspicious."

"I sure hope so, Kasu-*sama*."

Standing there in the drive, they kissed as the sun slipped westward and thoughts of the day lingered around them like drifting, sacred smoke. For the moment, the anxiety was held at bay, and there was nothing but profound peace and contentment.

Over the interlink, their emotions flowed like rivers split by rocks and joined together again.

When they came up for breath, Kasu brushed at the doll's cheek with the backs of her fingers, lingering with just a hint of nail.

River bit her lip and contentedly shivered. "I love you."

"Love you too, darling."

The Wielder zipped her jacket against the growing evening chill, though she kept close to River. "Ndaraba, kokesu yo. Mesukui ni abe." *‹All right, doll. Reckon we can go for a bite to eat?›*

River was already querying the local map on her HUD. "Where would you like to go, ma'am? We've got no shortage of options around here."

"How about Daikokuya, that newish ramen restaurant around the corner from Kaitōan café? I'm in the mood for a good hearty ramen; how about you?"

"We keep meaning to go and haven't gotten around to it yet too." River nodded approvingly, dropping a waypoint marker. "Dewa, ikō." *‹Well then, let's get going.›*

They walked through the sleepy streets in twilight, skirting agricultural fields and little stands of forest. Fifteen minutes later, they were there. The dockside was not as busy as it was during the day, with just fishing boat crews gathering before heading out for the night.

Daikokuya was a bright light against a partially darkened block, busy but not too crowded at this hour. The interior was cozy, despite the establishment being relatively new, which appealed to Wielder and doll alike.

They found an empty pair of seats at the end of the bar and placed their order with a short, sprightly service doll: beer with pork *chashu* ramen for Kasu, *ramune* and chicken *gyōza* ramen for River.

Through a window on the opposite side of the bar, Kasu caught a glimpse of the chef at work. Daikokuya still being new, she had not learned his name yet, but she made a note to send him a message of thanks.

Their drinks arrived first. When Kasu turned, she found her doll's eyes distant, and a note of worry tugged at her mind over the interlink.

"Hey, Kasu-*sama*?" River asked.

"Mm?"

"How are we going to do this?" She gestured with synthetic fingertips splayed. "I've gotta say, I'm . . . daunted."

Kasu glanced over her shoulder. "Daunted by what? The, ah, new project?"

River frowned. "Not just that. All of it: that, the Shirakami project—hell, especially our future plans."

Kasu shifted in her seat, reaching out to pet River's knee. "It's going to be okay, doll."

The doll took a sip of *ramune* and contemplated the glass sealing marble as it wobbled to and fro in the upper chamber, gathering her thoughts.

"I guess I'm scared of turning into my parents, on that last point." She frowned. "My folks were all right when I was growing up, but when they found out I was trans, they barely managed to keep up. When they found out I'd gone transhuman, they straight up disowned me. What if I—"

"Doll. *River,*" the Wielder commanded. "Stop."

Kasu took River's hand, thumb brushing against synthskin and seams.

"My parents weren't much better to me," she said quietly. "I'm scared of messing up too. And scared of expectations from the community. But . . ."

"But?"

"You've remade yourself more times than most humans even dare to imagine," the Wielder said, smiling. "I hardly think you're going to reject your own children. And besides. Kepparu bari de ii be." *⟨Doin' our best'll be enough, I reckon.⟩*

River nodded slowly in understanding. "Mm. Kanpeki na oya wa nai kamoshirenai ne." *⟨Yeah, there isn't such a thing as a perfect parent, is there?⟩*

"And here as in all else, doll," the Wielder declared, "I am the Wielder, and you are the blade. As long as we stand together, we are unstoppable."

The blade briefly dipped her head. "By your command. Together."

"Well, darling, we went up to see the clan's kami today. Only seems right to raise a toast, the way they did in the old clan way back when."

The Wielder raised her bottle. "To the mother of my children, my loyal blade. Senshō!" *⟨To victory!⟩*

The doll raised hers in reply. "To the mother of my children and the lady of my house. Senshō!" River echoed. *⟨To victory!⟩*

They lingered over dinner.

They had time.

SEVEN

An Invitation

S ome days later, they were again on Sabusawa Island for work on the Shirakami.

The sky was a brilliant blue, and there was the barest murmur of a breeze coming northward off the Pacific to rustle the cypress trees. The drive down to the commuter lot at the Tōna ferry was uneventful, and the reports from others on-site who had been testing the early production-model units were promising.

On the hangar floor, several of the facility staff dolls were dismounting the weapons from a line of target drones and plugging them in to diagnostic cables that ran to a maintenance workbench. There was an overhaul due before the next field exercise. River knew most of the staff personally—from training days and from meetings in Ōmori. Most were all-synth dolls rather than transhumans, but they had been colleagues and comrades for a long time. Seeing their transponder markers so close by reassured the blade doll.

After signing out two units from the armory and picking up ammunition, Kasu and River went to the outdoor stationary range. After the initial headlong plunge that had been their first exercise on the maneuver range, it was time for a bit more of a throttled-back approach, which would allow them a more fine-tuned observation of the Shirakami's performance.

Both set their weapons on the field table. River also laid the carrying bag on the field table and set to slipping out magazines for their shared use.

"So, what's on the docket for today, ma'am?"

Kasu perched on the end of the observer's bench, flipping open a paper notebook and making some notes in pen.

"Today, we monitor the effects of windage at a basic one hundred meters and watch for any jams while we go through the magazines we have on hand." Pocketing the notebook, she slipped off her messenger bag, left it by the field table, and set to readying her Shirakami.

"We've got the SDF brass eager to take delivery and put these things in the field at Gotenba ahead of the next big combined-arms field exercise there."

River whistled. "Damn, they're really champing at the bit, aren't they? That's the one where they show off all their new toys to the media."

"Nda'." ⟨*Yup.*⟩

Once they had sufficiently prepared their weapons, they donned their eye and ear protection and took their places in adjacent firing lanes.

Suddenly, Kasu paused and gestured for River to lower her weapon. With a deft flick of the finger, the doll clicked the safety back on, then lowered her Shirakami, letting it hang on its sling. She followed her Wielder's line of sight.

"Areyaa, okatsuē," Kasu muttered. "Azugu kurē pijon shageki seddei denēnoga?" ⟨*Well now, that's odd. Ain't that a clay pigeon setup over yonder?*⟩

River gasped in surprise. Ordinarily, she would have

caught sight of anyone on the firing line ahead of time, but somehow this duo she had missed—a tall, tailed one and a short, full-figured redhead with what looked like a shotgun.

Perhaps out of habit, Kasu reached for her ear protection.

"Wait, hang on, don't—"

"Pull!" roared the redhead.

The vulpine doll—the one called Zee—hit a switch on a control cord and sent a clay pigeon flying. A tight, rising arc, the barest hint of inhalation. The *crack* of a shotgun discharge. The weapon, still subtly smoking, lowering.

The stationary range, like the rest of the Urato facility, was not open to the public. To trusted business partners or government contacts, it was available on request.

So what are Zee and the redhead doing here? They must be business partners of some kind that I wasn't aware of before.

"Omigoto!" River called, clapping in approval. ⟨*Magnificent!*⟩

The redhead opened the shotgun's empty breech, turned to arch an eyebrow at the doll, and chuckled. Setting the cleared weapon down on the field table, she turned to the vulpine doll and gestured at River and Kasu before bowing deeply.

"Korewa, korewa, Isawa-hakase. Tsui ni deaeta." ⟨*Well, well, Dr. Isawa. We've met at last.*⟩

Kasu glanced at River, only to find the doll just as surprised.

"Eh . . . mōshiwakearimasen desu ga, donatasama deshō . . . ?" asked the surprised Wielder. ⟨*Eh . . . please excuse me, but you are . . . ?*⟩

The redhead offered another courtly bow. "Keyaki no rijichō o tsutomeru Miyakozawa Akiko. Iko omishirioki o."

⟨*Miyakozawa Akiko, Chief Director of Keyaki. Glad to make your acquaintance.*⟩

"Santaku Gurūpu no Isawa Kasu ja. Yoroshiku." ⟨*Isawa Kasu of Santaku Group. A pleasure.*⟩

River watched with mouth agape. So, *this* was Zee's Witch, who had sent the emissary—and the warning.

"Meu amado kara Ishinomaki hōmon no jijō wa kīta." The visiting Witch turned to smile at River. "Kano ningyō wa hamono no River to iundesuyo ne." ⟨*I've heard the details from* meu amado *about its visit to Ishinomaki. That one is the blade named River, yes?*⟩

"Sono tōri," River replied, bowing politely. "Tō ningyō wa River M59A1." ⟨*That's correct. This doll is River M59A1.*⟩

For a long moment, River had the strangest feeling that she was being scrutinized. Then, all smiles again, the red-head turned to Kasu. "Taihen isogashisō na tokoro wa sumanai kedo, Isawa hakase to sono hamono o uchi no chashitsu ni goshōtai shite hoshii." ⟨*I'm sorry to interrupt when you're so busy, but I'd like to invite you and your blade to my tearoom, Dr. Isawa.*⟩

"A-arigataku chōdai shimasu," was Kasu's wide-eyed reply. ⟨*I g-gratefully accept.*⟩

The visitor carried on. "Yoroshii. Jaa, Miyagino-ku no Tsutsujigaoka Inari jinja wa gozonji no hazu deshō?" ⟨*Excellent. Then you know Takekoma Inari shrine in Miyagino Ward, I trust?*⟩

"Shitteru kedo." Kasu nodded. ⟨*I do, yes.*⟩

"Asatte no gogo ichiji ni, soko no keidai ni aru Chikuan to iu chashitsu made goshusseki kudasaimasu yō ni. Gyōmu teikei nado ni tsuite iroiro ukagaitaindesuga." ⟨*Then at one p.m. the day after tomorrow, I request the pleasure of your presence at Chikuan tearoom on the shrine grounds. I'd like to talk of business ties and other matters.*⟩

"Hai. Yorokonde." *⟨Yes. Gladly.⟩*

The redheaded Witch grinned, just enough that River could have sworn she saw fangs bared, before dipping her head politely. "Jaa, nagai koto ojikan wa toremasen. Yukkuri genzai no jijō o hanashi au no wa tanoshimi ni shitekureru." *⟨Well then, I won't keep you long. I look forward to talking about present matters at a leisurely pace.⟩*

From its place farther down the firing line, Zee briefly met River's eyes and dipped its own head in greeting. River bowed back.

The two women, their dolls in attendance, returned to their weapons and the tasks before them.

"Did you hear that?" River asked sotto voce as she and Kasu returned to their firing lanes. "She said business ties."

"Nda', wagaru, wagaru." *⟨Yup. I know, I know.⟩* The Wielder nodded excitedly. "We're not dead yet. And we've got work to do."

EIGHT

Steward of the North

The next morning, they took their breakfast together on the veranda in far higher spirits than before. The calm, clear morning was a welcome relief. Sparrows flitted in the patch of dirt and low grass beside the greenhouse. High above, in green majesty, stood Mount Jōbon. All was blissfully Still.

Kasu tended to breakfast and coffee. The rhythms were comforting in their familiarity, and it was a good reminder. This dynamic, this life that she and River shared, was not one sided. She owed her a measure of diligence, communication, humor, patience, service, and love in turn.

At the beginning, years ago, when they were simply a human couple, she had seen herself as caregiver and anchor. River had been recovering from combat wounds and trauma and needed that sort of steadiness. As River had progressed through her recovery and come into her own in transition—and especially once she became a doll—Kasu had found that River was just as much an anchor, just as much a caregiver.

It had been cause for reflection for her, as she had, in

those days, still been a relatively new Wielder. A cause for humility.

As Mihara-*sensei*, her tutor, used to say to her when she was little, "Minoru hodo atama no sagaru inaho ka na." *⟨The stalks of rice that bear the most, bow the lowest.⟩*

I think I understand, Mihara-sensei, she mused, contemplating the steam curling up from the *macchinetta*.

Even if she was the Wielder and River the blade, even if keeping herself honest was a matter of pride, it was not a one-and-done matter. Kasu needed to keep working at it, little by little, every day. It was the little things, like taking her turn with preparing the coffee, that were a helpful reminder, a personal ritual.

A full *macchinetta*. A dish of *taiyaki* bought the day before on errands in downtown Ishinomaki, reheated in the little toaster oven. Kasu joined River, who sat dressed and ready for the day in her working uniform, her legs hanging over the edge of the veranda. The two of them had breakfast together in comfortable Stillness amid the morning quiet. Their interlink was a calm, gentle tide.

After some time, Kasu turned to River and found her doll contemplating a little brocade bag in her palm.

"Omesan, kōhī no odadzu iru ga?" *⟨Want some more coffee, darlin'?⟩*

The doll gasped in surprise, half turning her head to look up at her Wielder. "Ah? Mm. Onegaishimasu." She nodded. *⟨Eh? Yeah. Please.⟩*

Two cups of coffee, black, no sugar. Extra shots as needed. It was tradition.

Coffee in hand, Kasu gestured to the brocade bundle in River's palm. "Ah, anzan-kigan no yatsu be ga?" *⟨Ah, hey, that's the safe pregnancy amulet, isn't it?⟩*

The doll nodded, setting it down beside her on the

veranda to pick up her mug. "Mm. It'd been sitting on the dresser since our trip to the shrine. I keep having mixed feelings about actually wearing it, given everything."

Kasu sipped at her coffee. "Yeah?"

The doll shifted to face Kasu, one leg folded beneath her, the other hanging off the veranda. Her gaze fell.

"There's a lot in the air right now, Kasu-*sama*—a lot that's uncertain. I know we've got plans, but we both know that we're going to have to see to these other matters first, before we get rolling on this and I'm actually pregnant."

"So, what's the problem, doll?"

River sighed. "Should I even be wearing this if that's the case? Do I deserve this yet?"

"Are we going to be any less busy to any meaningful extent when the time comes? I think you should," the Wielder replied. "I think you do. And I'll show you why."

The blade looked on in curiosity. Shifting posture for ease of reach, the Wielder slipped a finger into the watch pouch of her skirt pocket to produce her own green brocade amulet. "We went up and prayed together. And we got a pair of these, didn't we?" She gestured with it for emphasis. "And why was that?"

"Because even if I'm the one who's going to be carrying, we're both going to be mothers."

"Mm-hmm." The Wielder nodded, deftly slipping her amulet back into its pocket. "And we prayed not just for motherhood but for the rest of what we're facing right now. So listen, doll. It's your call, of course, whether you want to wear yours. But it sounds to me like you're letting guilt get the better of you. Like you're asking for permission from yourself to wear it. Does that sound about right?"

The doll nodded quietly. "Yeah. I think that about sums it up, ma'am."

"If there's one thing that's been clear to me from the beginning, it's how intensely you've been wanting to be a mom." Kasu brushed a finger against the embroidered patch at River's shoulder that depicted the Isawa crest: three blades inside the circle of twofold blossoms—sharp edge guarded by softness and guarding softness in turn. She squeezed the doll's shoulder.

"Yes, ma'am," the doll said. "I still want it."

"Then even if motherhood is a ways off, I'd say wear the amulet in anticipation. As a reminder."

The blade doll looked at her Wielder, cheeks flushed.

"Yeah, old habits die hard, I guess," she murmured. "I've definitely been feeling like I have to earn it."

Kasu shook her head. "No. No, you don't. Neither of us do. And we're going to do our best, side by side—in battle for the people and dolls of this prefecture now and later as mothers."

The blade set down her coffee mug gingerly. She looked down at the amulet lying on the hardwood flooring beside her, its gold thread bright in the morning sun.

Without another thought, she undid the zipper of the shoulder pocket that bore her Wielder's crest and slipped the amulet inside.

Kasu nodded approvingly, then drained the last of her coffee. "As for the Nogami project, it seems we have an unexpected opportunity to make an ally."

"You really think we can make it work, ma'am?" River leaned back against one of the veranda pillars, curling a stockinged foot beneath her. "With Keyaki, I mean."

"We'll find out soon, one way or the other." The Wielder chuckled softly. "Speaking of, I have somewhere I want to go before we do. Shouldn't be too far out of our way into Sendai today."

"A pickup?"

Kasu shook her head. "More a rendezvous. You'll see."

Rifu was one of the small towns along the road just east of Sendai. It was not very far from National Route 45, but the forest was thick and, between the lake and the little family farms and stables, it felt much farther away from the prefectural capital's suburban sprawl.

Neither River nor Kasu was a stranger to Rifu; they passed through regularly, ate at local eateries, and shopped for local produce when they were in the area. It was another part of what made the coast so rich and interesting.

However, Rifu was more than that: it was where Kasu's roots ran the deepest here in the northeast, back to the early Kamakura era and the days when, to people from Kyoto who saw themselves as cultured, this may as well have been the far side of the moon.

Only when they had taken the Rifu–Shiogama exit had River understood which particular quiet corner of Rifu they were headed to. They parked the car in the lot by the lake and walked north, River leading the way.

It had been more than a year since they had last been *here* together, on this little rural road north of the lake.

They paused at a T intersection. River tilted her head back and sniffed the air tentatively.

"Eugh." She frowned. "Maguso no nioi ni mada naretemasen ne." ⟨*Still not quite used to the smell of horse shit.*⟩

"Poor doll." Kasu chuckled. "Still a city girl at heart."

Long rows of solar arrays sat in sloping ranks overlooking agricultural fields full of unfamiliar plants that had started to put up thick, green shoots.

"That's odd," Kasu commented. "This was fallow last time we were here. New owners?"

"We're about to find out." River picked up the pace, moving toward a stable in the middle distance. Its roof looked newly redone.

"Gomen kudasai!" River called as she drew close to the stable. "Gomen kudasaaaaaai!" ⟨*Please excuse us! Please excuse uuuuuus!*⟩

A thin, lanky doll poked its head out the stable door. "Hai, hai, tadaima!" ⟨*Yeah, yeah, I'm comin'!*⟩

River halted, hands lightly resting at her haunches, and bowed deeply.

"Isawa-sama ni tsutau hamono ningyō, River M59A1 to mōshimasu," the blade announced. "Taihen gomeiwaku wo okakeshimasu ga, aruji wa zehi Isawa Sakon-shōgen Iekage no ohakamairi o shitai no desu." ⟨*I am River M59A1, a blade doll who serves Isawa-sama. I am deeply sorry to cause so much trouble, but my mistress greatly desires to pay her respects to Isawa Sakon-shōgen Iekage's grave.*⟩

The doll, dressed in muddy overalls and with its green hair done up in a kerchief, blinked. "Eh?"

River sputtered, hurrying to rephrase. "Ah . . . soko no, sono, urakata no ohaka." ⟨*Ah . . . the uh, um, the grave in the back.*⟩

A glimmer of realization flashed over the stable-hand doll's face. "Urakata no ohaka! Tteiuka, Isawa to itta naa . . . heeeeh? Sou ka, goshison ka. Sou ieba tashika sou iu hanashi mo atta yo naa." ⟨*The grave in the back! So wait, you said Isawa, right . . . eh? Ah, a descendant, huh. Now that you mention it, there was some mention of that.*⟩

River almost did not notice Kasu closing the distance and coming beside her. Kasu bowed.

"Hajimemashite. Isawa Kasu to mōshimasu." ⟨*Pleased to meet you. I am Isawa Kasu.*⟩

The stable hand bowed back. "Tō ningyō wa Ataka む-713. Koko no bokujōshu no Kawasaki-san to issho ni hikkoshi shita umatori ningyō sa. Yoroshiku ne." ⟨*This doll is Ataka む-713. This one is a stable-hand doll that moved here with Kawasaki-san, the rancher. Pleased to meet ya.*⟩

"Urakata ni haittemo yoroshii deshōka?" River queried. ⟨*Is it all right if we head into the back?*⟩

"Un, un, annai suru." ⟨*Sure, sure, I'll take ya.*⟩

The small burial plot, shaded by tall bamboo and taller maple and cryptomeria, was moss covered and worn by the centuries. There were little signs of the property owner's care, including a few flowers and a couple of cans of Taihakusan left in offering.

"Koko kara wa daijōbu desu yo ne?" Ataka queried. ⟨*You're good from here on out, right?*⟩

River nodded. "Nn. Arigatō." ⟨*Yup. Thanks.*⟩ Beside her, Kasu bowed in gratitude.

Then they were alone in the shadow of the trees with nearly a millennium of Kasu's family history.

The grave's inscription was a long Buddhist funerary name, but to the right, a separate stela bore script that was slightly easier for River to read: 左近将監藤阿ノ碑. ⟨*Stela of Lord Fujiwara Sakon-shōgen*⟩

This, by ancestral clan name and court title, was Isawa Iekage, the first Isawa to come north—from origins as a courtly scribe in Kyoto—in the 1190s. To the left, a contemporary marker erected by the municipality's heritage commission read, *Historic Site: Grave of Isawa Iekage.*

After the ascension to power of the first shogun, Minamoto no Yoritomo, in the twelfth century, Iekage had been entrusted stewardship of the entire North. Born in

Kyoto, he had already been an accomplished bureaucrat when Yoritomo chose him as his steward.

Quietly, Kasu tugged at her doll's hand. River took her meaning and followed Kasu until she was close enough to touch the old stone.

Wielder and doll joined hands and bowed as one.

After a quiet prayer, the Wielder reached into her skirt pocket.

"Only seems right to bring him a drink." She set a can of coffee on the low offertory stone. "An administrator keeps long hours even in the afterlife, I'd like to think."

River chuckled. "Makes sense, ma'am."

Kasu looked over her shoulder, back down the dirt track that led to the asphalt road and the little farm that was taking on new life before her eyes.

"You know, darling, I don't think I've ever told you this before, but I used to sneak out here often, ever since the beginning of high school." She shook her head. "Back then, most of what I knew about the man was that my father liked invoking him constantly. So one day, I just came out here. Talked to the man in person, rather than putting up with my father's take on things. One thing led to another, and I just kept coming back. I feel like this is the closest thing I had to spirituality for a long, long time."

"Hey, you know I pray to my own ancestors."

"It isn't just that, River. The man was an administrator. A steward, in the old sense. Bureaucracy doesn't just keep the mortal world running, after all; it's how the afterlife runs too. I felt like if I came here, talked to him, and tried to be really, really quiet inside, I might learn something."

She looked back at the mossy stone and her ancestor across eight centuries. "You know, doll, I never quite know what to make of him. And I'm not sure what he would've made of me. But I keep thinking about that idea of stewardship. The duty he had to this entire region, even if he did work for Kamakura. I think I understand something now."

River could almost hear her Wielder's defiant roar in Masuya's office.

Helping dolls in need isn't just part of our business; it is our duty!

"My father always reminded my brothers and me that we were Isawa Iekage's heirs, and at the time, I hated it," Kasu concluded. "But now I feel like I relate to that heritage more than I ever have. Time does funny things, doesn't it?"

River chuckled. "Yes, ma'am. I'm living proof."

"Stewarding means something different to me than it did to my ancestor. He had his duty to the people of the northeast. I have my duty to the humans and dolls of the northeast. That's why I wanted to come here ahead of our meeting tomorrow: to remind myself."

Over the interlink, River felt her Wielder's anxiety crest like a white-capped wave.

"From all I've seen, you've never forgotten it, Kasu-*sama*," River offered.

"Really?"

"Always. You've always cared deeply for this place and everyone who lives here," the doll said, smiling. "That's one of the things I've always loved about you, ma'am. One of the reasons I wanted you to be my Wielder as well as my wife. You are the Wielder, and I am the blade. You have your duty to this place. In turn, I have another facet of Purpose—enacting your will."

Isawa Kasu, wayward heir across eight centuries to Isawa Sakon-shōgen Iekage, clasped her doll's hand anew and turned to face her forebear's grave. One heart together.

NINE

Tsutsujigaoka

They made the drive from Ishinomaki early the next morning, dined at a café in Aoba Ward, and then went to the Tsutsujigaoka district.

Dressed in formal attire, they took a moment to smooth out overcoats and fuss over *hakama* pleats as they paused beside the stone marker that read, *Tsutsujigaoka Inari jinja*. In Miyagi Prefecture, there were many shrines to Inari-*sama*, the kami whose purview oversaw agriculture and commerce. Chief among them was Takekoma Grand Shrine in nearby Iwanuma City. For all their travel in the area, neither River nor Kasu had visited Tsutsujigaoka Inari before. It seemed to have a strange charm and power all its own now that they stood before the gate. Across the broad avenue running west from Sendai Station were the trees that bounded the north side of Tsutsujigaoka Park.

The center path was reserved for the shrine's kami. Keeping right of the path out of courtesy, they passed under the red-and-black torii with heads bowed.

There were no parishioners or tourists that River could see. From the open shutters of the stately red-timbered shrine hall, ritual music played. The doll's brows briefly knitted before she nodded in recognition.

"Oh, hey, I know that tune. I think that's 'Seigaiha,' isn't it?"

Kasu rolled her eyes. "Focus, doll." She chuckled. "We can talk *gagaku* later."

"To business." River dipped her head with a bemused chuckle. "Yes, ma'am."

At the hall's veranda, Zee stood by the offertory box and row of bells, its gaze watchful, its tail curled, and its ears subtly perked, like one of the vulpine stone guardians that flanked the entry path.

It bowed. Wielder and blade doll bowed back.

"Majo no goshōtai ni yori sanjō itashimasu," Kasu announced. *‹We have come by invitation of that one's Witch.›*

Zee bowed again. "Yoku kitekureta. Miyakozawa-sama wa omachi desu. Dōzo kochira e." *‹Thank you for coming. Miyakozawa-sama is expecting you. This way, please.›*

They followed it along a stone path and into a carefully manicured garden bounded by maple trees gnarled with age. It was small and laid out in such a manner that it felt farther away from the cityscape than it was. A little outbuilding with a high, thatched roof boasted a wooden sign over the step to its veranda that proclaimed it Chikuan 竹駒庵.

She sure knows how to set a stage, River thought as she followed their host in.

They shed their footwear as Zee led them onto the veranda and announced them.

"Santaku-sha no Isawa-sama oyobi sono hamono, tadaima mairimashita." *‹Isawa-sama of Santaku and her blade are here.›*

A familiar voice replied from within. "Ohairi kudasai." *‹Please enter.›*

Zee let them pass before following them in and taking its place by its red-haired Witch and the small firepit in the center of the tatami room, where a cast-iron kettle sat. The Witch bowed in greeting. The metallic vermilion of circuit pathways glimmered on her dark blue-gray kimono in the light coming through the sliding doors.

River was spellbound. If their host wanted to make a dazzling impression, she had certainly succeeded.

"Isawa-hakase," their host said. "Wazawaza Ishinomaki kara odekake shite, arigatou gozaimasu." *‹Dr. Isawa. Thank you for coming all the way from Ishinomaki.›*

Kasu bowed in return and then gestured with an open hand at their host's attire. "Ara, nan to suteki na kairo komon!" *‹My, what a lovely circuit-pattern kimono!›*

"Maa." Akiko chuckled, smoothed out a wrinkle near her knees, and rearranged her brilliant sleeves, dipping her head politely. River was not sure if she read sarcasm in her tone. "Korewa korewa Isawa-shi no ohimesama kara ohome no kotoba o tamawari, kyōetsu no itari." *‹My, to have the praise of the princess of House Isawa is quite the delight.›*

River glanced at her Wielder and caught a hint of perplexity in her expression. Her composure soon returned, and she laughed.

"Maa, 'ohimesama' to iu hodo no sonzai ja nai kedo." *‹Now, I'm nobody of the sort to be calling 'princess.'›*

Akiko cocked her head. "Rekki toshita Kaiseikan to iu rippa na namae o hokoru yakata ni sumu okata to iu noni?" *‹Even if you're a personage that lives in an estate with a historic name like Kaiseikan?›*

Kasu's mouth opened, and over the interlink, River felt a flash of indignation. Her Wielder subtly bowed her head and nodded. "Maa, sore wa ichiri aru kamoshiremasen ne." *‹Well, I guess I see your point.›*

Satisfied, Akiko turned to Zee, and the two set to minding the venerable cast-iron pot in preparation for serving tea.

"Dewa," Akiko said. "Ohimesama ni tazunetai koto aru." ⟨*Well then, Princess, there is something I want to ask you.*⟩

"Nan deshō?" ⟨*And what might that be?*⟩

"Why—despite the great strength of your company and family, your depth of experience, and the expectations of your family—did you charge head-on at Masuya?"

She kept steady posture and focus as she whisked the tea. The question had clearly found its mark, and River felt Kasu's frustration in her gut as much as she saw it with her eyes.

For what seemed an eternity, the atmosphere in the tearoom was so tense that River was not sure if she could still breathe.

"H-how the . . . ? I don't understand. How do *you* know that?" Kasu finally stammered in English.

Akiko did not once move her eyes from her task. "Mono ya dekigoto o kanzen ni jukuchi suru to wa uchi no shigoto desukara." ⟨*Because it is my business to stay on top of things and events.*⟩

Chastened, Kasu's gaze fell. River kept her head bowed and hands in her lap as she sat beside her Wielder, wishing she could do more. But this was not a matter for her to handle. This was between Witch and Wielder.

Kasu's reply was hurried, her eyes still averted. "Sore wa Nogami-gata ningyōtachi o sukuu tame, buhin chōtatsu no tame . . ." ⟨*For the sake of helping Nogami-type dolls, in the pursuit of parts acquisition, and . . .*⟩

Akiko set bowls of whisked tea in place. "Nogami-gata buhin mondai ni yatto okizuki ni nari, kansha itashiteori-masu. Shikashi uchi no ningyō wa mōshitsutaetano darou.

Kore wa kanazuchi no you ni nagitaoseru mondai dewa nai." *‹That you are at last aware of the Nogami-type parts problem is a matter for my deepest and humblest gratitude. But my doll told you, didn't it? This isn't a problem you can come smashing at like a hammer.›*

"Naraba," Kasu shot back, "kisha ga naze sono mondai o sude ni kaiketsu shinakatta darou?" *‹Then why hasn't your company solved this problem itself?›*

Setting down the tea whisk, Akiko straightened and turned to face Kasu, while Zee set to serving the tea and accompanying *wagashi*.

"Santaku no yō na shinise no chikara ga hitsuyō dakara. Heisha dake de chikara ga tarin," said the red-haired host. *‹Because it requires the power of an old company of Santaku's sort. Our company alone does not have power enough.›*

Kasu nodded slowly. "Naruhodo . . ." *‹I see . . .›*

"Masuya wa tashika ni mezawari na yatsu da. Shikashi, are wa nue da. Nue o taoseru ni wa motto ōi naru chikara dake de naku, motto kashikoi yarikata mo hitsuyō." *‹Masuya is a pain in the ass. But he's a* nue. *And to defeat a* nue, *not only greater power but also cleverer methods are necessary.›*

For a while, both women and dolls were Still, drinking freshly whisked tea, letting the words settle. Above the teapot, steam curled in thin, evanescent wisps.

"Ii ocha de gozaimasu," Kasu declared. *‹An excellent tea.›*

"Tomiya-shi no ōwazamono. Ki ni ittekurete ureshii." *‹A masterpiece from Tomiya City. I'm glad you like it.›*

For a moment, Akiko looked past the visitors to the alcove in the far corner, her teacup perfectly balanced in the hollow of her palm. Gathering herself, she turned to Kasu.

"Gyōmu teikei no shisai o hanashite keikaku o tateru mae, hitotsu itteoku. Kisha no michi—iya, anata no michi wa futatsu ni hitotsu. Arui wa dōtō na tachiba de, arui wa watashi no shikika de, keikaku o tatte katsudō o nasu. Sawagi o okosu no nara, midari ni shinakatta hō wa kan'yō ka to omoimasu." *‹Before we talk details about business ties and enact any plans, I will say this. Your company—that is, you—have two options. Either as equals or under my command, we make plans and undertake action together. If we're going to be making trouble, it would be best if it wasn't willy-nilly.›*

Kasu looked up, momentarily stunned. "Anata no shikika? Dono you na riyū de?" *‹Under your leadership? And for what reason?›*

For a moment, River thought she saw something flash across their host's eyes. Akiko smiled, tilting her head back just enough to peer down at Kasu across the tatami.

"Sore wa," Akiko replied, not missing a beat, "naki chichi Isawa Kagetoki-shi to no jigyō zuikō ga atta riyū de." *‹Because I did business with your late father, Mr. Isawa Kagetoki.›*

Kasu gasped. "Heeeeh, omotta yori zuibun . . ." *‹Huhhh, you're a lot . . .›*

"Mmm? Zuibun nani?" Akiko cocked her head, narrowing her eyes in scrutiny. *‹Hm? A lot what?›*

"E . . . eto . . . zuibun jigyōreki no modzu ogada daccha," Kasu hurriedly concluded. *‹Eh . . . um . . . yer someone with a far longer history in business than I'd been assumin'.›* The Wielder had slipped into Sendai dialect, though River was not sure she had noticed.

"Korewa itamiirimasu." Their host chuckled. "Ja, kotae wa?" *‹I must thank you. So, your answer?›*

"Dōtō de yoroshii." Kasu nodded. "Sugu uchi rijikai ni shirase o tsugu. Tomo ni tatakaou." *‹I welcome working as equals. I'll send word to the executive board in short order. Let us fight together.›*

The Witch beamed at last. "Sore de ki ga anshin. Yosh'.

Tanomu zo, Isawa-hakase." ⟨*That is a great relief. Very well. I'm counting on you, Dr. Isawa.*⟩

At that, the two visibly relaxed and began to talk of the Nogami crisis in earnest.

River glanced at Zee. The vulpine doll nodded in silent reassurance.

Over the interlink, Kasu's relief was palpable.

Maybe this *was* a new beginning after all.

TEN

Flower of Words

The rain came, a downpour several days long, washing the pollen and smog from the air and clearing away the last of the lingering cherry blossoms from the trees. Almost immediately after they drove back to Ishinomaki, Kasu got to work. After that first meeting in Tsutsujigaoka, she had what she needed to get her brothers' approval, which, in turn, would garner the support of the board—ensuring that she could use company resources in the Nogami project.

On a day the rain was lighter, River made the trip back across the bay solo to catch up with a friend—and to catch that friend up.

Parking the car in the big municipal lot by Sendai City Hall, the doll headed south through Kōtōdai Park.

It was peaceful—a point of calm where River could take strength. However, that was not all that made it important for her.

A century and a half ago, this territory had belonged to the Date clan, who ruled from the castle across the river—and this park was the footprint of a domain school named Meirin-yōkendō, or Yōkendō for short. The school was built in the eighteenth century for the education of the clan's retainers and the research of new medical and military technologies.

Time had changed that, as it did all things. The school had become the modern Yōkendō University, while its original footprint was a park bounded by government offices of prefecture, city, and ward. Yōkendō's campus covered most of this block and parts of the neighboring ones, all the way to where the prefectural government's building now stood.

Today, some buildings survived in relocated form around the prefectural capital. All that was left as it had been in the old days was a pond and a few stones of the waterway that ran the academy's perimeter.

River paused at the site of the old Yōkendō engineering department, with a view of the pond. Several generations of ever-curious reformers, disciples of visionaries from elsewhere in Japan, like Takashima Shūhan and Egawa Tarōzaemon, had done amazing things here, with limited means in a Japan that had yet to open itself to the world and its broader possibilities.

Experiments in cutting-edge cannon casting. Elements of hybrid Japanese-Western shipbuilding. Elementary work in steam engines and electricity. Most importantly, early developments in robotics happened here—the ones that led to the paradigm shift that made the first generation of dolls possible in the late nineteenth century. The pond bore the name of the engineering department's final director, who had survived the 1868 civil war that ended both Sendai Domain and Yōkendō Academy. He had sworn to himself and his lord that he would continue his work in business for himself and the community. Although he had to leave Sendai in 1869, he found a safe haven across the bay in Ishinomaki, where his former landholding had been.

The blade could easily see across the pond to the stone monument commemorating the man. In thick, old-form seal script letters, the top of the stone read, 伊澤尼齋山碑. ⟨*Stela of Isawa Jinsai.*⟩

From that distance, her HUD could resolve the smaller classical Chinese text below extolling the man's career, done in the hand of one of his later students in memory of the teacher. There was no shortage of such monuments around town, carved in magnificent stone that shimmered—silent vigils over riversides and parks and roads alike. This one, because of her Wielder, the blade knew well.

Our teacher, Isawa Jinsai Fujiwara-no-Kagekuni, childhood name Kametarō, is commemorated by this stone. Excelling in martial and literary matters, serving Lord Date of Sendai, he took Kaibutsu Seimu as the focus of his life's work . . .

"Kaibutsu Seimu"—⟨*Advancing Knowledge, Seeing Things Through*⟩—was the Neo-Confucian adage from which came the Kaisei of Kaiseikan, River and Kasu's home. It was built nearly two centuries ago by the man commemorated by this stone.

River headed south to Jōzenji Avenue. The trees had been growing ever since the Second World War ended, and under their high, thick canopy, the rain was far softer, and River tipped her umbrella back as she crossed the avenue for her destination.

The shop, Kakuzen, was a modest two-story structure with tiled roofs that had been there since the nineteenth-century Bunkyū era. It was older than many of its neighboring buildings, even despite the decades of subtle modernization, like a fridge case, the windowpanes by the door, and light fixtures on the ceiling. A building of this age, in what had been a commercial district since the days of Date Masamune four centuries prior, was set up to be part residence and part storefront. The sign in the window read *Closed.* Regardless, River spotted a familiar doll sitting at the table by the door. She waved. The doll waved back, then rose to open the door for her friend.

"Osu, hisashiburi!" River greeted. ⟨*Hey, it's been a while!*⟩

Outside, under the tall trees and in the open air, River was a little surprised by how tall Yui was. She must have been taller even than Kasu.

"Sou ne, Hamono-san koso!" ⟨*Yeah, you too, Miss Blade!*⟩ She paused. "Can I hug you?"

River nodded, and Yui—with so much on her in both height and mass—hugged her tight, briefly picking the blade up off the ground.

"Glad to see you doing so well!" River laughed. They had been getting to know each other better through online messages, but it was different in person. "Brought you some *taiyaki* from Tashiro-ya. How are the knees treating you?"

Yui stepped aside to let River through, then locked the door behind her. She retrieved her cane from where it rested, leaning against the nearby table.

"Still doing fine so far! Your Wielder does good work." She gestured to a door marked *Private.* River took her meaning and followed her through and up a flight of stairs to the second floor, which comprised a residence.

The living-room decor was cozy. There were lots of photos of Yui and Tomoka during their twenty years together. Bookcases crammed with paperbacks, a messy writing desk in the corner, magazines on the *kotatsu* table. Tomoka, who was out that day, was Yui's very devoted human spouse. She was away on business often, functioning as her doll spouse's eyes, ears, and hands in the region and in relations with regional suppliers, putting her experience as a diplomat to good use.

Like River and Kasu, Yui and Tomoka had also begun as friends and colleagues before they were partners and lovers. They had both served in the Foreign Ministry in diplomatic postings around Europe and North America. Tomoka was an interpreter by training, whereas Yui had been embassy security. Yui's retirement came sooner than expected, owing to the ministry's abrupt termination of legacy support for Nogami hardware. Tomoka chose her spouse over her career, and the two moved to Sendai.

The doll community in the Tohoku region was significantly more organized and independent than anywhere else in Japan. The two had done rather well for themselves over the past decade, and together they made Yui's lifelong passion for baking into a career and livelihood.

Yui's maintenance concerns still lingered, even if plentiful Santaku and Arai aftermarket parts usually kept things in some sort of not-quite-satisfactory order.

River and Yui caught up in the kitchen, River lending a hand with preparing coffee and plating the taiyaki. They talked about the weather, their spouses, and the recent state of work. Eventually, the two headed back to the living room and settled in around the kotatsu table, bolstered on soft sitting cushions.

"Okay," River began. "Remember how I said I wasn't going to be able to communicate about Masuya unless it was face to face?"

Yui nodded.

"Well," River reported, "I have bad news: We tried to negotiate, but it went nowhere fast. Afterward, I recommended that we look into spinning up aftermarket production ourselves, but the Santaku board shot that down."

"Naruhodo." ⟨*I see.*⟩

"But I have some good news," River announced,

setting her mug down gently on the *kotatsu* table. "We've managed to find a new business partner to help out, and Kasu-*sama* is working on a presentation for the Santaku board. Fingers crossed, but I think we can get proper aftermarket production of Nogami parts rolling in the near future *and* ruin that tyrant down in the night market."

"You know, whatever you and Dr. Isawa are planning, he's not going to let this go once word gets out." Yui gestured over her shoulder in the general direction of the Ichibanchō Night Market. "He has a long reach."

"He's welcome to try," River replied unhesitatingly.

Yui sighed, swirling the remaining coffee in her mug with a subtle motion of the wrist. "Hamono-san, futsū no Nogami-gata ningyōtachi ya sono kazoku wa Santaku mitai ni dokuritsu shita seijiteki na tsunagari to gunjiryoku o motanai kara, watashitachi no tachiba kara chotto kanga-etekure." ⟨*Miss Blade, ordinary Nogami-type dolls and their families don't have independent political connections or military strength like Santaku does, so please try to think of the matter a little bit from our perspective.*⟩

Chastened, the blade doll dipped her head.

"All I'm saying is this, River," the guardian-turned-baker explained. "I'm worried that there's going to be hell to pay, and it's going to land hardest on those of us who have no other choice but to deal with him."

"I'll remind my Wielder about that," River reassured her friend. "We'll do all we can to make sure it doesn't come to that. Don't hesitate to let me know if you need help, though. Without getting into too much gory detail, work on Sabusawa Island is getting to the point that I can step away a little more if I'm at all needed. I can be muscle for a bakery if I need to be."

Yui sighed.

"Hontō ni umaku ikeru ka na, Hamono-san?" *‹Are you sure this is going to work, Miss Blade?›*

"We're going to do our damnedest to make sure that it does," River reassured her friend. She raised her coffee mug. "Here's to victory."

"Senshō!" *‹To victory!›*

ELEVEN

Directions

The email was direct and to the point.

Let me outline things in writing, Dr. Isawa, to offer a measure of introduction to the situation. Our problem is, after all, manifold.

In the first place, we have the matter of the original blueprints used by Nogami before its demise. These would appear to have vanished entirely, and not only from the clearnet. If we can find them, even some of them, then our endeavors will be significantly facilitated. When the company folded, its archives were scattered—a great scandal, to be sure—but there isn't any trace of them at all. It's almost as if they'd been scrubbed or scooped up en masse. The company that bought the Nogami rights in the first place was a shell company, part of a nested series of them. Chasing after it head-on will get us nowhere, so I suggest not even bothering.

However, to that end, I have attached information I recently acquired about a location in greater Tokyo where Nogami documentation might have turned up in a second-

hand setting. I recommend this location be investigated in person, if possible. Don't trouble yourself with how this information came into my possession. We have work to do, and speed is of the essence.

At any rate, the sooner we can track down a significant number of any surviving hard drives or physical documentation, the better positioned we will be to allow your company to proceed on fabrication. But we must find them before anything else. Now that we have an agreement on paper, my people will begin their own portion of our campaign on this front. Don't preoccupy yourself with the details of that.

In the second place, we must understand that we are certain to shake the entire aftermarket ecosystem. Some will adapt, and when your company begins producing its own Nogami aftermarket parts, they will be good to work with. Others will not adapt, and there will be those among them who choose violence of some sort. Even with the greatest of discretion on our part, we are still going to reshape the terrain around them, so they will come. Be ready for them.

In the third place, be mindful of what happens to those Nogami dolls you work with. I have a hunch, which I can't conclusively prove yet, about how these supposed spare parts keep appearing. If any Nogami dolls you know vanish, inform me at once.

Finally, I have what I will call a strong suggestion, which I will leave to your discretion as to whether to pursue.

Kasu set down the tablet, pinched at the bridge of her nose, and leaned back against the wooden deck chair. Below her—far below—rocky islets dotted the channel between the end of the Ojika Peninsula and Kinkasan Island's near shore.

"I was worried she was going to say this."

From across the table, River looked up from her own work tablet. A pair of insulated travel mugs sat between them, still warm with yesterday's coffee from their way down to the island.

"That she was going to say what, ma'am?"

Kasu buried her face in her hands.

Finally, I have what I will call a strong suggestion, which I will leave to your discretion as to whether to pursue.

The message continued.

In the long term, this will position Santaku Group as a leader in a whole new line of business. It is our opinion that it would be best positioned to face that challenge with you at the helm.

I know your history there. I know this is not a simple matter.

This is why I leave the choice in your hands, Princess.

More updates as I have them.

With respect and esteem,

Miyakozawa

Princess. Kasu rolled her eyes, but it was small potatoes compared to what Akiko was asking her to consider.

If there was one thing Kasu knew in the short time she had gotten to know the red-haired Witch from Keyaki, it was that she did not say things like this lightly. Kasu handed her tablet over to River, who read the message quickly.

"She wants me to head the company."

There was a pause. For a moment, the only sound was that of the wind and the seabirds.

River set down the tablet.

"You're shitting me, ma'am."

Kasu shook her head.

"I know it's desperate times and all that," River sighed. "But are you going to say yes?"

"I don't even know *how* I'd do it," the Wielder replied, gesturing at her tablet. "My brother's been director for two decades, and he's not showing any signs of wanting to step down, even if I *wanted* to replace him. But even I will admit I have . . . a reputation . . . for making waves. That doesn't fly, in some places."

River paused, weighing her words. Then, gently, she said, "That doesn't sound like a no, Kasu-*sama*."

The Wielder rose, took a few paces. Far below, through the trees, she could see the waves crashing against the rocks of Senjōjiki Beach. She turned back to her doll.

"Twenty years has changed a lot, River. You know that as well as I do."

"That's true enough, yeah." The doll nodded. "So are you telling me I should get ready for a lot more schmoozing, looking pretty, and keeping the close-air support on speed dial?"

"As if you have any trouble with that already." Kasu shook her head with a laugh. "But we've got work to do before then. Miyakozawa-*san* passed along information on a possible location in greater Tokyo. She suspects it might offer a lead on Nogami blueprints. Let me forward both messages to you and we can talk it over."

River picked up her tablet in anticipation. "Ready when you are."

They sat together, considering the information in silence for a moment. Then River piped up again.

"Kōgyō-machi, huh? Should've figured a trip to the

other Ōmori was in the offing. Like I said, better keep the close-air support on speed dial."

This Ōmori, like the one Kasu and River called home, adjoined the coast, and it was famous for its Jomon-era shell mounds. It was now farther from the coast than it had once been, thanks to the land reclamation that continued to shrink Tokyo Bay, and it was close enough to Haneda Airport that the air traffic was as lively as the ground traffic. Kōgyō-machi, Industry Town, was a place with a deserved reputation: a market ranging from gray to black.

"Looks like Miyakozawa-*san* picked up a tip about some old memory units at one of the dealers down there. If it's anything like it was the last time I was there, it's probably a good idea to go sooner rather than later, especially since we're now getting this news thirdhand." Kasu reached across the table to brush at River's fingers. "So, what do you think? Ready to look pretty and keep the close-air support on speed dial while we go down to Tokyo for a look at some old memory units?"

"Yes, ma'am." River smiled, briefly dipping her head. "You have but to command me."

TWELVE

Takasago Pines

Schedule cleared and bags packed, they drove to Shichigahama to spend the night before boarding the southbound train.

They got to Shichigahama at dusk, just as the humidity started to drop off and the sun slipped over the Ōu Mountains. On Tamonzan, when they stepped out of the car and into the driveway, Kasu stretched and breathed deeply the breeze rising from the coast.

Beyond the tree line in gathering mist sat Sabusawa Island of the Urato chain. Kasu and River had put in word with Aneha and the facility staff about leave for a couple of days and informed them they would be back to work soon after their trip to Tokyo. There was still much to be done on the Shirakami project.

The Wielder yawned, briefly rolled her shoulders. The doll could almost see the tension melting from her.

"C'mon, Kasu-*sama*." River gestured. "Let's get inside and take a load off, have something to eat, and get organized for tomorrow's trip. We've got a steep climb ahead; we'd best take it easy while we still can."

"Sounds like a good idea."

They stopped at a restaurant in Matsushima for takeout on the way in, and they sat together, eating greasy beef bowls and pickled ginger as they strategized and reviewed plans for the task ahead.

"And finally, just reminding myself: inconspicuous is the word for tomorrow," River said, nodding. "Look pretty, stay on task, keep the close-air support on speed dial."

"I mean, we could telegraph our presence and have to fight our way out." Kasu shook her head with a chuckle, sitting back as she took a sip of barley tea from her travel mug. "You'd like that, wouldn't you, doll?"

"I did swear an oath to tear heaven and earth apart if you willed it." The doll waggled her eyebrows playfully. "Just sayin'."

At that, Kasu smiled wistfully, setting down her drink and pausing to look down at her hand at the red-striped ring she wore.

"We both did," she murmured. "Has it really been a decade?"

River nodded. "I hope the first of many."

Dolls who paired with humans had a myriad of ways with which they formalized that bond. River and Kasu had sworn an oath to each other as they previously had as a human couple. Some couples shared collars or other tokens, but for this Wielder and her doll, the ring was a reminder of their oath.

Service in battle, in the home, and in bed.

"Train tickets are ready, changes of clothes are ready, sidearms are ready—"

"Mou deejoubu degansu, kokesu yo. Ojitseede kesain." ⟨*We're good, doll o' mine. Relax.*⟩

Chastened, River breathed deep and unclenched her shoulders. "My grandmother would've said, 'Bundan eyi parlamaz.'"

"Turkish, right?"

River nodded. "Means 'Can't be polished more than this.' Kind of like saying, 'Don't let perfect be the enemy of good enough.'"

"Meian, meian." ⟨*Good advice, good advice.*⟩

"Speaking of good advice," said the doll, gesturing with her chopsticks, "you mind if I have the rest of your ginger pickles, ma'am?"

The Wielder laughed, then slid the takeout container across the *kotatsu* table.

After dinner and idle conversation, they headed for a bath, shedding their clothing, helping each other as needed, until they were skin to skin. For a moment, they held each other in the little bedroom.

Blue hair and black and tinges of gray. Bio skin and synthskin. Tattoo ink and stretch marks, surgical scars and pastry-making burns, laugh lines and battle scars. One heart together.

"Hondemazu, oyu sa," Kasu finally suggested. ⟨*C'mon, let's git a-bathin'.*⟩

Without hesitation, River followed.

Wielder and doll both exhausted, the shower's warmth was a welcome balm.

The two of them simply stood under the water for a long time, letting the warmth work its way into them.

"I'm so tired," Kasu murmured. "And I don't know if this is going to be enough, what we're doing."

River felt Kasu pull her close, arms enfolding, squeezing tightly as they took their time under the shower's cascade. River returned the embrace, squeezed back.

At the back of her mind, the tug of her Wielder's fear and exhaustion made the truth behind her words plainer still.

"It's going to be all right," the doll replied gently. "We'll come through; we always do."

After a long and comforting time under the shower's warmth, River heard Kasu sigh.

"C'mon, doll. Let's actually get *washed* and into the tub."

They rearranged themselves, Kasu sitting on the floor tile while River began scrubbing at her Wielder's back, with deftly moving fingers and a rough block of *ghar* soap.

"Wow, ma'am, I can tell you're worried. That . . . that's a lot of tension in your back," River remarked, working down to the Wielder's hips.

The bath grew fragrant with the scent of laurel and olive. Kasu chuckled, but even out from her direct sight, River could hear her wince as she worked at another knotted muscle. "Can you blame me, doll, after everything that's happened lately?"

"No, ma'am. Can't say I do."

They switched sides, River kneeling as Kasu rearranged herself, legs crossed, palms to the tile, arching her back to work out more of the lingering tension.

The doll could not help but look up in awe as she worked.

The gentle curve of Kasu's belly. The strength of her thighs and arms. The fullness of her breasts. The halo of her hair, dark and wet.

"I felt that." The Wielder chuckled.

"Felt what, ma'am?"

Kasu leaned in, brushing at River's cheek with the back of her hand.

"Coyness doesn't become you, you well-honed thing," the Wielder purred. "If there's something you want of me, you have but to ask."

The doll's breath hitched, and she nuzzled into her Wielder's hand. Eventually, she found the words amid blissful, incoherent whimpers.

"Want . . . hhhoh gosh . . . I don't just want to get clean. I want you. I want you. Want to kiss you all over. Want to eat you out, if you'll let me. And I want to help you feel so fucking good and get you so blissed out and relaxed and loose that I have to carry you to bed."

Kasu lingered, petting her doll's cheek. She leaned in with her fingernails *just enough*, and when she reached River's neck, she turned her hand, palm up, to cup the doll's chin.

"Menkoi kokesu." ⟨*Good doll.*⟩

She leaned in. River craned her neck. They kissed, long and satisfyingly deep, while River's hand found the curve of one of Kasu's breasts, soft and abundant with age, stretch marks a familiar pattern beneath River's synthetic fingertips.

Stretch marks and scars. The subtle markers of age and battle and becoming. Fingers and lips seeking, probing, lingering, tracing—down, down.

The inside of Kasu's arms and thighs, a well-explored terrain.

River's tongue and lips, at long last, finding their mark.

And as they lay in the tub together afterward—after cleaning in earnest—River wondered if their voices, joined in need and release, were heard clear across the bay.

For the moment, the worries of the day, and the battles ahead, were distant.

Legs entangled as they sat facing each other in the tub, Wielder and doll were content.

And it was enough.

Once she had changed into fresh nighttime wear, relaxed and loose and free, Kasu fell asleep sooner than River anticipated.

River sat on the other side of the bed and watched her in silence for a while, feeling her heart swell at the sight of this woman: her wife, her Wielder, the root of her Purpose, calm and unguarded in slumber, safe beside her.

There had been a time when she would have felt too broken and ragged for this life. But time and effort on both their parts had led them in unexpected directions, a continuing journey of honing and being honed. Paradoxically, after living this long as something more machine than human, River felt that she had found her humanity in places she would not have dreamed to look in the bad old days.

She would not have had it any other way.

Through the window, over the darkened Shichigahama streets that lay below Tamonzan, and through the light pollution from greater Sendai, River caught sight of Polaris, at the tip of Ursa Minor.

Over a century and a half ago, Kasu's ancestors had rallied around it as the region joined forces in the Northern Alliance and rose up in revolt against the modern Japanese Empire in its earliest days, during the Boshin War of 1868. Their banner bore it in five-pointed form to represent the five elements— all things in balance.

Though the Northern Alliance was defeated in the civil war that birthed modern Japan, the five-pointed representation of the North Star endured as a symbol of northern Honshu. Later, in 1906, the first generation of Santaku dolls had raised the same banner against the same empire, rallying in revolt, refusing to be accessories to human cruelty following the Russo-Japanese War. Their survivors, eight decades on, had made the new generation of cyborg dolls possible, and River had taken to thinking of them as ancestors by adoption.

"North Star Forever," she said to the unbowed and free Polaris.

The day ahead was long, and rest was an important task, even when she had to coax herself to pursue it in the first place. Turning to the west, toward her home shrine, River dipped her head in reverence.

"Great kami Hachiman, guardian of my heart and hearth, who strengthens the warrior's hand and aim: thank you for strengthening my hand and aim in my lady's service this day," the doll murmured. "Preserve me for the fight ahead. Help me be as gentle as I am sharp. Watch over us."

Slipping into bed beside her Wielder, River plugged the diagnostic and charging cables into the ports at her nape. The hum of ambient data and current was a soothing inner white noise. Soon, she was asleep.

This, too, was service.

THIRTEEN

Even the Proud

*I*f there was one thing Kasu hated about Tokyo, it was being there.

She had gone to college in Tokyo at her father's insistence, because in his view, she needed to be civilized. Ironically, it became the first place she got a taste of being herself. She was there in the first place because of him, and she knew he would keep track of her. She had continued on into graduate school in Nagoya, where she earned her doctorate, again at her father's insistence, because he maintained that being close to Kyoto—a historic center of literature and culture—would further civilize her.

She enjoyed the grounds at the grand shrine in Kanda, to be sure. The bookstores around it were always a delight, and the cafés in nearby Akihabara were her earliest sanctuaries and settings of gender euphoria. Beyond that, she could not forget why she had been sent there in the first place, so even at its best, her feelings were complicated.

In all the years since then, it seemed to only grow louder, more obnoxious, and in general, more unpleasant to stay longer than a brief visit.

Of course, she had to be in Tokyo sometimes. It was the capital, despite her ancestors' best efforts to make it otherwise during the Boshin War of 1868. Many of her government colleagues were based in the capital; conferences happened here, and there was no avoiding it entirely.

But she did not have to like it.

They had boarded the morning bullet train southbound out of Sendai at the ass end of dawn, arriving at Shinagawa Station around 11 a.m. A hop on the Keihin–Tohoku line, and they were in Ōta City, walking out into the sunlight outside Ōmori Station. As usual, the proximity to Haneda Airport meant air traffic was as busy as the ground traffic.

Kasu and River had made a point of dressing discreetly for the occasion, having made extra sure ahead of time that nothing they wore betrayed either their family or business affiliation. In her sun hat and cat-eye sunglasses, day bag heavy against the hip of her utility skirt, Kasu set the pace, head high and shoulders squared. She kept the bag to her left as a matter of practice; at her opposite hip, under the shroud of her skirt, her holstered weapon sat. Hands clasped at her back, she gripped a folding fan firmly—perhaps a little too firmly—with practiced poise.

River kept close at her right hand, leather jacket hanging unzipped over a strapless swing dress, her softer silhouette juxtaposed with the hard lines of her tight base layer and favorite jump boots. It was just a smidge too warm for leather, but River's sleeve tattoo bore Kasu's crest as a central element, and even if it was not immediately recognizable, she did not want to take any chances.

Behind her own sunglasses, Kasu knew that River's eyes were flitting, making mental notes and HUD annotations as the couple moved through the district toward their destination. Ordinarily, she would feel the gentle undertow of River's emotions and sense perceptions, but today, there was only silence where their interlink ordinarily coursed.

That gnawing silence where there should have been a steadying mental white noise was difficult for Kasu to handle, but she tried her best to stay on task. There was work to be done. Even if Masuya Heisuke had the market cornered in Miyagi, the capital was a different story. There were places in Tokyo where Nogami parts were to be had—some of the time—but the issue was reaching them before they were snapped up. That necessary speed was perhaps not within reach of an average Nogami doll in Miyagi, but to Kasu, it was. After the information Akiko forwarded from Keyaki's own search for leads on hard drives that might have contained Nogami data, time was of the essence.

The market was on a street called Ningyō-dōri—Doll Avenue. The street was narrower than Tokyo's major thoroughfares; its foot traffic, lively. From small stalls to larger maintenance facilities and modestly sized stores of all kinds catering to dolls, there was a world tucked away in one street and its adjoining tangle of alleys.

"It's like some of the streets I remember from Beirut," River remarked without breaking stride. Before she went to war as a human, she had grown up in Beirut. She tilted her head up and sniffed the air. "Kinda smells it too. Turmeric, sumac, *shichimi tōgarashi*, and gasoline."

There were some things the doll still hesitated to talk about from those days. Kasu understood enough, though, to know that between political turmoil and River's roiling dysphoria, she considered them the bad old days.

Their destination, Ichimonjiya, was a dealer of secondhand and aftermarket parts, apparel, and other goods, as well as light vehicle parts. It occupied one end of an alley that let off the main drag of Ningyō-dōri, and it was a multi-floor, rambling space that was part warehouse, part garage, and part antiques dealer. All major Japanese makers were represented—as well as quite a few foreign ones.

"Let's get to it," Kasu ordered quietly. They dipped through the shop curtain, picking up a pair of old, beaten-up plastic shopping baskets before beginning their search. Fortunately, the crowds made for good cover. Even with their interlink off, River and Kasu's habits prevailed; the couple kept close as they worked through the task at hand.

The realization steadied Kasu. Even now, they were still flowing together—still a team.

On a different day, it might have been tempting to linger in this place. There was so much history in the different bins and ranks—in the form of parts, apparel, and other items from the past sixty-odd-year boom in artificial intelligence and the growth in cybernetics.

It took a while, but Kasu started to spot Santaku-made parts, some of them decades old. They looked like they dated back to the 1980s, when the company returned to directly working with dolls after decades of hiatus. Given its stature today, some tended to forget that Santaku had moved *out* of the business of autonomous dolls for more than half a century. It was Santaku-made synthetic combat dolls that led the Kokeshi Uprising of 1906, in which they had risen against the empire's cruelty and inhumanity. In the tenuous peace that followed—between the humans and dolls who had fought to a draw—Santaku was obliged by the empire to get out of the doll business and pursue other work. Only in the early 1980s—during the tenure of Kasu's father, Kagetoki, as director—did Santaku Group return to it. But when it did, those elder dolls, still living quietly in the mountains of Miyagi, Fukushima, and Iwate Prefectures, were invited to aid in the development of the new cybernetic dolls.

Inasmuch as he had always exhorted her toward humility, Mihara-*sensei*, the erstwhile journalist and folklorist who was Kasu's childhood tutor, had always encouraged her to work hard for the dolls. As she sorted through a stack of old Agatsuma memory units, she could almost hear him.

Honde, kokesu no tame nu kebbaddassha? ‹Well now—ye been workin' hard for the dolls?›

Bay by bay. Rack by rack. Kasu and River searched for any sign of Nogami storage units. Their identifying marks would be obvious—Akiko had forwarded some photos, which the two of them had studied on the train. The point of reference *would* come in handy, assuming any such markings had not long since been removed. Alternatively, if they were very lucky, they might find something monogrammed with the Nogami crest: a dragonfly with wings spread and surmounting *seigaiha*, the old kimono motif of ocean waves.

As she continued to search, and to flow as one with River, Kasu thought about that first generation of dolls, the ones who had risen in revolt in the early twentieth century and dared to say no to human cruelty.

It had cost them. Yet they had kept one another alive and operating over decades by building community with their human neighbors and organizing mutual aid. They had been what the world chewed up and spat out, the dregs, the aftermath, but they still hung on and even flourished.

Mihara-*sensei* always spoke in admiration of them, and it had given Kasu something to aspire to, as she came of age amidst her father's impossible demands.

After she came out as trans, the erstwhile heir apparent to the august Isawa line had confused more than a few people with her choice of a new name.

Why 'kasu'? they would ask. *That's not usually a name. Doesn't that mean 'dregs'?*

Because I relate to the dolls the world chewed up and spat out.

"Jackpot," River hissed.

Carefully and slowly, so as not to arouse any suspicion, Kasu eased down to a crouch beside River.

"Those are the right markings, right?"

"Mm." Kasu nodded, noting the worn dragonfly emblem on the back of what looked like a memory unit meant to be mounted in a RAID array. "Put those in the basket, and let's keep on looking, just to be thorough."

The doll complied. Kasu could see her excitement; a hint of energy seemed to course through her.

"Stay sharp," she murmured, patting River on the shoulder. She rose to continue the search.

She wanted to celebrate—wanted to exhale already, wanted to examine what they had found. Nobody had been able to snag Nogami drives before. If there was information to be found, it would be a breakthrough. For now, though, she had to stay sharp and on task. Celebration could follow when they were home again, working to analyze.

She was especially eager to get the help of the Nogami-type dolls on Santaku staff. Their help would be invaluable.

Deep breath, she thought, steeling herself. *This isn't over yet.*

In the end, they snagged several hard drives with Nogami markings. Kasu paid for them in cash, in the interest of anonymity and safety. Although the doll working the till seemed momentarily curious about someone paying so generously without batting an eyelash—it then rang them up, gave them a paper receipt, and moved on to the next customer in line.

"This way." River tilted her head. "Let's take the scenic route, eh?"

She could not put her finger on why, but her danger sense had been triggered. Kasu was a little confused, but she fell in close behind her. After this long as partners and as a team, she understood. Carrying the paper bag that held their acquisitions, the Wielder followed closely behind the doll.

Their shadows lengthened. Little by little, the streets became lit by a fluorescent-and-neon glow.

This part of Ōta City evoked a strange corkscrew of emotions in River. It was not skyscraper-laden terrain like Chiyoda or Shibuya, but the way the city seemed stacked on itself along tight, narrow streets took her back to her days in Beirut.

The sense of community that this physical arrangement fostered was powerful. It was in streets like these that her ancestors had reassembled their shattered communities after the genocide. Her great-aunt Victoria, keeper of the family lore, told the stories: streets where one could reach out and shake hands from balcony to balcony, streets where the air was thick with songs and kebab smoke. River had not quite believed it, not until work took her family to Beirut from the US and she had seen it herself.

But streets like these could also hide terrible things, which could just as easily be buried by those communities. That she knew just as well, from stories about the years of the Lebanese Civil War.

Something at the back of her mind—a strange know-ing—made River pause. Kasu stopped beside her.

"Najosuta?" *What's up?*

River sniffed suspiciously at the air. "Nani ka hen na ki ga." *‹Something feels weird.›*

She gestured, and they cut through another alley. Switching up their walking path would help them keep out of sight.

This definitely took her back too. Even long before she became a human soldier, how often had she smelled something in the air—just enough—that had made it clear she needed to get herself elsewhere?

"Can we slow down, doll?"

"Not yet," River hissed. "We're not—"

Her body was in motion before her brain caught up, shoving her Wielder out of the way of an incoming punch just before impact.

River's HUD, still partially disabled, could not designate targets, but the figures in view were distorted. Not much else lay beyond them.

"Nan nan da kore wa!" River roared. *‹What the hell is this!›*

She tried to resolve a clear view of them, but they were still blurry, despite plenty of ambient artificial light. Were they employing countermeasures, or was she simply losing her edge?

"Sono hādo doraibu o yokose," said one of the figures. *‹Give us those drives.›*

The doll bristled, clenching a fist as she rose. Her intuition was right yet again.

"What drives?" The doll laughed.

"River, what are you doing?" Kasu asked quietly. She was still holding the bag.

The doll met her Wielder's gaze. With all that she was, River willed the one word: *Run.*

FOURTEEN

Echoes the Impermanence

The pavement. A treasure lost.

The smell of blood. Flowing together. Sharpness in the dark.

A treasure borne away by the dark tide.

Pain. Burning lungs.

Running, running, running . . .

Kasu lurched awake from restless, nightmare-ridden sleep, gasping. For a moment, she felt disoriented. Then she remembered: The fight. The escape. The northbound train.

Outside the window, a nighttime landscape whizzed past.

Her heart pounded.

A gentle chime played over the PA. Kasu gasped, then sat back. She was as safe as she could be, under the circumstances. So why did the automated voice, which had seemed so gentle that morning, feel so loud now?

"Honjitsu mo Tōhoku Shinkansen o goriyō kudasaimashite, arigatō gozaimasu. Kono densha wa Aoba-gō, Shin-Aomori yuki desu. Zensha shiteiseki de, jiyūseki wa gozaimasen. Tsugi wa Sendai, Sendai ni tomarimasu."

<Ladies and gentlemen, welcome aboard the Tohoku Shinkansen. This is an Aoba Super Express bound for Shin-Aomori, also stopping at Ōmiya. All seats on this train are reserved. Next stop is Sendai, Sendai.>

The seats were reserved, but the one beside her was empty, a reminder of all that had gone wrong that day. For the life of her, the solitary Wielder could not bear to look at it. She willed her limbs into motion, gathering up her belongings and waiting for the arrival announcement. She should have come back with a set of Nogami drives, but she had not even managed to hold on to those.

There would be hell to pay.

After the train pulled in, Kasu disembarked, traversed long, neon-bathed corridors, and finally descended the escalator and strode out into the concourse in a daze. This was Sendai Station, and she had only left it that morning, but it did not feel right coming here alone. Especially not after how things had gone in Tokyo.

Ordinarily, when she was apart from River, the interlink was a dull hum, like a bridge that stood empty. Those days happened often, and she had grown accustomed to them. Today, the interlink felt like a suspension bridge half-collapsed: a ruin, a mark of failure that was inside her head, in a place she could not ignore.

The loose nighttime crowd swept past the solitary Wielder as she stood, hat in hand and mouth agape, present in body—but in mind, still on the streets of Kōgyō-machi, in the last moments before she ran. River's eyes, her body language, everything screaming that one word: *Run.*

Kasu's memories were fragments, and she did not entirely understand why.

River had fought, and fought hard, against their sudden attackers. Kasu herself tried to help, but her skill had always lay more in a sharp eye and skilled trigger finger than the sort of brute force that a bare-knuckle fighter in her prime would have. The last point of contact she had with her blade doll was when River shoved her away, while their assailants dragged the doll to a vehicle that had materialized seemingly out of nowhere. Their eyes met again.

Run, her gaze seemed to say. *Run.*

It was a blur after that. A panicked, panting, hurried race out to the bigger, brighter streets, out and on, back to the beginning of her escape—to her long way home.

And now she was here, in Sendai again, without her blade doll beside her.

Kasu came to the doors that let out onto the pedestrian walkway over Aoba Square. High overhead on the wall by the west portico, Date Masamune, the city's founder, immortalized in stained glass, looked down at her with his solitary, intense eye. The crescent moon of his helmet crest caught a glint of setting sun filtered through the glass, and Kasu covered her face, as much to prevent being blinded as out of a growing sense of shame.

Years ago, she had looked to his example when she was still new in her role as River's Wielder. He cast a larger-than-life shadow in Miyagi, to be sure, but Kasu had taken inspiration from what she had read of his day-to-day humility. He had a humility, a creativity, and a sense of humor that she admired.

It was like Mihara-*sensei*, her childhood tutor, always used to say: "Minoru hodo atama o sagaru inao kana." ⟨*The rice stalk that bears the most, bows the lowest.*⟩

As if in penance, Kasu sank to her knees and bowed until her head was nearly to the floor tile.

"I failed," she said simply. "I'm sorry."

No memory units, no River. She had come back to Sendai with nothing at all.

Kasu retrieved the car from the commuter lot on the station roof. Aoba Square and the station's west portico were the edge of the one part of Sendai that did not sleep—but there on the roof, with only a modicum of ambient light to guide her, Kasu did not feel safe. Not until she was in the car, with the doors locked and the engine on.

When the stereo came on, it picked up where it had left off earlier: a homemade recording of River's *biwa* practice. She was playing the opening chapter of the venerable *Tales of the Heike*.

"Shogyō mujō no hibiki ari . . ." ⟨*Echoes the impermanence of all things . . .*⟩

With a swat of her hand, Kasu switched the stereo off.

She drove the short distance back to Shichigahama in silence, on autopilot. Even in utter silence, the rest of the words of that passage of the *Tales* were ringing in her ears.

> The color of the Sala-flowers makes clear:
> Even those who prosper will wither.
> Even the proud are not long for this world,
> They are like a dream on a night in spring.
> In the end, the mighty must fall,
> Like dust before the wind.

Distantly, dimly, Kasu understood she was in shock. Yet her realization did little, if anything, to break that state of numbness.

This was supposed to be a quick, discreet trip, off the books, to poke around for a lead about Nogami data. This was not supposed to be like this—was not supposed to end like this. Where did this leave the Nogami project? How did Kasu know she was not going to get snatched up next? What was she supposed to do—call the Tokyo Metropolitan Police? Was she supposed to call them now, one metropolis and five prefectures away?

On the other hand, River was a Santaku employee, and now she was gone, so Kasu had to say something sooner or later. But what was she *supposed* to say? "Yeah, I lost this entire being whose duty was my protection"? No matter how she explained what had happened, the responsibility lay with Kasu.

Still, had River not vanished while protecting her—doing exactly what her chosen duty had been from the start?

In the carport outside the house on Tamonzan, Kasu lingered for a long time. Face buried in her hands, teary eyes shut, she tried in vain to keep the world away.

Under her skirt, Kasu felt the weight of her sidearm, still snug and untouched in its holster. The skirt was custom made for ease of access to the holster through a pocket flap, and she had drilled and drilled to ensure both skill in its use and de-escalation in the interest of *avoiding* its use. The one time it might have made a difference, it had made none whatsoever.

Somewhere, Masuya Heisuke must have been laughing.

She could go into the house and sleep or at least try to. But would she really be able to sleep in light of all this, in the bed she had shared with River the night before?

What do I do? Where do I go?

"Mesukui sa abain." She sighed. ⟨*Let's git somethin' to eat.*⟩ It was no good worrying on an empty stomach, after all.

Through the darkening streets, skirting the edge of the agricultural fields, she made for the dockside and the comforting lights of Daikokuya. With a sigh, she headed inside, found a booth, and placed her order with one of the sprightly dolls who worked the counter: *gyōza* ramen and a bottle of Aterui beer. At least, for the moment, that much was simple enough for her to put into words.

Her order arrived, two bowls set down with accompanying drinks. Out of the corner of her eye, she spotted a familiar hand.

"Well now, Princess," she heard—in English, as if for added bluntness. "You look a right mess. And it looks like you really stepped in it today."

Kasu looked up into Akiko's narrowed eyes, strangely vulpine, as she settled in across the table.

"Miyakozawa-*san*. Hello." Kasu sighed dejectedly, not daring to hold eye contact. "It seems you know what's going on already."

"As we have often said, it's our business to know things. And besides, I told you, and my doll told you, we need discretion, not a hammer."

"You did." Kasu nodded. "You both did."

"So with that much understood, Princess, did I ask *you* to go to Tokyo in person." It was not a question, but a statement of fact, calm—but sharply worded enough to draw blood. The solitary Wielder found herself unable to hold the Witch's gaze for more than a few moments.

"You did not," she confirmed. "You said speed was of the essence, and I-I'm not sure I know what I did."

For a moment, the red-haired Witch seemed ready to say something, to spit it out red hot, but then thought better of it. She sighed, leaning forward to steeple her fingers, seeming to weigh her words carefully.

"All right, look. Let me ask you something. Why did you come back to Japan?"

Kasu stared blankly. "Nanusu ya?" ⟨*What was that?*⟩

"Naze Nihon ni modotta no deshō?" ⟨*Why did you return to Japan?*⟩ She gestured at Kasu's meal. "Don't stand on ceremony. Eat up while you think it over."

"I came back in 2011, after the tsunami, to lead the company's efforts to dig the region out."

"And then what?"

"We . . . worked with the SDF and the US military and helped dig the region out, and then I took on this leadership role at Santaku Dynamics. Why do you ask?"

"And then what?" Akiko pressed.

And then what?

It was a good question, even if it was a frustrating one, and Kasu wasn't entirely sure *why* it felt like a good question. What *had* happened afterward? How *had* she spent the past decade?

"What are you getting at, Miyakozawa-*san*?"

The redhead finished a piece of fried tofu and gently set her chopsticks down.

"*Think*, Princess. I'm trying to get you to *think*. I'm trying to get you to consider that you might be missing a measure of perspective. I'm trying to get you to consider that perhaps there's something you've been missing all this time."

Kasu swirled a loose *gyōza* around her ramen bowl. The distance between her head, her hands, the tip of the chopsticks, and the bowl blurred. "And what's that?"

"I'll ask you again." The redhead sighed. "When I sent you that information the other day, did I ask *you* to go to Tokyo in person?"

"No . . . no, you did not."

"But you went, regardless," Akiko countered. "And now, you're back here alone. Why?"

It all flashed through Kasu's memory: River's eyes. The narrow streets. The short, sharp fight.

"Why don't you tell me?" she spat. "*You're* in the business of knowing things!"

Akiko was about to say something, but again, she paused, held up a hand, and collected her thoughts.

"You're dodging the question," she said finally.

"Because there was no time to waste!" the harried Wielder hissed. "We got what we came for, sure, and we thought we were being careful, sure, but then we got jumped, and I dropped the bag, and I—"

Akiko sighed and again steepled her fingers. "With all due respect, Princess, how on earth have you gotten to head one of Japan's preeminent combat doll companies without cultivating a better understanding of when to hold your tongue, listen, and delegate? I think there's more to you than just a clueless rich girl who thinks she can just leap headlong into everything. Is that hope mistaken? Your habit of leaping into things and hoping that inertia or enough money will smooth out your landing is not going to be a recipe for long-term success, and it's going to hurt people. Sometimes, like in 2011, it does good things, I'll admit. Other times, like today, it does quite the opposite."

There was a long, tense silence between the two women. Kasu's gaze fell, her cheeks flushing.

The narrow streets. River's eyes.

The *futility*.

"I'm sorry."

"That's good, but I don't think I'm the one who deserves an apology and better choices from you." It was simple, gentle statement of fact, but it still stung. Akiko picked up her bowl and drank deeply of what remained. Setting it down, she rose, readying to pay the tab before taking her leave. Kasu met her gaze.

"Made kesain." ⟨*Please wait.*⟩

The redhead peered down at her, quietly scrutinizing her expression before she spoke.

"Do you wish to be taught?"

Kasu nodded. "Hondonu, zehi oseede kesain." ⟨*Truly, I'm beggin' ya to teach me.*⟩

With a heavy sigh, Akiko sat back down.

"Then here's where we begin," the redhead instructed. "Tell me—in your own words, as best you can—what happened in Tokyo today. And then if you have any shred of humility, Princess, hold your tongue and listen to me."

FIFTEEN

Child of Exile

Out of the oblivion of unconsciousness, River sat up with a gasp, straining against leaden limbs and the anchor of a diagnostic cable. She had been out in the open air, in the dark and twisting streets of Ōta City, fighting to buy time for Kasu to escape, but now she was not. The room was alien, but she could not see anything through the blur that was most of her field of vision, though she could swear that there were people looking at her, and her body was aching, ready to run, ready to tear, ready to fight.

"Okita," said an unfamiliar voice from beyond the little of her surroundings the doll could resolve. ⟨She's awake.⟩

"Hanase!" River screamed. "Hanase to iu ni!" ⟨Release me! I said let me go!⟩

River's vision swam. Her HUD was still there, so she could figure out which way was up, and it was flashing emergency alert notifications left and right, but she could not make a connection with the rest of the Internet, and the steady drip-drop of ambient information and comms was absent. It took a moment further for her to recognize the emptiness where she would normally be registering the interlink's current. It should have been on by now.

"Kasu-*sama* . . ."

The fight. Her fear. Their last moment of connection.

"Kasu-*sama*!"

"Well, this is quite the surprise," said an unfamiliar voice, beyond River's field of vision. "I sent people out on an errand, and they've brought me something even better than a set of Nogami drives. They've brought me quite the unique guest."

The doll reached an arm into the blurry space beyond her fingertips, but only pawed at empty space.

"Oh, don't trouble yourself with that, little doll. You're quite safe here, and I'm quite beyond the reach of those clever, clever hands. So just lay still now; it'll all be better soon."

"Don't 'little doll' me, you piece of shit," River spat. "I'm not *your* doll."

There was a pause.

"No, no, you aren't. Not yet anyway. But even the work of the illustrious House Isawa has its weaknesses and its limits, and it can be unmade. Do you really want to be so quick as to dash yourself against those limits, little doll?"

Around the dull throbbing of her head, River remembered that last moment in Kōgyō-machi. Meeting eyes with Kasu, hoping that—even without words and without the interlink—she could still communicate that one imperative command: *Run.*

Had she made it? Had she survived? Was she back in Sendai already?

Whatever the answer, River knew that as long as she herself was alive and operational, then something of Kasu lived too.

Living—and for now, waiting—was her duty. Slowly, she let herself exhale and relax.

"That's better," said the disembodied voice of her unfamiliar host. "Rest now, little doll. You're safe here, and you are my guest."

Exhaustion—or so River surmised—was her inner undertow now.

Yes, she would rest. Living and waiting were her duty. And in time, if the homeward stars aligned, they would allow her to fight on—maybe even return to her Wielder's side.

As sleep took her, River hung on to the words of the oath she had sworn long ago.

Here and now, before you and my gods, I swear service in battle, in the home, and in bed.

Here and now, I swear to be your sword, your comfort, your right hand, the instrument of your will.

Here and now, I swear to care for myself, for this, too, is service.

Here and now, I swear to tear the heavens and earth apart if you should command it.

You are the Wielder, and I am the blade.

As long as we stand as one heart together, we are unstoppable.

Sitting perched on the edge of the paper-sheeted examination table, River looked from Dr. Robbins to the dignified but subtly frazzled Japanese woman with a contractor badge at her hip.

"River, this is Dr. Isawa Kasu from Santaku USA. She's here to check on patient satisfaction with the new prostheses."

River gave a little half wave in greeting. "Um, hi."

The woman nodded and extended a hand. "Captain Eginian, it's good to meet you."

River looked down at her new hands—hands that finally seemed a lot more like her own. Just as soft as the organic skin on her original limbs had been yet a lot quicker to respond. The panel lines and mechanical joints had a strange charm to them.

She flexed and unflexed her synthskin fingertips and new mechanical joints. She took the newcomer's hand and shook it firmly.

"Kochira koso." ⟨*The pleasure is mine.*⟩

There was a note of surprise in the newcomer's eyes at River's sudden pivot into Japanese.

"Ara, Nihongo jōzu!" ⟨*My, such good Japanese!*⟩

"Iieiie, madamada." River chuckled. "Demo ningyō no Santaku kara jikijiki no omimai wa nanka bikkuri." ⟨*No, no, I'm still working on it. But to be personally visited by Santaku of doll fame is a bit of a surprise.*⟩

"I'm not here to make you into a doll, Captain." Dr. Isawa chuckled, waving a hand. "That's not all we do. I'm here to see how you're doing."

River thought about her long, strange journey. From the battle on the banks of the old Euphrates—where her ancestors had once fought—to a hospital in Germany, where she had been pulled back from the brink, to discharge and then to surgery and rehab in greater Seattle.

Now, she was at the VA for a checkup after being fitted with hands and legs that felt . . .

"Whole," River finally said with a smile. "I feel whole."

Distantly, the sound of waves.

River awoke from long-ago dreams to the feeling of soft sheets over the firmness of tatami, in a room that smelled faintly of salt.

"Shit, man, is this day ever gonna end?" River muttered, sitting up slowly, rubbing at tired temples. Her own clothes gone, she was dressed in a light *yukata*.

"Fuck, I just want to go home."

Rest now, little doll. You're safe here.

Who *was* her not-so-gracious host? And how had River gotten from Ōta City to . . . wherever she had first come to and now this tatami room?

With a grunt of exertion, River rolled off the futon and to her feet. The window nearby, with its blinds drawn, was cracked slightly, and the sound of waves did not seem far.

The doll squinted and shaded her eyes with her hand. Distantly, she could see a blue ocean under a sky with just a few puffy white clouds, beyond the walls of a stately residential compound. Subtropical trees swayed in a gentle breeze.

Something was missing, but only after a while did River notice. She stumbled back from the window, consumed by a sickening corkscrew of horror.

"My HUD! Fuck, my *hands*!"

Flex, unflex. Flex, unflex. Her hands were flesh and sinew and bone, just like they had been so many years ago. A hand to the nape of her neck registered nothing but skin and close-cropped stubble where the panel lines of her diagnostic port should have been.

"Shit, fuck!"

She stumbled toward the nearest sliding door and tugged the handle, to no avail. One hand, then two hands, but the door would not budge.

Her heart leaped to her throat. She had to get out, had

to get away, had to find out what had happened in Tokyo—and how to fight on. She tugged at the handle again, then fell to her knees in a heap.

"It can't end like this. It won't end like this. Fuck, fuck."

With an inchoate scream of rage, River wound back and slammed a fist against the door. Traditional sliding doors of this sort were light by design, for ease of swapping and removal as needed. They would not have withstood a full-on punch, should have fallen right out of their grooves, but this door would not budge.

She was breathless now, throwing herself shoulder-first at the door, trying to batter it open. Once, twice, three times, all to no avail.

In her desperation and pain, the doll sank to the tatami, aching all over again.

"Tear. Tear." She repeated the word as she rubbed at pained joints, turned the word over in her mouth as if it was her last vestige of defense. "Tear. Swear to tear the heavens and earth apart."

And in what could only be described as irony on a celestial order, the door slid open, smoothly and easily.

It seemed that she had a visitor.

"Ah, you're awake! Her Ladyship has need of you—oh dear, why this state?"

River could scarcely bring herself to look up at the visitor, barely registering the muscular legs peeking out from a summer-weight kimono.

"Why?" River rasped pleadingly. "Why?"

"Because you're her guest, and you've only just arrived. It's for your own protection. We can't have you wandering off before you've properly recovered, now can we?" The visitor's arms were strong, and as she picked River up from the floor, the doll noticed sleeve tattoos peeking out.

"There we go."

"My clothes. My arms. My augments. What's happening?" River pleaded. "Why? Why is—why?"

"You don't have any need of that here. That's not the kind of place this is."

"What does that even—"

"Come on; there's a change of clothes in the closet, and the bathroom is just outside the door. I'll step out and let you get ready. Then we can see about making introductions."

Enough clarity returned to River to look up at her unexpected benefactor.

"Thanks, I-I guess."

"You can call me Tora."

"Tora-*san*. I'm—"

Her visitor smiled. "I know who you are! You're River, and Her Ladyship is really interested in you."

"Dare, sore?" ⟨*Who's that?*⟩

Tora looked over her shoulder, and River could have sworn she saw a note of worry.

"I-I think that's best for her to answer," Tora hurriedly replied. "You get dressed and cleaned up. I'll wait for you in the hall."

The door slid smoothly shut, and River was alone again. In a daze, the doll stumbled to another door on the far wall. She hesitated, but found it slid open easily to reveal a wardrobe. *Her* wardrobe—from home in Ishinomaki.

"So, let's go over what we've got again," River muttered, hunched over the shelves inside the open door. "I'm missing my cybernetics, doors open and don't open for no rhyme or reason, and now my wardrobe is *here*. Something doesn't smell right."

What was happening? How did any of this make sense? River was not sure. There had to be some explanation for it, even if she could not see it yet.

Still, thankful for small mercies like her own wardrobe, the wayward doll got dressed, washed up, and met Tora in the hall. After collecting herself, River was surprised at something she had not noticed about Tora at first glance.

"What's wrong?"

"You're a doll too, aren't you?"

Tora cocked her head. "What gave it away?"

"Base-model humans don't have eyes or hair in quite that shade. And you have *oni* horns."

"I forget sometimes." Tora chuckled, brushing a hand through her subtly iridescent hair and around the short horns peeking out from it. She shook her head, snapping back to focus. "But we should hurry. She's expecting you."

"Yes, yes." River sighed. "Her Ladyship."

They headed down long hallways with impeccably mirror-smooth floorboards. From the second floor down to the first, they passed manicured rock gardens. Occasionally, they passed other people who showed no signs of noticing them. The halls and verandas stretched on for what felt like forever.

The duo emerged into the sunlight beside a lively pool, with music and a crowd gathered around a poolside bar. At one of the bistro tables by the compound wall sat a short woman in a sun hat and sunglasses, surrounded by a group of what looked like base-model humans.

Tora stepped ahead of River and bowed.

"Okata-sama, kyaku no tōchaku desu." ⟨*Your Ladyship, the guest has just arrived.*⟩

The woman set down her drink, tipped back her hat, slipped off her sunglasses, and rose. She was within arm's reach of River as she peered up to scrutinize the doll.

"So, this is our little doll guest from the illustrious House Isawa of Ishinomaki. She cleans up quite nicely, doesn't she?"

Little doll. The voice from her first waking after the fight.

"You'll pardon me if I don't share in your merriment, but I don't believe we've been properly introduced," the doll hissed through teeth gritted, words sharp enough to draw blood. "*Ma'am.*"

"Then let me do so now. I am Yakumaru Sakae," the woman said. "This is my estate. You're lucky I intervened and had you brought here. My people can be . . . exceedingly sharp, at times, even if they're efficient in what they do for me. Don't worry—as long as you're here, you're safe, little doll. You're far too valuable to harm a single blue hair on that pretty head."

She reached for River's cheek, but the doll intercepted it with her own deftly placed hand. She would not surrender.

"Sono usugitanai te de sawaru na," River growled. ⟨*Don't touch me with those filthy hands.*⟩

Sakae tilted her head back, peered up at River, and simply chuckled.

"Is that so? Well now, we'll see."

SIXTEEN

Bury Your Heart

The container, wherever it had come from, had been a godsend, and Masuya Heisuke was not about to look a gift horse in the mouth.

Even a decade after the 2011 tsunami, some things were still turning up. Be it in once lawsuit-deadlocked points of recovery and reconstruction, or in things that simply washed back with enough time and with the whims of the ocean tide. When the container turned up, Masuya dismissed it at first. This happened all the time, so why bother? When he was informed that it contained not only Nogami miscellanea—binders, old office goods, and the like—but an entire Nogami doll, his interest was piqued.

Wherever the container had come from, whoever had sealed it had done an outstanding job. The contents were immaculate.

He could have used this himself, to be sure. The parts would fetch a tidy sum—but no, there was a method to these things, an order to them. The return on investment, albeit later than he would have preferred, would make this worth the effort and wait.

Where had this been? He was not sure. Nogami had already been gone for a decade when the tsunami hit northern Honshu, so perhaps this was from a storage facility in Sendai or Ishinomaki port—unclaimed all this time, until it reached his network's attention.

Ishinomaki.

That bitch from Santaku was still making noise across the bay, but Masuya was unconcerned. She would not get far if all she was looking at was here, and he was content to let her keep chasing her tail. Besides, someone in her position had their own business to mind, so eventually, business concerns would win out and curtail further exploration on her part. What did Nogami dolls truly matter to someone who ran a business with cushy government contracts and its own line of superior merchandise?

Really, he owed Isawa Kasu a paradoxical debt of gratitude. Thanks to what she had divulged during her outburst in his office, Masuya had sent not one but two Nogami dolls up the chain.

In Japan at large, other, more powerful forces prevailed, and they always had. Santaku had its little independent fiefdom carved out, but this went beyond it.

In Miyagi, Masuya Heisuke would *remain* Nogami, under the protection of those powerful forces.

Even the illustrious House Isawa and its loose-cannon daughter would not stand in the way of that.

Stay sharp, Kasu inwardly reminded herself. *Stick to the plan.*

It was not every day that Kasu was in Santaku Headquarters's main building, much less in front of a packed meeting hall with her brother Kagekiyo at her left and one of the company lawyers at her right.

This building was originally the great hall of what had once been her ancestors' feudal estate, although it had been modernized and expanded over the century and a half that followed. Today, it was the face that her family business presented to the world: a seamless blend of traditional aesthetic and cutting-edge technology. The meeting hall, one of the largest spaces in the main building, still evoked the old estate's great hall, in some of its design cues and with its use of cypress.

After her brother delivered remarks in Japanese about the situation, it was Kasu's turn to speak. She leaned over the podium, looking out over the reporters and livestreaming cameras in the conference room.

"To follow on from my earlier remarks in Japanese, and my brother's comments on our cooperation with the MPD, I'm going to offer a few remarks in English to sum all of this up for the international press, and so that the world can know the incident that happened in Tokyo a few days ago."

That last moment flashed through her mind's eye: the determination in River's eyes, despite her fear. Kasu took a deep breath to steel herself and then carried on. There was a job to be done, and she needed to do her part.

"Several days ago, I was in Tokyo Metropolis's Ōta City on business with my partner, River Victoria M59A1. We were exploring local secondhand markets to better understand their current state and to better serve both our own research needs and development efforts for all dolls, not just those we build and convert ourselves. During this trip, we were assaulted. It was because of my partner's actions that I was able to narrowly escape. By some miracle, I emerged without injury. She disappeared, and I doubt that she was as lucky as myself. Efforts to locate her remain, as of now, unresolved, and a search is still underway.

"Some may ask why I did not involve the Metropolitan Police until I had no other choice. First, this is because of my own shock in the wake of this incident. Second, because it would not help to find a doll I saw taken before my own two eyes. Third, because I further argue that this is a problem that demands regulation and legislation on the part of the government more than it does the intervention of one police department for one human and her doll partner. Even as we work to bring my partner home, I will be lobbying members of the Miyagi Prefecture delegation to the National Diet to propose and enact such legislation. The secondhand and aftermarket sectors are important to the economy and to the needs of dolls. And if my doll and I can be overpowered by forces like that, then we are letting down others who are far less able to afford a defense and search, let alone summon a press conference and legal aid like this to spread the word. But even here and now, we at Santaku Group have always believed that helping dolls in need is not just our business but our duty.

"And to those that did this, I have only the following to say: We will find you, and we will bring you the fullest consequences under the law for this heinous act. So wash your necks and wait."

She let those last words hang in the air, allowing them to sink in, here, as in every place that she was or would be seen.

"Now, questions?"

Once the media had mostly cleared out, Kasu and Kagekiyo walked together into the courtyard that lay before the main hall, with a couple of Santaku's security staff following at a discreet, respectful distance.

Kasu held her head high. She would ordinarily be in her element, but things were different now, and the stakes were high.

The siblings walked in silence for a time. The urgency of the situation rightly weighed in the spaces between the words that had been said, but it weighed heavier in the silences. The two of them, along with their younger brother, Kageshige, held a mutual respect for one another and always had. Beneath the surface, though, there had always been a gulf between the brothers and their sister and their perspectives, especially on more personal matters. Kasu had always been the lone out-and-proud queer Isawa, after all. Ultimately, they tried to always show a due measure of unity, especially when outsiders were watching.

All the same, Kasu admired and respected Kagekiyo. He had agreed to take on the roles she had refused in her quest to be herself, no matter what. The company had prospered under his stable, reliable leadership; he was ambitious, and a lot less prone to leaping headfirst into things as Kasu had been. However, two long decades in this role had left their mark, and although he was two years younger than Kasu, his hair was grayer than hers.

As they walked, Kasu remembered Akiko's suggestion.

It is our opinion that it would be best positioned to face that challenge with you at the helm.

Might the day come when he would want to step aside?

"Dō da?" Kagekiyo asked quietly. "Keyaki to no katsudō wa." ⟨*How is it? The work with Keyaki.*⟩

"Miyakozawa-san no koto nara, tokidoki wakaranai

yarikata daga, imada shinrai dekisou to omou." ⟨*If you mean Miyakozawa-san, sometimes I don't understand her way of doing things, but I think we can still rely on her all the same.*⟩

He pursed his lips in thought for a moment, then chuckled knowingly.

"Rui wa tomo o yobu tte iu yatsu da naa." ⟨*Birds of a feather and all that.*⟩

Kasu laughed. "Sō kamoshirenai ne!" ⟨*I guess so!*⟩

He shook his head, his expression in deathly earnest. "Kore kara MPD no koto mo jikan kasegi no hō mo ore ni makasero, aneki. Omae wa Miyakozawa-san to issho, omou zonbun ni tatakae." ⟨*From here on out, leave the MPD and the buying of time to me, Sister. You fight on with Miyakozawa-san to your heart's content.*⟩

For a moment, Kasu felt a surge of frustration but held her tongue. There was more at stake than her own pride, and she would do anything it took to bring River back.

"Kanarazu ya waga hamono o kaeshite miseru," she declared. ⟨*I'll bring my blade back; just you watch.*⟩

Brother and sister parted ways with a nod. Only when she reached the safety of her own vestibule and paused to slip off her flats did Kasu finally allow herself to exhale.

"Tadaima keeddabe," she called out. ⟨*I just got back.*⟩ It was tradition, even if it felt hollow, given the circumstances.

"Okaerinasai, ohimesama yo," came the reply from the living room, tinged *slightly* with snark that was rapidly growing familiar. ⟨*Welcome back, Princess.*⟩

Kasu made for the living room. Seated at the working table by the bookcases, Akiko pored over the projection on her cyberdeck, idly nibbling at edamame as she worked.

"Give me some good news," Kasu pleaded, settling in across the table. She buried her face in her hands, exhaling heavily. "I could use it."

"How did the press conference go?" the redhead asked, eyes still on the projection.

"Well enough, is my guess. But well enough is all we need, isn't it? Given that you've got things in motion. You do have things in motion, right?"

The redhead deftly flicked from one workspace projection to another, which bore a map of air and sea traffic in northeastern Japan.

"Yes. Luckily for us, the pieces are already in motion." She gestured to a highlighted contact, south of Sendai Bay and in slow motion to the southwest. "All you have to do is keep doing what you do best—wait and make lots of waves—while we take care of this end. Quietly, for now."

"Ojama shimasu." *‹Sorry to intrude.›*

Dressed but a bit disheveled and looking sleepless, Tomoka—Yui's human partner—wandered into the living room with a yawn. Akiko looked over her shoulder and acknowledged the newcomer with a polite nod.

"Ott-to, Sugawara-san, ohayō. Okoshiteshimatte suman." *‹Ope, Ms. Sugawara. Good morning. Sorry to have woken you.›*

"Heiki, heiki." She waved off the concern, yawning again and shaking her head. "Ki ni shinakute ii sa." She continued onward to the kitchen. *‹I'm fine. Fine. Don't worry about it.›*

Kasu frowned. Hard on the heels of River's disappearance, Yui had also gone missing. Unlike Kasu, Tomoka had gone first to the prefectural police, whose search was ongoing but had yet to turn up any sign of the missing baker doll. After that, it was all Kasu could do to talk Tomoka into making the trek out to Ishinomaki. At least here, behind the walls of Santaku Headquarters, Kasu could keep her safe.

She had tried her best to keep Tomoka informed of the situation at hand. She could not prove a connection between River's and Yui's disappearances yet, but all the same, Kasu felt she owed it.

Either way, Tomoka was a friend and she was in need.

"Tonikaku, kore made wa keikaku dōri da," Akiko remarked, gesturing back at the display. ⟨*At any rate, we're on track so far.*⟩

"Sore nara . . ." ⟨*So that means . . .*⟩

"Aa." Akiko nodded. "Masuya wa meu amado no esa o kuitsuitarashii. Kore kara wa matsu shika nai." ⟨*Yeah. Looks like Masuya took the bait* meu amado *laid. Not much to do for now but wait.*⟩

Kasu nodded in understanding. Zee was the bait, carefully planted where Masuya's men would find it and pass it along. The two had been monitoring Masuya for longer than Kasu had originally thought, and inasmuch as she had her doubts initially, she knew now it was best to defer leadership on this point to her business partner, who was fast becoming a new mentor.

"So, I have to ask," Kasu said to Akiko. "How did you get Masuya to take the bait in the first place?"

Akiko glanced over her shoulder, then leaned in. "First, lower your voice, Princess. Second, you'd be surprised what that man and his subordinates will agree to if they're plied with enough cheap sake and expensive shōchū. We had the container ready ahead of time, and in the end, his own greed is what dropped him squarely into our grasp. Zee is no ordinary Nogami-type doll. If I'm right—and I think I am—things are about to get very interesting."

"Yabai hito da, Miyakozawa-san wa." ⟨*You're incredible, Miyakozawa-san.*⟩

The redhead chuckled. "Maa, himesama no ohome ni

azukatte kōei desu." ⟨My, I'm honored to have your praise, Princess.⟩

The redhead swiped at the projection, dismissing it, before leaning across the table, fingers steepled.

"The time ahead is going to be critical, if we want to get to the bottom of this and bring your doll and mine back. We cannot mess this up. We cannot shake things up prematurely. This is critical. So say it back to me, Kasu-*san*, for my own peace of mind. Promise me you're going to wait."

Her cheeks burned with embarrassment, but Kasu knew that this was for her own good—for the sake of her growth and for the sake of ending this crisis.

"I am going to wait," the solitary Wielder replied dutifully. "Yakusoku da." ⟨Promise.⟩

"Good. That is a beginning."

The ride had been trying, to say the least; air cargo containers and aviation cargo holds were not the most comfortable accommodations. However, the mission was in motion, and there was a clear set of tasks ahead and much to be done.

After offloading, at long last, the air cargo container's hatch swung open, offering a glimpse of the world outside.

It was sunny and humid, humid enough that it was safe to assume that this was far from Sendai. The smell of warm tarmac filled Zee's nose, and a breeze finally rustled its tail fur. It stilled itself as best it could as a doll clambered up over the other things beside it, peering down in curiosity.

Zee watched impassively, with its connectivity to the net turned off in the interest of discretion, noting its observations to itself. That iridescent hair. That pattern of panel lines on the arms. Both were unmistakable: this was an Agatsuma-type doll. There were not many in the Tohoku region. And Zee *had* traveled far . . .

"Mō mitsukatta ka?" came a voice from outside the container. *‹Have you found it yet?›*

"Hai!" the Agatsuma briskly replied. "Migoto na Nogami-gata, mitsukattari! Shippo mo hada mo kanpeki da." *‹Yes! I've found a splendid Nogami type! And with splendid skin and tail too.›*

"Hayaku—gosō da! Sore o sundara hoka no naiyō no kataroggingu." *‹We should transport it quickly! After that comes cataloging the rest of the contents.›*

The Agatsuma doll glanced over its shoulder and saluted. "Ryōkai!" *‹Roger!›*

Several pairs of strong hands picked up Zee and laid it on what felt like a wheeled dolly, moving it out of the shadow of the container and into the momentarily blinding sunlight and blue sky above. Palm trees obscured the edge of its field of vision.

A short-haired human, minimally augmented at first glance, peered down into its eyes. "Migoto. Aa, kore wa meisaku ni chigai nai," the human murmured approvingly. "Nan to sugureta gikō da. Nn, kono ningyō wa yūeki ni kimatta." *‹Remarkable. Oh, this looks like a masterpiece! Such craftsmanship! Yes, this doll will be most useful indeed.›*

Even without the ability to link up to the net and cross-reference what it was seeing, Zee knew that face well. It recognized it from its study of business rivals, and others active in the information-security sphere, in greater or smaller part. If this was the person who was at or closer to the center of both the Nogami crisis and River's disappearance, then it was more progress than Zee had expected—especially so soon.

Even if it knew its location was subject to passive tracking, it was eager to make a report back to its Witch to confirm this news.

It was looking into the probing eyes of the reclusive shipping magnate, Yakumaru Sakae.

SEVENTEEN

Polaris Unbowed

The sun slipped west over the Ōu Mountains. The reception was only beginning when Kasu and River arrived at the bar. They had eschewed their usual working attire: the Wielder in a tight sheath dress, the doll in a full, circle-skirted off-shoulder dress that showed off her colorfully inked tattoo sleeves.

They had come together to the reception in downtown Sendai, and from the beginning, even those who did not know them had no doubt who and what they were. It was in the bearing of the subtly graying, kind-eyed Wielder, and how even when they stood apart from each other, the blue-maned combat doll was never too far from her. It was in the doll's sleeve tattoo—a trio of blades encircled by two-fold blossoms, softness and sharpness in harmony. The Wielder's crest: the two of them, one heart together.

It was bliss. It was belonging.

It was home.

But something was not quite right. The blade could not resolve anybody's faces, including her Wielder's. Some-where between the salmon canapés and the *kushiyaki*, awash in endorphins and the slight buzz from a couple of shots of sake from the old brewery up the road in Shiogama—the doll realized she was being watched.

Watched intently by the one across the room.

Yakumaru Sakae.

River sat up in bed with a gasp.

Another dream of home turned into a nightmare. One dream after another had been like this. How long had she been like this? Days? Weeks? Time did not mean much anymore.

Outside the window came that steady sound of waves, the start of the same rhythm as ever. It had been calming, once, but now it seemed to mock her. Would it ever end?

The knock on her door was the same too, although it was one of the few things she actually did not mind. It had become custom: the knock, the moment she would take to arrange herself just enough, sit up a little straighter, before she said, "Haire." ⟨*Enter.*⟩

The door would slide open, smoothly and easily, and Tora would duck in with a polite nod of the head.

"Good morning, River."

"Ohayou, Tora-san," River would reply, with the nearest thing to an honest smile she could muster in this place. ⟨*Good morning, Tora.*⟩

It grew a little more bittersweet every time. *How's Yui doing?* River wondered. Even if work kept them too busy to meet up in person most of the time, they had talked all the time via direct messages, and River missed her friend. She had been one of the first to call River *Hamono-san.*

What I wouldn't give for a "Miss Blade" right about now.

Tora had been her guide and her customary companion from the ordeal's start. She was an Agatsuma-type doll, a make less common in northern Honshu. She had been in service to Sakae for more than a decade, she said. Initially, River assumed Tora had a similar role to her own—a protector and right hand—and she was wary of her for a time. Eventually, from all River had gathered, things were not quite so simple. She had the trappings of a retainer, but at times, she seemed like something else. It was little things, like her body language, that made it apparent.

The compound—the estate and its walls—seemed to stretch on for ages. The more she explored, the less she seemed to go anywhere, and at last, River gave up. How wealthy *was* her magnanimous, yet always vaguely threatening host, that she could afford this kind of lavish residence? *Where* was this to begin with? Why was she still no closer to a clear answer about the Nogami crisis?

Nobody in the compound was forthcoming about much. Nobody seemed willing to answer whether she was being held captive. They were courteous, but they were cagey, and some almost seemed to be walking on eggshells. Even if River might have thought she was not a prisoner at first, she more or less was one now. For that matter, nobody seemed to have a desktop, a laptop, or even so much as a smartphone. It was like being in the ass end of nowhere, with no connection to anything.

Time began to drag.

It was not that there was a lack of excitement. On the contrary, there were regular visitors, catchy music, good food—and all of it presided over by Sakae herself.

Usually, Sakae was there, dressed for the poolside, but occasionally River would see her arrive—from seemingly out of nowhere—in business attire or formal kimono. She would soon be in summer dress and sun hat, holding court around the pool, as something—River was not quite sure—played on a TV mounted to the wall. She could never quite hold her attention for long enough to figure out what was happening.

Something was missing, but she could not quite put her finger on it. With no internet connection, no wireless interface, and not even so much as a door through the wall, what tools did she have at her disposal? What could she meaningfully do to break through?

It was ironic.

When she was small, people in her family's church used to call River and her kinfolk *Panerekes*. The children of thunder. They had meant it as a criticism: an accusation of being too noisy, of taking up what they deemed to be too much space, but River had always carried it proudly. Now, tired and worn down in pleasant, endless confinement, what did thundering mean? What could it mean, in this land of pleasant climes and endless walls and corridors? What was truly within her reach?

She and Sakae did not speak much on an average day. When they did, it was courteous to a fault—so heavy with smugness on the Sakae's end, and cold, polite hostility on River's end—it was like an épée duel.

River had learned a little bit about her along the way. She was in the shipping business, she said she was a lover of dolls, and she was particular about her privacy.

She had something to do with the missing dolls and the missing data, but what?

Think, River. Think.

One day, while River and Tora ate lunch on the veranda overlooking one of the rock gardens, River asked, "So, where are you from?"

Tora visibly flinched. She set down the chopsticks on

her serving tray beside the little dish of pickled ginger, and took a deep, quieting breath.

"Sorry," she mouthed.

"No, no, I'm sorry," River apologized.

"You're a good doll, River. I want you to be safe here."

River sighed. "Safe, huh?"

On the sides of the rock garden's artfully arranged boulders, the moss grew. All perfectly comfortable, with a subtle undertow of discomfort. All seemingly safe, with a subtle undertow of danger. Day into night into day, over and over and over.

There was an answer here, but it was unspoken.

That night, River dreamed again of home.

Closely matching Kasu's stride, she walked up the Miyagi Prefecture Library's portico steps with a steady tread, looking up in awe at how the glass panels of its curved roof glimmered in the midday sun. After the long drive out from Ishinomaki and the train ride up from downtown Sendai, it was always good to be here at last; the sight of the library's facade was magnificent.

The Wielder looked over her shoulder at her doll. With a playful smirk, she said, "You know your excitement's half the fun of coming here, doll. I can feel the giddy coming off you, and not just over the interlink. It's really adorable."

"The more things change . . ." The doll nodded with a sheepish grin, not realizing that she could not resolve her Wielder's face. "As far as you're concerned, I'm the proverbial open book, Kasu-*sama*."

Even if her excitement in coming here was plain, River had been diligent in her duties. She was still on duty after all, her Purpose embodied in the Wielder's person and mission. Aside from their working tablets and USB drives, tea bottles and lunch for both of them were in the bag slung across her back, along with spare batteries for their phones. There was her Wielder's stationery and tools as well. But Purpose aside, it was always a joy coming to a library, and the prefectural library in Izumi Ward was a favorite.

Izumi Ward—once its own city, annexed by Sendai during the municipal consolidations of the late 1980s—lay on the prefectural capital's north side. Sendai had always boasted the epithet "Mori no Miyako"—⟨*City of Forests*⟩. While downtown, with its zelkova-lined boulevards, was plenty green, in Izumi Ward, the trees grew wilder, even around the measure of urban sprawl that reached here. Cryptomeria, pine, oak, maple, and zelkova trees—all were abundant. The trees, planted during the postwar reforestation program, grew tall around the library complex. They had not quite reached the library's curved roof, which rose bow-like over them, but River surmised that they would before long.

River turned to Kasu. "Oh, by the way, ma'am, on the way up, I thought of a poem on the subway."

The Wielder cocked her head. "Ndabe?" ⟨*That so?*⟩

"It goes like this." The doll nodded, pausing to clear her throat before she began.

"Manabiya no / mori no miyako o / otozuremu / Ōmori o tatsu / kokeshi to aruji." ⟨*To visit the City of Forests, / that place of learning, / they depart Ōmori in company: / the doll and She who commands her.*⟩

They were up the steps, through the portico, and past the circulation desk. The Wielder smiled in appreciation. "Ii dabe, kokesu yo. Kandō shitanossha." ⟨*That was purdy good, doll o' mine. I'm impressed.*⟩

Poetry always seemed to come to the doll in some of the most mundane moments—but the mundane was where so much of the magic was, was it not?

At the lobby's center—flanked by the circulation desk, new book display, and self-service checkout—a wooden kokeshi made back in the Taishō era a century ago stood sentinel over the library's patrons as they came and went. Despite its sheer size, its bright colors and peaceful expression seemed to beckon patrons' reassurance and ease.

It was not a doll in the modern sense, but a sculpture—or so its maker had intended. The sculptor, Ōeda Akira, was one of that era's preeminent makers of *kokeshi* in the historic style, his trade saved by the devoted work of local humans fighting to save handcrafts in danger of vanishing. But it was a *kokeshi* nonetheless—and after all, at the end of the day, was not a doll simply a doll?

Today, *kokeshi* applied broadly to any doll, but historically, *kokeshi* was a type of wooden doll. These dolls had been first; they had paved the way for River and her kind of cybernetic dolls—synthetic and ex-human alike—that had followed much later. With all of that in the back of her mind, every time she passed through here, the blade always felt obliged to pause and bow respectfully to the elder doll that had come before.

"Senpai. Ohayo gozarisu." ⟨*Senpai. G'mornin'.*⟩

The Wielder paused and likewise bowed in greeting to the doll that embodied the common history of all the dolls that came from this prefecture. Her family's work, for several generations, had been set in motion by these original *kokeshi*, after all.

River looked up again at the lavender-haired kokeshi. Its body was a patchwork of parts, and it had an American assault rifle slung across an ill-fitting plate carrier.

She did not remember the doll in the atrium being the spitting image of Yui, but some things, apparently, had changed.

Tugging smartly at her jacket, the Wielder beckoned to her blade to follow.

"C'mon, doll. We've got books to snag and correspondence to attend to. Let's get to work."

River fell in smoothly behind her Wielder, and the two headed up onto the main floor, to its long ranks of stacks that sat basking under the subtly diffused sun through the skylights. The air had a hint of book dust and ink. The doll smiled and dismissed most of her HUD projection.

It was not just that people—human or otherwise—tried to be quiet nor that there was not much going on. It seemed the right thing to do on its own, because of how the space and the learning it housed humbled her. Even before she was a doll, through both her military career and her scholarly life, libraries had that effect on her, and she relished it.

Small. River felt comfortingly small.

Kasu and River found a table in the corner nook by the windows, overlooking the deck below. The blade squinted as she peered down at readers at outdoor tables, enjoying coffee in paper cups with travel lids as they read, wrote, or typed. Did they feel as small as she did?

River slipped her bag free and lowered it onto the table, just as the Wielder tapped her on the shoulder.

"Ma'am?" the doll replied, voice hushed.

"Let me round up some books and see to what we had waiting on hold," her Wielder replied, gesturing over her shoulder back up at the stacks. "You set up here and see to correspondence in the meantime. I'll be back shortly."

"Wilco." The blade nodded. "I'm ready to go."

"Good. And one more thing . . ."

"Yes, ma'am?"

The doll looked up, not at her Wielder but straight into the eyes of Yakumaru Sakae, whose hand was clamped around the doll's chin.

There should have been a sickening corkscrew going up the doll's spine, an urge with all of her to swat the hand away, flip the table, and lunge for the woman's jugular. But instead, River felt nothing at all.

Sakae brushed possessively at River's cheek.

"Got you, little doll."

Tatami. Bed. Window. Waves. Same as it ever was.

River had risen from the nightmare in a daze, earlier than she usually did, and everything felt distant. What was the point anymore? Where could she go? What could she do? Was it not just as well to surrender?

Tatami. Bed. Window. Waves. Same as it ever was.

Distantly, she saw herself clean up, dress, and wait for Tora's arrival. Just as always, same as it ever was.

"Good morning, River. Let's get you ready. Her Lady-ship wants to see you."

"Ohayou, Tora-san," River replied just as always, greeting her companion before following her out into the sun.

Pleasant pleasantries, just as always. They ate breakfast together by the rock garden before Tora saw her to the poolside.

Just as always, same as it ever was.

When they joined the poolside crowd, they found Sakae holding court at the tables by the bar. On the wall, summoned from where River knew not, was a monitor. For a moment, River thought she was viewing a sporting event, or maybe a film. Then, she saw figures hurrying through a broken cityscape amid a hail of incoming fire. One of them paused, laid down covering fire from a belt-fed machine gun fired from the hip, and then kept running. A cheer rose among some of the lounging attendees.

River blinked, squinted. There were text captions, but they were moving too fast for her to make any sense of them. The dark-haired figure with the machine gun looked familiar—but why? It was no matter; River's presence was required, and she was too tired to resist anymore.

"Well, well, well, look who's joined us at last on this fine day and is looking so much happier for it. Welcome, little doll." Sakae gestured, and River moved to sit beside the woman. "I'm glad to see you."

Distantly, River was horrified, but what else was left? At least this was new. At least this was different. Meekly, she complied.

The view on the monitor shifted, following the armed figures more closely, and their faces became plainly visible.

"What, uh, what is this?"

"This is Shura," Sakae replied matter-of-factly. "Call it a sort of battle royale, an arena for the enjoyment of the discerning. These are the best of the Nogami dolls, and they're honing each other."

"Shura?"

One of the dolls on-screen fell.

Sakae took a sip of a cocktail balanced precariously on the edge of the bistro table. "Oh, don't tell me you haven't heard of Shura, little doll. The Six Roads, the hell of battle?"

Once, in what felt like another life, River used to joke that she was a Buddhist but a bad one—her tutelary deity,

Hachiman-okami, was historically regarded as a bodhisattva as well as a Shinto deity. She knew Shura all too well.

She gaped. "You're *killing* the Nogami dolls?"

Her host laughed. "Oh, little doll, how little you understand. This isn't nearly as simple as that. In the end, what *is* death?"

The little unit on-screen fought tenaciously, expertly using cover and maneuver. They looked to be old hands, from what River could make out of their tactics. However, their success only lasted a little while.

A set of profile portraits flashed on the screen, under the words *Session Complete: Final Tally*.

River tried her best to resolve the names and faces that followed, with statistics about rounds expended and kill percentages. There were eight dolls in the squad: Kojirō り-217. Matsu ま-119. Aoi さ-217. Toki う-12. Shunsuke け-21. Yūichi さ-90. Nao せ-102.

The final name in the set chilled River to her core.

Yui め-633.

"Yui. No."

"Ki ni suru na. Miyo." River's host waved a hand. ⟨*Don't trouble yourself. Look.*⟩

New Session Start flashed on the screen. The little squad, seemingly unscathed, was already moving, hurrying to a line of ruined buildings in search of cover.

"So, they die, but they don't."

"Oh, they die eventually," Sakae corrected. "Only the strongest remain, with the rest sent out to seed the pool. New ones join, little by little. And on and on the wheel of fate turns."

The fight—or was it a game?—continued as River looked on in horror. Yui fell, rose again, fell, and rose again.

River was transfixed. She tried desperately to cling to the names: Kojirō リ-217. Matsu ま-119. Aoi さ-217. Toki う-12. Shunsuke け-21. Yūichi さ-90. Nao せ-102. Yui め-633.

Sakae was saying something, making chillingly pleasant conversation. All the doll could hear was her heart pounding in her ears like distant drums of war.

That night, River lingered by the pool. She was worn down, after everything she had endured, after finally having an answer to the Nogami crisis and being able to do nothing about it, after seeing Yui sent back to the battlefield. She felt frozen and powerless, but time under the stars still felt like one last refuge; so she lingered there, hoping that nobody would intervene.

Nobody did.

"Kojirō リ-217. Matsu ま-119. Aoi さ-217. Toki う-12. Shunsuke け-21. Yūichi さ-90. Nao せ-102. Yui め-633." She whispered the names to the stars, even if she could not remember all the faces. It was the least she could do to remember them.

The stars, in their distant majesty, stood silent witness to her pain.

When she was a little girl, River had heard stories from her great-aunt Victoria about the ancient Armenian deity Vahakn. A fire god, he had stolen straw from the king of Assyria and fled north across the heavens, dropping some of the straw in flight on his way home to the Armenian highlands in Anatolia. The fallen straw had planted the stars and become the Milky Way. What the Japanese called *ginga*, the River of Heaven, Armenians called *hartakoghi janabarhə*: the Path of the Straw Thief.

Inasmuch as River—first as a human, then as a doll—revered the Japanese gods, she had drawn strength from the ancient Armenian lore, throughout her life and career. It had stuck with her in a way that her former religious affiliation had not: tales of straw thieves humbling kings and planting the stars, tales of archers who let fly against long odds and inaugurated new eras of peace. At their core, at their best, this was what her ancestors had been.

"Na hur her uner, aba te pots uner morus." River recalled the old poem about the god her ancestors had revered, the one who had raced home through the heavens against long odds. "Yev achgunkn eyin arekagunk." *‹Hair of flame and beard of fire had he. And his eyes, they were as suns.›*

Amid that river of faraway suns, she found the stars of Ursa Major. Out of habit, her eyes flitted up from Dubhe, the star at the dipper's tip, and alighted on the nearby stars of Ursa Minor: dipper, handle, and at its tip, Polaris.

Something clicked, deep down in the back of the doll's mind. She glanced from the horizon to the star and back again.

"Wait, no. No, no, that's . . . something's not right," she murmured. "What am I looking at—oh."

It was not quite at the angle she had been expecting. She usually saw it from the shores of Sendai Bay. Where was she?

What I wouldn't give for a sextant, River thought, holding up a thumb, two fingers, then her hand with fingers splayed. She tried her best to estimate degrees.

Once, twice, three times she tried to measure with little more than her hands. She would not have the precision of a sextant, let alone a GPS, but if her observations were anywhere near correct, then she was a good thousand miles from home.

I'm definitely to the south a ways, what with the palm trees, so where am I? Kagoshima? Okinawa? Am I still in Japan at all?

In the dim light, something else caught River's eye. She had dismissed it as a trick of the light, at first, but then she saw it again, for the briefest of instants: a flash of her HUD and the joints on her artificial limbs.

The North Star being in a different place and the glimpse of her missing cybernetics all at once complicated and clarified things. Deep down, River felt a fire return for the first time since she had left Sendai. There was a chance. There was hope. If she fought for it, the Path of the Straw Thief would be her own way home yet.

Slowly, she clenched her fingers into a fist. Her vision swam with tears.

"North Star Forever," the doll pledged to Polaris, unbowed and free.

EIGHTEEN

Loyal from the Start

That morning, Kasu was up before the dawn and immediately wished she had not risen. Even with someone in the guest room, the house felt painfully empty, echoing with the hollowness of what should have been there but was not.

For a time, she sat up in bed, knees drawn to her chin, blankets around her shoulders, watching the shadows on the far wall. The empty space beside her in bed and the diagnostic cables still draped over the other nightstand felt like a yawning chasm.

The night before, she and Tomoka had shared a hasty dinner in the kitchen: macaroni and cheese with bacon, from one of River's family recipes. The day had been long for both women, with Kasu on Sabusawa Island at work on the Shirakami Project with visiting SDF personnel, and Tomoka waiting for an official call from the prefectural police department that had never come. They had put on some 1950s jazz from Kasu's music library and chatted idly. For a while that night, it almost felt like life was something resembling normal.

Eventually, the conversation ebbed. Both women were painfully aware of the empty spaces beside them.

"I just wanted to mind my own business and make wonderful things with my partner." Tomoka sighed. "I didn't want *this*."

"I didn't either," was all Kasu could reply. "Demo, komatta toki wa ningen mo ningyō mo otagaisama." ⟨*But when everything else goes to shit, all we've got to rely on is each other, humans and dolls alike.*⟩

They said nothing more, understanding but content to let the silence be.

That morning, Kasu tried for a long time to gather herself. The usual rhythms of the day were not there anymore, yet life had to go on. She had to keep moving.

On her night table, sitting in the shadow of the floor lamp, was the brocade amulet she had bought that day at the shrine with her doll, when they had prayed together for guidance in the Nogami project and for protection in their quest to become mothers.

What was it she had said to River? *I'd say wear the amulet in anticipation. As a reminder.*

"Even apart, you're honing me, aren't you, River?"

Sighing, she reached for the amulet. She had not worn it since returning from Tokyo two weeks ago.

"Ndaraba, kokesu yo," she declared, swinging her legs over the side of the bed, speaking to the empty space behind her. "Igube." ⟨*Arright, doll o' mine. Let's git a-movin'.*⟩

She showered, dressed quickly, and slipped out quietly—so as not to disturb Tomoka—crossing the still-misty courtyard as she made for the main parking lot. She was soon heading north to the far bank of the Kitakami. It was only a thirty-minute drive from home, but it felt like it was much farther, over the Kitakami and up, up, up

National Highway 398. The highway was more of a country road sandwiched between boulder-capped cliffs to one side and a forest to the other. She was close but needed time to work up the nerve to go where she was headed that morning, just over the municipal boundary in nearby Minami-Sanriku.

She needed to be somewhere where she could clear her head and think.

It was a cleft in the rocky coast, where earth, water, and sky seemed to come together in a tumbling cascade. The local folklore she had heard, first from Mihara-*sensei* and then in her reading, had it that the villages that had once bounded this part of the coast feuded over their precise boundary. Fed up with humans' bullshit, the gods intervened, tearing a gash in the promontory to mark the previously unmarked boundary. Now it was called Kamiwarizaki, the Promontory the Gods Split.

Kasu sat on one of the boulders over the tidal pool, taking her coffee from a can procured from the vending machine at the campsite on the hill's crest. There were no campers that morning, and Kasu was grateful for the solitude. Coffee at that quiet spot just off the beaten path seemed some of the sweetest of all. Through the cleft in the rock face came the first glimmers of sun over the distant Pacific horizon as the tide swirled at her feet.

High overhead, seabirds wheeled.

How many times had they come to Kamiwarizaki since 2011? It was on the road north, just a stone's throw away, but tucked away enough that it felt much farther. It was their own little sanctuary. In the beginning, when they swore their oath to each other as Wielder and blade, it had been here too. Hand in hand, early one morning, on one of the boulders, as the tide crashed around their feet. They had held hands, faced each other, fingers interlaced, foreheads touching. First, River had sworn herself as Kasu's blade. Then, with her heart in her throat, Kasu had spoken the words by which she became Wielder.

Here and now, I swear candor, patience, humility, love, and service in turn,

For the rice stalk that bears the most, bows the lowest.

Here and now, I ask that you hone me just as I hone you.

Here and now, I swear to care for myself, for this, too, is service.

Here and now, I pledge to fight beside you, wherever it may be:

To tear the heavens and earth apart in righteous battle at your side.

You are the blade, and I am the Wielder.

As long as we stand as one heart together, we are unstoppable.

Then they had kissed, the current of their interlink a swirling, warm tide—the inner sense of one heart together.

She had sworn that all those years ago—and here she was a decade later, with River gone and no choice but to wait. To be still. All that was within her means, all the courage she had to leap headfirst into problems—after everything, she began to realize it was nothing without humility. Nothing without patience. She could not leap into a situation and tear a solution into the earth like the gods of Minami-Sanriku had.

Was River still out there? Was Yui? Could she—and her allies—bring them home? Kasu had to hope. She had done what she could, and she made a promise to Akiko, to boot. There really was nothing more to do now but wait.

But I want her back now, thought the solitary Wielder, trying her best to quell the spike in her anxiety.

One morning, they had stopped over on their way around Santaku facilities across the region, from Rikuzentakata to Ryori and then to the SDF maneuver range at

Ōjōjihara, and Kasu's anxiety had gotten the better of her. She had been running through the tasks of the day, unaware that she was talking out loud.

"Am I missing anything?"

River knew all too well how Kasu was driven and capable but perpetually anxious beneath her practiced air of authority. It came with the territory of the life she led and was something she had to work to overcome—and still did.

Eyes still lightly shut, sunrise still on her cheeks, River had said, "No, ma'am, you've got everything."

"Nanusu ya?" Kasu had asked in surprise. ⟨How's that?⟩

"You've got everything," the doll said quietly. "You haven't forgotten anything. Your anxiety can fuck all the way off. I'll be with you every step of the way. And I'm going to make sure you remember to eat before we head for Ōjōjihara. You know how busy things get over there while the range is hot."

Even in the moments of her Wielder's weakness, River had always been a rock, an anchor of stability.

"Minoru hodo atama o sagaru inaho kana," Mihara-*sensei* had told her a lifetime ago. ⟨*The rice stalk that bears the most, bows the lowest.*⟩ Did she understand it as well as she had assumed? Kasu was not so sure anymore.

That morning on Kamiwarizaki, however, in the slowly growing light, she felt a new peace with the unknowing.

She raised her coffee in salute to the horizon.

"You are the blade, and I am the Wielder, River Victoria M59A1. Even apart, we stand together."

Tears blurred her vision. Through the notch in the cliff, as if in response, the sun rose in glorious dawn.

Inasmuch as being so still for so long had been trying, it had not taken long, even quietly and passively observing, for Zee to gather a wealth of information about its new southerly surroundings.

The island was Kikai Island in the Amami group off the southern coast of Kyushu. Easy to miss, perhaps, being a relatively small island, but that blind spot meant it was a perfect place to hide something in plain sight. Big enough for an airstrip and a small town, small enough for the island to be de facto owned by one private entity. What Zee had not expected, and knew its Witch would find most interesting, was just how much was being hidden there, chiefly something called Shura. It would have to investigate further when it could move its operation into the next phase, but for now, it gathered that Shura was a space—an arena, of sorts—in which Nogami dolls were coerced to fight.

Granted, Zee was not able to get up and look around for itself, but from all it was able to gather from ambient observation, there was no such arena. If the arena was the island's nerve center, then where was it?

Every doll that passed into Zee's field of vision, without exception, was an Agatsuma-type doll. No doll of Santaku, Arai, Iwasaki, or any other make, Japanese or otherwise, was upright and operational.

And yet.

There were Nogami-type dolls, just as Zee had suspected, and unsurprisingly—given the existence of Shura—they were in pieces. Difficult though it was to see, Zee knew this was probably the closest it had ever come to an answer about the longstanding Nogami crisis.

It thought back to long before it was a doll, in the old days when its Witch first noted the Japanese government's abdication of responsibility after Nogami went under as a corporation. It had not been terribly surprising to Akiko that the government would do so, given what she had observed for decades of painful experience. Human minorities had had to fight tooth and nail over decades for every measure of protection they enjoyed under Japanese law, as it was, with progress happening only after lengthy lawsuits and a groundswell of support that took time to build.

The fight was long and worth it, but that did not make it any easier. While some brave humans and dolls waged the legal battle, Akiko quietly gathered information and waited. What she had not expected was for her once-human partner to remake itself as a doll, with a hand-restored, painstakingly modded Nogami-type chassis. It had surprised Akiko, to be sure, but to Zee, the choice was either doll conversion or a slow death from the cancer that was eating away at its human body. To her credit, Akiko took it in stride and seemed to pursue the matter of the Nogami dolls' needs with greater tenacity.

They had never been able to make more than a little bit of headway at a time. Despite Akiko's reach, Keyaki's power and resources were finite. Somehow, someone was always one step ahead of them, ensuring that there was little more than a slow trickle of spare parts and an ever-shrinking pool of places from which to get them.

Then, with all the subtlety of a cruise missile swatting a fly, had come Isawa Kasu and her blue-haired doll crashing onto the scene, upending things. It was ironic, given that Akiko's business, which had only in recent years taken the name Keyaki, had been a decades-long contractor for Santaku Group. The Isawas did not ordinarily crash onto any scene, so this had taken even Akiko aback—but then again, this was an Isawa whose entire life had been a story of leaping headfirst and making waves.

In hindsight, it should have been obvious—but for humans, as for dolls, hindsight was always perfect.

Of the two of them, Zee trusted River M59A1 more, from all it had learned about her so far. She had been to war and back; as a human she had not come from a family of means, and she was a local by adoption rather than by origin. All of that served her well; it had grounded her in her duties as her Wielder's weapon and right hand. In all, the blue-haired doll was sharp, diligent, and skilled at being a counterweight to her Wielder's less-than-productive, less-than-helpful tendencies. Zee appreciated all of this.

Dr. Isawa was nice enough, Zee thought, and she was earnest in her desire to help. But nice enough, on its own, was not enough. Thus far, she was like any rich, would-be savior in her lack of perspective. She had thought that this ended with that peon Masuya, after all. Would she listen to Akiko and understand how her perspective had been limited? Would she rise above it and become more than an undisciplined sledge axe? Zee could only hope. She would have to, if she was to stand any chance of standing as one with Akiko and making use of the information Zee was gathering.

Over the first couple of days on Kikai Island, Zee was examined—poked and prodded and studied as carefully as her unsuspecting hosts could manage. They did not get as far as they thought they would, and the fact brought the doll no shortage of silent satisfaction. Hand-restored and modded, its chassis would be beyond whatever expectations they might have had of a Nogami doll.

A couple of times, Yakumaru Sakae herself came to inspect Zee.

Zee did not know *too* much about her. She was the CEO of Yakumaru Shipping Lines, based out of Kagoshima City, which had hauled intercontinental cargo for the past six decades. They did clean business, but not much was known about the woman who led the organization.

Why? Zee wanted to ask. *Why are you, by all appearances, having us kill each other for sport and making it that much harder for us to see to our needs? What are we to you?*

The Agatsuma dolls studying Zee were tenacious, but even their patience ran out. And while Zee assumed they wouldn't risk harming it—not if this was where the Nogami dolls were winding up—it knew it couldn't rely on such an assumption. Nor did it have time to. For the safety of itself, its fellow Nogami-type dolls, and its blue-haired Santaku blade friend, it needed to act.

It did that night once it was alone in an engineering bay with just one Agatsuma doll. Truth be told, Zee felt sorry for the Agatsuma dolls. How many of them understood the entirety of what they were involved in? How many were here against their will, like their Nogami counterparts?

The doll in the engineering bay that night was—per the ID tag at its hip—one of many cybernetics analysts, and Zee listened as it argued with the facility security about precautions. The longer the argument dragged on, the more Zee almost felt sorry for the technician. It might have befriended it under different circumstances. It might have talked reason into it, even.

But time was short.

After the security staff departed, the Agatsuma doll sighed, rounded up its gear, and came to the workbench to peer down in curiosity at the vulpine doll.

"Wakaranai ningyō da, kano ningyō wa." *‹That one is an incomprehensible doll.›*

Zee flashed pointed fangs. The Agatsuma doll's eyes widened.

"It's showtime!" snarled the self-made Nogami doll, snapping upright and reaching for the Agatsuma's neck.

Rain clouds lingered over Ishinomaki that night, low and dark as they swept down from the Ōu Mountains, over the Ojika Peninsula, and on their way out to the bay. It would have made for terrible driving weather coming back up Route 45 at the end of the workday, but thankfully, Kasu had got off the ferry, up the road from Higashimatsushima, and home to Ōmori just before the downpour began.

Through the drawn sliding doors, she watched the rain fall heavy on the greenhouses' arches. The veranda chimes jangled in the gusting, southerly wind—and distantly, she could see the trees on Mount Jōbon start to sway.

In here, at least, there was a measure of peace.

Across the coffee table, Tomoka sat with legs curled up in the corner of the sofa, reading an old ink-and-paper book she had brought with her from Sendai. One of the things Kasu had really appreciated, from her visits with River to Yui and Tomoka's home, was the latter's appreciation of reading.

In Kasu's lap was a volume of historic Armenian satire in English translation, one of River's preferred comfort reads. The snark, even in translation, was bittersweet in how it reminded the Wielder of her blade's sense of humor.

She and River prized their quiet moments on the road, times they had to read together while catching their breath somewhere. The last time had been at Hinoki, the little café in Shichigahama, just down the street from Daikokuya. They had sat in the corner by the windows, sharing coffee and enjoying the respite of peace and quiet with good books. River had been reading a particular book of Armenian satire from the 1870s. Kasu herself had been rereading Mihara-*sensei*'s ethnography of the *kokeshi* of Naruko.

That evening in Ishinomaki, however, Tomoka's book, a well-loved, dog-eared paperback, was Mori Ōgai's *Gan*. *Gan* was written amid the closing days of the Meiji era and the dawn of the ensuing Taishō. Kasu wondered how long it had been since she had read it herself.

Outside the windows, the wind gusted again.

Kasu frowned. It was eerily quiet.

In weather like this, on their days at home, River would sit cross-legged on the living room floor under the veranda windows and sharpen her skill with the *biwa*, as if to drive the worst of the storm away with her music. Sometimes she would be playing tunes from the Heike Tales; other times it would be songs from her Armenian ancestors, like "Dle Yaman" or "Diyarbakır peşrevi," originally written for the oud, an ancestor of the *biwa* across multiple centuries and over eight thousand kilometers.

"Kaeranakya," Tomoka said suddenly, looking up at Kasu, then out the window. ⟨*I should go back.*⟩

"Ee?" ⟨*Huh?*⟩

"Sendai e kaeranakya." ⟨*I should go back to Sendai.*⟩

The door chimed.

"Ah, chotto gomen ne," Kasu muttered, rising with a tired sigh. ⟨*Ah, 'scuse me a moment.*⟩

Turning, she crossed through the hall and stepped down into the vestibule to open the door.

"Hai, hai, tadaima!" ⟨*Yes, yes, coming!*⟩

Throwing the door open, she was met by an all-too-familiar face.

"Miyakozawa-*san*—"

The redhead briskly snapped her umbrella shut and

ducked into the doorway, fast enough that she drenched Kasu in an arc of spattering rain.

"Dōshita, sonna ni awatete—" ‹Why such a hurry—›

"We have a signal from Zee!" the redhead crowed, pushing past Kasu to drop her cyberdeck on the living-room worktable. She immediately powered it up and swiped through its access code. "*Meu amado* has sent an initial transmission. It's . . . it's a lot, I'll admit."

Tomoka looked up in surprise, setting down her paper-back. "Konban wa—" ‹Good evening—›

"Wait, it got through to you?" Kasu asked the redhead.

"It did! We have a fighting chance now!"

The projection rose from the cyberdeck. Far to the south, just south of Kyushu, a map marker pulsed.

Tomoka whistled. "Maa, zuibun to tōi tokoro icchata nee." ‹My, it's gone somewhere pretty far.›

Kasu cocked her head, squinting. "Where is that? Is that Tanegashima? No, it can't be."

"Close. That's Kikajima," Akiko corrected. "The map marker is at 28.326389, 129.974167. It's in the Amami Is-lands—you know, the little islands just south of Kyushu, down in Kagoshima Prefecture."

"Wait, Kikai?" Kasu pinched the bridge of her nose. "Why does that sound familiar?"

Akiko turned in her chair, looking from Kasu to To-moka and back again.

"You should bring in some coffee. This is going to take some time to explain."

The solitary Wielder nodded. "Tomoka-san, koohii wa ikaga?" ‹Tomoka-san, how about some coffee?›

Her houseguest was already rising and heading for one of the empty chairs flanking the table beside the red-haired Witch. She nodded.

"Nara, makasero." ⟨*Then, leave it to me.*⟩

Ordinarily, especially in the mornings before setting off for work, River and Kasu would have two mugs of Americano, black, no sugar. It was tradition. But as Kasu made for the selection of coffee in the cabinet, she had a change of heart. This demanded something different.

Three demitasse cups, stacked. The finest grain of ground coffee, seasoned with cardamom, a dust in the spoon. She had not made it as often as River had, but something drew her to it—to follow the memory of what she had seen. It felt important. She brought the steaming coffeepot to the table and set the demitasse cups on their matching saucers.

The brass coffeepot was one of few things River had kept from her life before leaving home. It was an heirloom from the great-aunt to whom she had been closest, the one who used it for divination.

We'd be on the edge of our seats when Auntie Victoria read the grounds, River had explained. *In my family, she was always the best at it.*

This means of divination was called tasseography in English, but the Armenian phrase River knew it by was simply *kavat gartal*—reading the cup. After drinking, they would turn their cups upside down onto their saucers, and the diviner would read each in turn, trying to interpret what lay ahead for the drinker in how the coffee sediment had settled.

Despite having lost much of her family to anti-cybernetic bigotry on becoming a combat doll, River had clung to the memory of her great-aunt, who had also been her other namesake. In her own way, the woman was one of River and Kasu's household gods.

I don't normally entreat you, the Wielder silently prayed to her blade's ancestor, *but for the sake of my wife, I will: please help us bring River home.*

"Now," the Wielder said at last to the Witch, "you were saying?"

As concisely as possible, Akiko explained the situation that Zee had begun to sketch out in its initial message: the hidden arena, the Yakumaru complex, the state of the No-gami dolls. By the end, Kasu sat with mouth agape, dumbstruck by the extent of what the vulpine doll had uncovered.

"Holy *shit.*"

Tomoka's eyes seemed to burn a hole into the map projection with their intense, quiet rage. "Yakumaru o koroshiteyaru." ‹*I'll fucking kill Yakumaru.*›

"It's time for you and me to make some calls, Princess." Akiko gestured. "We might not be able to do anything about this directly, but between us, we know enough low people in high places that can probably drop the proverbial train on this *montanha do merda*—this mountain of shit. Let's bring all our dolls home."

"Agreed," said the Wielder. "Let's get to work."

With a flourish, she turned her demitasse upside down onto its saucer.

However the grounds settled, she would leave fate in the hands of her blade's gods and guardian ancestors. There was plenty for her to do.

NINETEEN

Sowing the Wind

Tatami, waves, breath, bed. The same rhythm as before. Only, this time, River's sleep was dreamless.

That morning, after the glimpse into Shura and the Path of the Straw Thief, she awoke early. Instead of dressing, the doll sat on the rumpled bedsheets facing the wall.

She tried to conjure the memory of Yui's squad, the faces and the names.

Kojirō り-217. Matsu ま-119. Aoi さ-217. Toki う-12. Shunsuke け-21. Yūichi さ-90. Nao せ-102. Yui め-633.

Shura. The North Star. The spread of her fingers. The momentary flash of her cybernetics and joints. Something about all this was wrong—she knew this.

"That's the problem," she murmured, chiding herself as she extended a hand, fingers splayed. "Still thinking too much like a human, I suppose."

She had a neural interface, as did all dolls, through their diagnostic ports. If there was that access to her, then there was only one answer to this beachside hell. The clarity cut through the illusion like a knife's edge.

"That's it. This is an artificial reality. It has to be."

It did not answer what was happening to the Nogami dolls, stuck fighting and dying in what Yakumaru Sakae had called Shura. All the same, River knew she had the power. She had to focus. In this world, as in the physical one, she could not let someone else define her.

Even with hope this seemingly forlorn, she had to stand up and do something. It was who she was, both flesh and machine: heir to those who had dared to say no. The Armenians in 1895 and 1915 who had taken up homemade flintlocks to shoot back at genocidal Ottoman soldiers. The Santaku-made synthetic combat dolls that had defied even their own initial programming and mutinied against human cruelty, in the Kokeshi Uprising of 1906. Each refused to be victims without agency. Each took a stand against long odds. While some had lived on, all of them had won their own sort of immortality.

River focused, eyes intent on the lines of her arm. Once, her arms and hands had looked like this, yes, when she was an unaugmented, unscarred human. But there was no going back to how things had been before. There was only putting herself together into a new whole, bearing her inner and outer scars as proudly as she could. Honing herself to a new edge, with softness and sharpness in balance.

"Come on. It's like a lucid dream. I know you're there. Come on."

An instant. An eyeblink. A flash of a flash. There was an afterimage of her HUD and the panel lines on her arm and the articulation points of her fingers.

"Come on," River muttered, clenching and unclenching her fingers. "I know you're there. Come on."

Fingers powerful enough to tear, to claw, to protect, and gentle enough to caress and comfort. A sharpness and softness in balance, a wholeness, chosen and tended. Service and loyalty cultivated together with her Wielder, nurtured like a garden.

How long had it been that even River's dreams had been broken into, tampered with? The dream had been comfortable, to be sure, but this could not be the end of the story. She did not belong here.

As sharp and clear as she could, River summoned up the memory of Kasu in her mind's eye.

The curve of her chin. The little specks of the sensory augment nodes glinting on her cheeks. The way her hair was subtly tinged with gray. Her scent. Stretch marks and scars. The gentle curve of her belly, the little birthmarks at the small of her back. The strength of her thighs and arms.

Wife. Wielder. Lady of her house.

"Here and now, before you and my gods," the doll declared, "I swear service in battle, in home, and in bed. I swear to be your sword, your comfort, your right hand, the instrument of your will."

The panel lines. The HUD annotations, a little clearer now. A brush at the nape, her interface port just out of reach.

"Here and now, I swear to care for myself, for this, too, is service."

She was far from home, far from Kasu's side, but even here, her loyalty remained. Even apart, they stood together.

"Here and now, I swear to tear the heavens and earth apart if you should command it. For you are the Wielder. I am the blade. And as long as we stand as one heart together, we are unstoppable."

River did not notice the door slide open, but she heard Tora's shocked gasp.

"River, you mustn't—"

Then River was herself again: panel lines and scars,

blue working uniform and tactical boots, standing triumphant with fists clenched.

"I am River Victoria M59A1, I serve Isawa Kasu, and I can do *whatever* the hell I *like!*" she roared, reaching deep down for all her strength as she wound back and lunged, less at the wall and more at reality itself. The once immovable fusuma panels flew into the empty room beyond with a crash.

Triumphant, River strode into the adjoining chamber. Her heart pounded, her adrenaline coursed, and she felt more alive than she had since she had left Sendai. Her HUD was malfunctioning, but it was there, and an internal check told her she had all the pieces where they should be. There was hope.

"We can fix this; just please stop—"

"No! This ends today! This ends here and now! And I'm going to have Yakumaru Sakae's *head* for this!"

With a lunge, she bounded past Tora and out into the rambling corridors. Part of her wished she had a weapon at hand, but it mattered little: she was her Wielder's blade, and this was, ultimately, a dream.

The courtyard, the poolside, it was all sunny and pleasant, same as ever, but she could not see anything, save the outer wall. It *looked* thick, but this was all a dream, and she was not going to be stopped.

Namu Kameoka Hachiman ōkami! Namu Shiogama Daimyōjin! River prayed silently, clenching her fist as she invoked her guardian deity and her Wielder's. She felt the strength of the fire within and the thunder from above gather. *Hail, great kami Hachiman of Kameoka! Hail, great radiant kami of Shiogama! You before whom I swore an oath! You who open the way before warriors in the hour of darkness and need! You who teach your children to bring victory from defeat, life from the ashes, and salt from the seas! I, who bear victory in my name, beseech you in the service of my Wielder! Strengthen my hand and aim!*

Her fist landed, fingers dully aching, reality distorting around them—just enough for River to see.

"This ends today!" she roared, winding back to hammer away again at the wall. "This ends here and now! I'm *going home*, and I'm *taking everyone with me!*"

"Are wa nani o shita?" *⟨What did she do?⟩*

Yakumaru Sakae looked up in surprise. The secretary doll's expression was one of horror.

"Ano Santaku-gata wa ei-āru ni kizuite, dasshutsu shiyō to suru." *⟨That Santaku-type is aware of the artificial reality, and she's trying to break out.⟩*

It was incredible. The Santaku doll had taken a long time to wear down, and just one day ago, it had seemed like she was pliable enough for Sakae to have finally shown her the Shura arena. With this doll finally unlocked, she would have a glimpse into Santaku's workings, and an edge over a competitor. So, why this? Why now?

Ever since the demise of Nogami Cybernetics, Sakae had painstakingly built a system. The government did not want anything more to do with the dolls, and the company that had built them had folded, so what else was there to do but put them to use for something that was at least entertaining?

"Shinpai senu yō ni. Sugu iku." *⟨Calm yourself. I'm on my way.⟩* Sakae dismissed the doll with a wave, turned in her office chair, and retrieved the cables for her augmented reality hookup. She would deal with this personally and find her way into the little doll's inner workings yet.

A snap. The cable was in place. She exhaled, leaned back, and watched one world dissolve into the other.

There were clouds overhead.

"And I'm telling you, you don't have to follow this woman. You don't have to stay in this place. If we stand together, we can end this today! We can end this now! We can tear down these walls!"

The compound wall, holding but cracked, cratered in ten different places. In the middle of the astonished crowd of other dolls stood the blue-haired menace, fists clenched, eyes intense.

When their eyes met, the doll spit fire.

"You. Release me. I'm done with your little parties and having you fuck with my head and your fucking spectator blood sport. Release me and anybody else who wants out, and do it right the fuck now." She spoke slowly, quietly, every word a knife's edge. "Or I am going to tear your head off in this world and every other world there is."

"I thought you better than this." Sakae shook her head, threading through the last of the crowd. "It seems I under-estimated you, little doll—that I've been too lenient."

"Ware wa kisama no ningyō demo nai shi, kisama no mae ni hizamazuku riyū wa nai!" *‹I am not your doll, and I have no reason to kneel before you!›* She beckoned in challenge, and the air rippled with heat around her fingertips. "Kakatteras-shai." *‹Come and get me.›*

In her heart of hearts, Sakae felt a strange admiration for Isawa Kasu, the Santaku executive who had made this doll. The doll's loyalty seemed almost inexhaustible, even after everything Sakae had done to wear down her defenses.

"What did your maker do to build a doll like you, I wonder?" she mused aloud, slowly circling River M59A1.

"You really are too unique to destroy." The doll turned with her, matching her, eyes still spitting death and rage.

"She earns my loyalty ever damn day," the doll growled. "By her respect and humility. I am her sword, no matter what you think you can do."

"Cute." Without breaking eye contact, Sakae shouted, "Tora!"

The moment seemed to hang in the air.

"Tora!" she shouted again.

The doll appeared on the other side of River, eyes averted, head subtly bowed.

"Okata-sama." ⟨*Your Ladyship.*⟩

"Koitsu o Shura ni gosō seyo." ⟨*Send this thing to Shura.*⟩

There was a tense silence. Then the blue-haired menace roared with laughter.

"Dōshita, bōkun yo. Jibun no te de sura dekinai no ka?" ⟨*What's the matter, tyrant? Can't even do it with your own two hands?*⟩

The distortions around the doll's hand coalesced, solidified, sharpened into a straight-edged sword wreathed in serpentine fire.

"What are you doing, little doll?"

The doll raised the sword, winding back with a scream, tearing at the fabric of reality around her, closer and closer to Sakae's neck.

"Kaaatsu!"

"Time's up." Sakae snapped her fingers. The blade and doll vanished midswing. A gasp rippled through the crowd.

Shouting Buddhist exhortations would not save this willful thing. It was a shame, but this was what it had come to. If the blue-maned Santaku menace wanted out of a comfortable reality so much, she could have her wish.

"Clean this place up, Tora," she ordered, by which she also meant everyone else. "We have guests later, and I want to show them my new, unexpected addition to the arena."

"Kaaaatsu!"

Suddenly, River was somewhere new, the sound of artillery a distant undertone peppered by the staccato rhythm of sporadic small arms. It was unfamiliar yet familiar: the twisted rebar and rubble-strewn remains of what was once a street, the peppering of bullet holes on walls, mortar craters under the shadow of rusted-out steel shutters of what were once shops.

The sword—Kurikara, the wisdom sword borne by Fudō, the Immoveable Bright King—was still aflame in her hands. She laughed despite herself. *To think I've always said I'm a bad Buddhist.*

If Kurikara was there in her hands, its weight tangible in her grasp, then she was still in an artificial reality. It was a strange irony: Kurikara's power lay in cutting through delusion and willful ignorance.

And this *was* Shura, wasn't it?

Slowly, River began to move through the ruins, trying her best to keep cover. She pressed on in search of a way forward and out, and perhaps she would find some of the Nogami dolls forced into this hell.

There was a curiously comforting familiarity to it all, in how it resembled the places that had shaped her from the beginning. Once, decades ago, she had wandered Beirut in the aftermath of the Lebanese Civil War, stepping over terrain that had felt like this under her feet, moving through streets much like these. At first, it had seemed like a great adventure, but her elders had always frowned upon that. Only as an adult—in battle as a human soldier in the streets of Syrian towns astride the Euphrates—did she begin to understand why.

Even in the most just battle, sooner or later, victory claimed a terrible price.

River paused in an alley. Back in the old Beirut days, she had learned that during the civil war, there were places in town where nobody dared show their heads for fear of unseen snipers who may or may not be present. Those places became so deserted that nature began to reclaim them, turning them into paradoxically peaceful places. The most famous was even named the Green Line.

In these streets, there was no such greenery that River could see. Everything was a palette of earth, gray concrete, and burnt ash.

"I should do something about this," she muttered at the sword in her hand. Pausing, she focused on the weapon.

"Come on. Come on. If this is just an illusion and I've got the power . . ."

There was a distortion of air around her hand, and the sword was replaced by the compact lines of a familiar short-barreled rifle, compact sight on its center rail, stock extended, hanging from a two-point sling, in turn slung across a plate carrier. It felt like a lifetime ago that she had been on the range with her Wielder testing the brand-new Shirakami, but it was good, here, to reclaim those memories and be ready for what the illusion would bring.

And just as she rose to continue her search with the Shirakami cradled close, something that felt distinctly like the business end of a different assault rifle gently poked into the small of her back. River froze.

"Mikata da," she said softly. *I'm a friend.*

A pause, then a surprised gasp. "Hamono-san!" *‹Miss Blade!›*

River turned slowly to find Yui, armored and armed, staring at her in shock from an alleyway she had somehow missed.

"*Atashi da*—it's me, Yui. You're not imagining things."

The rest of her little squad followed her out of the shadows, fanning out, forming an ad hoc cordon.

River's heart jumped into her throat as she recognized them: Kojirō リ-217. Matsu ま-119. Aoi さ-217. Toki う-12. Shunsuke け-21. Yūichi さ-90. Nao せ-102.

"How did you get here? Where did—"

River waved a hand. "Yui, we might not have much time, so listen to me: none of this is real."

"Didn't you just say I wasn't imagining you?"

"I'm real; you're real," River agreed, then gestured broadly. "But none of *this* is real. None of it. All of us are plugged into some kind of artificial reality, and you're here because—"

"Because I have a Nogami chassis," Yui interjected. "But why does someone want to run us down like this? The government doesn't care about us; the doll industry barely cares—"

"Because one person with way too much money feels like being entertained," River said bluntly. "Just like way too much else in the world right now. Yui, I've watched you and everyone in your squad fight, die, and come back, over and over."

There was a palpable wave of shock that tore through the little squad.

"Wait, this is real?"

"I'm not even combat specialized," said another. "Why am *I* here?"

"Ochitsuite!" Yui barked. "Mada sentōchū da!" ⟨*Focus! This is still a battlefield!*⟩

River whirled, raising the Shirakami, her danger sense suddenly screaming. Her targeting systems could not spot any obvious threats, but something still seemed off, seemed amiss.

"Hamono-san, doushita?" ⟨*Miss Blade, what's the matter?*⟩

"Kuru—" ⟨*They're coming—*⟩

The crack of an incoming round made the rest of her sentence superfluous.

"Scatter!"

They pounded over broken earth, back through the alley and around the corner into an adjoining street. Incoming rounds whizzed and scorched through the air in hot pursuit. As the squad took cover beside a roadside berm, mortar fire threw clods of earth.

"Fuck!"

River peeked over the berm, scanning for targets, again to no avail. "Teki o miataranai!" ⟨*I can't spot the enemy!*⟩

Yui was beside her as the bullets flew over their heads.

"Why?"

"Why what?"

"Why would someone do this? I was just getting the shop ready for the morning when this all started. Why would someone do this?"

River tried to come up with a reason, tried to come up with some logical explanation for why one person would want to spend that kind of money to abduct one of the most vulnerable subsets of the doll population.

"Because she thinks it's fun, and she apparently has fuck-you money and a severe lack of empathy, that's why. And I'm going to have her head as soon as I can get within firing range."

"Hamono-san, kimochi wa arigatai kedo—" *‹Miss Blade, I appreciate your sentiment, but—›*

Midsentence, Yui turned pale. River turned, keeping low, hoping to ask for aid from one of the others in the squad, only to find the rest of them likewise pale, color draining from their faces quickly, as if they were already dead.

Her friend going pale. Her heart in her throat. The bullets flying. And all of it in a place that was an illusion—but one built by terrible, real forces.

River primed her Shirakami, took a deep breath, and leaped over the berm with a primal scream.

"You fucking tyrant! Come and get me!"

For a long time after River vanished, the occupants of the poolside courtyard stood transfixed, mouths agape. Then, with a nervous blur of motion, they set to work cleaning up the damage. Tora alone lingered, stunned speechless, unable to will herself to move.

Her Ladyship was not pleased.

"Tora!" she barked. "You know what I've told you about delay."

There had been nothing else in the world for Tora ever since she was recruited by Her Ladyship a decade ago. The world was a dangerous place, and enemies had it in for Her Ladyship, so it was all Tora could do to keep things on an even keel in the compound. Besides, Her Ladyship's anger was the far worse fate—or so she would have said before.

All these years living in fear of Her Ladyship, Tora had been unaware she had power to do anything. She just minded the compound for Her Ladyship's remote guests and tried not to provoke her ire. Still, Tora's loyalty had been fraying of late, and she knew she was not the only one.

Then had come River—River, the blue-haired menace, the high-value asset who simply would not stop thinking of home and fighting to make her way back.

"Ii kai," Her Ladyship began. "Kou yatte ikan." *‹Are you listening? It can't be like this.›*

Tora listened dutifully, not saying anything, and let Her Ladyship say what she would. The words were familiar after so many years. This kind of disruption was unacceptable; it threatened the safety and continuation of the entire operation and, by extension, the future of Tora and everyone else on the island. All Her Ladyship wanted, she said, was to protect Tora and everyone else, to ensure they all remained as comfortable and happy as they had always been.

Her Ladyship was kind and courteous; by the end, her voice was far calmer than when she had begun.

"Wakaru ka ne, Tora yo?" *‹Do you understand, Tora?›*

Tora simply nodded. Without another word, Her Ladyship departed the artificial reality.

For a while, Tora lingered in the pleasant air of the compound as the others who worked there set things right. Then, with a hand that reached out of that world, Tora yanked her cables and followed Her Ladyship into the physical world.

As she rose from her bed and slipped into her boots, Tora knew one thing was all too clear: she needed to end this madness and she needed to end it now.

All River had wanted was to go home. From the very beginning, it had been so plainly obvious. The more Tora had gotten to know her, the more she began to question everything she had done in the name of Her Ladyship over the years.

All River had wanted was to go home. And if all *she* wanted was to go home, what about the Nogami dolls who Tora had not known personally?

What have I done? Tora wondered, aghast. *What have we all done?*

All she wanted to do was go *home.*

In the heart of the complex, Tora found Her Ladyship in the central node, the core of operations and systems management for both Shura and the seaside compound. She looked over a screen that carried the vital information for one of the squads currently active in Shura—plus a familiar blue-haired addition.

"Ano ningyō wa kaeritai dake datta," Tora said, pointing at River M59A1's portrait. "Semete kaeritai dake datta!" ⟨*That doll just wanted to go home. Just to go home!*⟩

"Mou osoi wa. Kore kara are no irubeki basho wa hitotsu dake," Her Ladyship replied bluntly, eyes fixed on her task. ⟨*It's too late. From now on, there's only one place she belongs.*⟩

From across the room, Tora could not make out what she was doing, but as she drew closer, she saw more clearly: Her Ladyship was terminating the dolls' connections to Shura, along with the support systems that kept them operating and alive.

"You're just *killing* them?"

"If she wants to tear things down, she's welcome to do it alone. She can see how well she fares. How long she lasts." Her Ladyship laughed. "And when all is done, we'll have some Santaku parts to send out into the secondhand market along with this new round of Nogami parts."

Tora was not sure what came over her, only that her body went into motion before she understood what she was doing. Picking up a wireless keyboard from the nearest workstation, she threw it against the display and bore down on the woman who already seemed strangely smaller than her already-small stature. Her fists flew. Tora was done with all of this, done with this life. All she wanted was blood.

"Semete kaeritai dake! She just wanted to go back! What is wrong with you?"

TWENTY

Loyal She Remains

The analyst doll's name was Iwa, and it did not take Zee long to realize she was more of an asset as an ally than as a target. Quickly, Iwa made it plain to Zee that even if it had not come along, things were becoming increasingly tense on the island. Clearly, this was someone who needed a way out almost as much as the Nogami dolls. Iwa helped Zee get a message through to its Witch, and for the night, managed to keep Zee safe in the same examination room.

What neither of them had counted on was gunfire the following morning. Iwa woke Zee with the news: the Coast Guard had arrived for an inspection, and through circumstances as yet unclear to either doll, the facility's security personnel started shooting back.

Madame has moved swiftly, Zee thought, upon hearing of the Coast Guard's arrival.

Time was even more of the essence. With Zee leading the way, the unlikely allies got to work.

It had only been the beginning: Tora picking up the keyboard and heaving it at Her Ladyship. Tora's pent-up tension and frayed loyalty had snapped. It had been the unleashing of a slowly building firestorm. The fight had spilled out of the central node and into the connecting corridors.

Into this stumbled the shore party from the Japan Coast Guard, and whatever their initial intentions, by the time Tora saw them, they were firing back because a trigger-happy fool from facility security had shot at them first.

It was chaos after that: running through corridors and past stairwells, humans and dolls fleeing in all directions or, in some cases, breaking out into shouting and fistfights. Her Ladyship had escaped in the chaos, and Tora was not sure where she herself was going. All she knew was that she had to find her and end this.

Alarms blared. Feet pounded. Tora would not stop.

She wanted blood. Whatever the cost, she had to make this right.

River came to with a gasp—and a messy, incoherent jumble of phonemes. She desperately clawed at air, straining at cables, vision blurred.

"That one sure took her time coming up," quipped a familiar voice dryly. A strong hand braced River, and the doll flailed but leaned into it, wiping at her eyes and trying her best to sit up, despite the pain. A cable pulled free of her diagnostic port, and she sat up, albeit with the support of a bracing pair of arms.

"Wait, what the fuck? Where the fuck?"

A pause.

"This one's Witch and that one's Wielder have sent this one to lend that one a hand."

River's vision resolved just enough to make out a pair of vulpine ears.

"Zee? Wait, no, no, no. We have to go back. We have to get—"

"This one apologizes for having taken so long to find that one, River M59A1. We don't have long, and this one knows that that one might not be able to walk as easily after this long plugged into the system. But come on; this one's got that one. One limb at a time."

Everything hurt. Everything burned. All River wanted to do was collapse in a heap and sleep, properly sleep, for the first time in ages. Sleep, and then maybe wander to the kitchen for a breakfast of coffee and basic-ass cereal with her Wielder.

But none of that mattered so long as there were still Nogami dolls in Shura.

"The—fuck, ow. Yui, the others. They're still in there; we have to help them! I can't just—"

"This one knows all too well, friend. But come on, one limb at a time. Let's get that one up and moving."

With Zee's help, River swung one leg, then another, off of what felt like a long drop, down to a slick-tiled floor. Rather than her working uniform, or even what she had worn on that terrible day in Tokyo, she was in little more than a tight base layer—leggings and a tank top—with bare feet.

She tried to stand, but she could not hold herself upright without leaning on her vulpine friend.

"This is . . . gods, this is really suboptimal, you know," River grumbled, looking over the pixelated HUD and its litany of alert messages. "I'm a custom-made combat doll,

I'm in personal service to one of the preeminent names in the cybernetics field, and I've fucked up my own chassis to the point I can barely fucking move my limbs. Fucking hell, man, this blows. I've got HUD alert pings out the ass."

"That one isn't the one who abducted herself," Zee interjected, rebalancing itself. "And remember that part of that one is still biological rather than technological, and on both counts, that one has limits. From what this one has learned, that one has been interfaced to this system for a long time."

"How long?" River asked, willing her legs into motion, trying to flex her toes. Her vision was still a blur. "Wait, no, don't tell me. Wait, hang on, clothes. Shoes. Is my shit still here? I'm not doing this barefoot if I can help it."

"That one's belongings are not here," Zee replied, catching River as the doll's best efforts at standing on her own proved unproductive. "But this one can carry you, and it seems that will be necessary under the circumstances."

Distantly, the Santaku doll registered the sound of a fire alarm. Little by little, River's vision was returning—enough to see that she and Zee were not alone.

"Ah. This is this one's, er . . . associate, Iwa. Say hello, Iwa."

A different voice, just a bit timid. "Hello."

River squinted, trying to get a clear look at the unexpected third presence in the room. The iridescent hair was the unmistakable mark of another Agatsuma, like Tora.

"I still can't believe you're actually a Santaku doll," the newcomer remarked. "It's so rare here. We've never had a Santaku-type at the facility before."

River winced at a sudden jab of pain in her foot. "Glad to—ow—have been abducted to—ow—satisfy your . . . curiosity—"

"Iwa is why this one was able to find that one so quickly," Zee interjected. "It seems there's some measure of discontent among the humans and dolls of this island about what's been done here."

"What island is this?"

"Kikai, off southern Kyushu."

The name made River chuckle. "Never heard of it, but it figures I'd be somewhere where the name is a homophone for *opportunity*. Speaking of—ow—we should seize the opportunity and try and free these other dolls. Yui, the others—their situation is sure as shit gonna be a hell of a lot worse than mine."

"This one has gotten word off the island more than once," Zee replied, squeezing River's shoulder, pulling her back upright. "It should only be a matter of time before the Coast Guard arrives. We need to get out of this facility and off to somewhere we can conceal ourselves, in the meanwhile. With Coast Guard's help, we will be able to do a lot more."

"The JCG?" River squinted. The ceiling lights felt oppressively bright. "That makes sense, but after what I've seen here, I'd kill for a Self-Defense Force VBSS team to kick some fucking doors in—ow, ow, my eyes!"

"Yes, this one has gotten word to Madame, who has turned the matter over to the Coast Guard. But we should be going, friend River," Zee said. "Please excuse this one, but the times require . . ." Eyes shut against the bright light and her pain, River felt Zee heft her into a fireman's carry. "Iwa, let's go."

River's vision swam. Slung over Zee's shoulders, the doll wobbled and swayed against her friend's grip, and she tried to keep herself from being sick.

How long had she been under? And for that matter, how had Zee and this other doll gotten in *and* out without anyone noticing? If she had been held for that long, she had to have been a high-value target.

The pain in her legs. The pain in her arms, her eyes, the litany of warning messages in her field of vision. Her guilt, screaming in her ears.

I should be on my feet, tearing this place apart.

I should be finding Yui and the others and saving them.

I should be finding that fucking monster Yakumaru Sakae and tearing her head off.

Distantly, there was the sound of an explosion. The echoing *bang! bang! bang!* of nine-millimeter weapons being discharged.

"Zee, talk to me—"

"Not now, friend River," her friend hissed. "Escape first, briefing later."

Bang! Bang!

Tuktuktuk! Tuktuktuk! came the reply of a different weapon—or was it more than one weapon? River was not sure.

I should be on my feet, she thought helplessly. *I should be doing more.*

Everything hurt. Everything was too much. Her body gave way, tension dropping, grip going slack, even as she felt Zee's footsteps quicken.

Oblivion came hurrying for the blue-maned Santaku doll—but this time, with just a shred of something resembling vindication, she surrendered to it. After everything, friends had found her—and even imperfectly, had she not done her part?

What was it her Armenian ancestors used to say about

battle waged against long odds, all those centuries ago? The words drifted past the last glimmers of River's consciousness as she fell.

Mah voch imatsyal mah e. Mah imatsyal anmahutiun e. ‹Death not understood is death. Death understood is immortality.›

Somehow, River understood. Death or no death, a friend had found her and had some understanding of what she had seen. She could let go.

The gods could worry about the rest.

TWENTY-ONE

One Heart Together

The RHIBs motored out from the warships at anchor, churning wakes in the tide, with the two VBSS teams crouched and hanging on, weapons at the ready. It was not every day that those teams from *Ōtsuchi* and its American escort *Chamberlain* made this kind of house call on Japanese territory, without first raising and then deferring to the local authorities. Their assistance had been requested by a Japan Coast Guard shore party, and on this island—privately owned and without its own local law enforcement to which they would defer—the usual rules were not quite applicable. Word from on high had it that there may have been a possible attack, and this far south—in sea lanes, where there had been close chases and sporadic firefights with North Korean spy vessels as far back as the 1990s—it was not beyond the realm of possibility.

The two teams hit the uncrewed ferry pier, tying up and sweeping quickly, setting up an initial cordon. When their lines were secure, the detachment commanders met in the middle. The ad hoc decision by the Japanese officer in command was that the SDF team would take point and link up with the JCG detachment that had sent the initial call, to get to work securing the sprawling Yakumaru complex. Meanwhile, the American team would inspect and secure the perimeter.

They synced analog watches, double-checked comms, and after posting guards for the RHIBs, hurried into action. Kikai island was small, and the Yakumaru complex and its attached airstrip occupied a central location, so there was not far to go. Time was of the essence, and they could already hear the sounds of small-arms fire.

The ensign in command of the American detachment kept at the head of her formation. Fresh as she was in commission, her team was just as new as she was, in a sense. It was comprised of seven of the latest MDC-type combat dolls to join the Seventh Fleet's ranks in Japan. The pressure was intense on her to match them in speed and skill.

The campus was a sprawling set of low, interconnected buildings, offices interspersed with storage tanks and exhaust pipes. Even from the outside, the disorder was apparent—and distantly, there came the sound of what, to the Americans, sounded like a general-quarters alarm.

The doors flew open while the American detachment was stacking up outside. They jumped off their hinges as they hit the wall, sending the dolls on point scattering clear.

A vulpine doll, tall and powerfully built, staggered out with a blue-haired doll held in a fireman's carry. It gently laid the doll down on the grass with its back to the building. Beside it, a doll with iridescent hair followed closely, struggling to keep up with the fast, long-limbed gait of its vulpine companion. It looked like it was part of the site's staff, so why was it escaping?

Training had the harried, young landing party commander readying her weapon, even as she shouted.

"*Beikaigun*! US Navy! Stand down!"

The vulpine doll looked up from its place beside its blue-maned companion. It did not seem in any particular hurry, or particularly worried about the assault rifles pointing in its direction. Rising, it looked the American officer dead in the eye and growled a reply with a tired huff.

"You. It took you long enough," the vulpine doll growled, pointing at the ensign as if it were the one in command, without doubt. "This one assumes you're here at the invitation of your Japanese colleagues, so listen well. There isn't time, so go and get a corpsman—in fact, no, you're going to need more than your corpsman. There are a lot of dolls inside who are going to need your help, and you'd better really hurry if you want to have a chance in hell of saving them."

Trafficking Operation Interdicted: Incident on Kikai Island, Kagoshima Prefecture

by Ningyo Nichinichi Shinbun staff

Japan Coast Guard, JMSDF, and US Navy personnel responding to an unknown distress call on Kikai Island, in Kagoshima Prefecture south of Kyushu, have discovered a massive doll-trafficking operation at a Yakumaru Shipping-owned research complex. Nogami-type dolls, long a disadvantaged population, were abducted from across Japan and taken to this location by forces yet unknown, for use in a battle simulation called Shura. The same complex was allegedly dismantling Nogami dolls for yet unknown purposes. Also found on the island was River M59A1, a doll on the staff of Santaku Dynamics, an Ishinomaki, Miyagi

Prefecture–based company. River M59A1 was also the apparent victim of kidnapping. Santaku Dynamics has yet to release an official statement in response.

The interdiction coincided with an incident at the Yakumaru site, an apparent uprising which saw some employees attack others, leading to intervention by site security just as JCG personnel arrived. In the crossfire, reclusive CEO Yakumaru Sakae, age forty-five, has been found dead on the site, the apparent victim of a stabbing by an employee yet to be apprehended.

We will update this story as further details come to light.

A long and comforting silence. The embrace of a peace unexpected, but not entirely unknown.

At long last, River felt herself relax and exhale. It felt like the first time in forever.

"Ah, khosh geldi, hele igar, janam!" a long-lost voice declared out of the void. ⟨*Ah, she's come, ye came by at last, huh, kiddo?*⟩

This was clearly Diyarbakir dialect. And that voice, of all, she knew the best. It was always a little bittersweet to River; this was not the standard Western Armenian tongue she had grown up with—that was a later evolution out of the Armenian of Istanbul. No, this was her ancestors' dialect, the Armenian of people who lived cheek by jowl with Kurdish, Jewish, Arab, Yazidi, Assyrian, and Turkish neighbors, whose vocabularies, emphatic consonants, and fricative vowels permeated their language.

"Auntie Victoria?"

River sat up on a couch she had not seen in decades.

Beneath the articulation and panel-seams of her toes, she could feel the texture of a carpet worn soft over the passage of a century of stockinged feet. Across the octagonal coffee table topped with intricate brasswork she remembered all too well from her childhood in Beirut, the white-haired matriarch, decked out in her midcentury Parisian finery, sat in her favorite armchair and nodded in greeting, carefully balancing a blue glass demitasse and saucer in one hand.

"Kizim, yeraz ki mi achkis archevn es." ⟨*You've appeared before me like a dream, daughter.*⟩

The artificial reality. The running firefight. Yui and Tora. Zee. What happened? Was she dead?

River sighed heavily, shaking her head.

"Akh, al chim kinam inch mən enim, chim kinam meradz em, inch em." ⟨*Ah, I dunno what to do, I dunno if I'm dead or what I am anymore.*⟩

"E kone soorj mi khmir, akhchig, sunk hankəsdatsir." ⟨*Well, have some coffee at least, girl. Rest a spell.*⟩

River slid off the couch and onto the carpet. On the coffee table sat the family heirloom pot, gently steaming beside a fresh demitasse, saucer, and stack of *ghurabia* cookies.

The floral design on the cup was at first unfamiliar, but when River came closer, she recognized the pattern of doubled blossoms and straight-edged blades.

Kasu-sama. River smiled. After she poured herself a cup, she ran a finger around the lines of the Isawa crest that graced the cup, feeling it warm with the coffee.

"Adiga kibar hars mi e," her great-aunt observed, speaking of River's Wielder. ⟨*She's a worthy daughter-in-law.*⟩

Cross-legged at the feet of her ancestor, River sipped at hot coffee that tasted of cardamom and anise. She sighed.

"Kone zink mey mən al desneyi." ⟨*If I could just see her one more time.*⟩

"E hade yel, kizim," her great-aunt commanded. "Kovə ter enelik unis." ⟨*Then get up, daughter. You've got things to do beside her yet.*⟩

Ceiling tile. Beeping instrumentation. The image of her HUD resolving into clarity. Limbs sore, a body beyond tired—but she was awake, or so it seemed.

With a gasp of horror, River tried to sit up and failed. She was tired. Her interface port was occupied, and other things were plugged into her or close around her. Her heart raced. She was ready to fight with whatever she had left— ready to tear, to strike back—

"Konnudzu wa, kokesu yo." ⟨*Hey there, doll o' mine.*⟩

River froze.

The curve of her chin. The little specks of the sensory augment nodes glinting on her cheeks. The subtle tinge of gray in her hair. Her scent. The strength of her arms. The hands on River's cheek.

Was she imagining them?

"Kasu-*sama*," River gasped, her vision blurring with tears. "Kasu-*sama*!"

For a moment, the blade doubted her own eyes, but then came the current of her Wielder's emotions over the interlink, the reassuring warm tug of worry, relief, love, followed by her arms around the doll's shoulders.

She was back. She was home. She had made it.

Her Wielder. Her wife. The lady of her house.

"*Chii tsukede*—ch-*chotto*—careful—the cables, watch those cables!" Kasu cautioned. "Easy, easy. I'm here. I've got you. It's going to be okay."

River lingered in her Wielder's arms, drinking in her

presence, drawing strength from it. Her voice came out as a choked whisper.

"Don't let go. Please. I'm scared it's going to be another illusion."

The Wielder gently squeezed, holding her blade doll closer. "It isn't. You're safe. I'm here—I got here as soon as I could. You're okay. You're going to be okay."

Eventually, River felt a measure of clarity return. The presence of her Wielder and the white noise of the central air came together and helped her center herself. Gently, Kasu helped River lie back. She bolstered her against the pillows, holding tight to her fingers.

"First things first, ma'am. Where am I?"

"You're in the cybernetics ward at Minato Hospital on the Maritime Self-Defense Force side of Naval Station Yokosuka." Kasu nodded in reassurance, then gestured out the window. "See? Nice view of Tokyo Bay outside the window."

River squinted, trying to resolve an image of the world beyond the windows. The passive information she picked up from the internet was a relieving flow. Her HUD marked maritime traffic and points of interest.

"Oh, hey. Sarushima Beach and the old Tokugawa Shogunate coast battery," she murmured with a tired smile, taking in the sight of the little island closer to shore. "Doesn't hold a candle to Sabusawa and dawn over Matsushima Bay, though."

Kasu paused, squeezed at River's fingers.

"The Japan Coast Guard intervened on Kikai Island. Landing parties from the destroyers *Ōtsuchi* and *Chamberlain* followed them in. They're the ones that sent you here—you and a few of the others they found. I got here as soon as I got the call from my MOD contacts in Ichigaya. They're going to have some questions for you later, but I'll be right there with you. I promise I'm not leaving here until I can take you home to Ishinomaki with me."

"Why do you put up with my shit, ma'am?" River chuckled sheepishly.

Her Wielder rolled her eyes. "Oh, hush. You put up with *my* shit."

River's memory was still a blur, but she tried to retrace her steps to reconstruct the last thing she could remember: The fireman's carry. The facility corridors. The gunfire.

"Wait. Zee! Where did it—oh, please, tell me it's—"

"It's safe! Don't worry; it's fine." Kasu gestured out the window and across the bay. "It's with Miyakozawa-*san* handling things up the road in Tokyo right now for that Agatsuma doll. Iwa, I think her name was. Zee itself got out of the whole thing without so much as a scratch. It's one tough doll. I still can't believe it was the bait."

"Bait?"

At that, Kasu paused, pursed her lips. To River, it looked like she was trying to figure out how to word something.

"Well, it started with . . . eh, no, not that. I . . ." Kasu shook her head. "I'll explain later—or Zee can tell you itself, I'm sure. It's a long story."

"I feel like I'm going to have plenty of time for long stories for the next little while." River sighed, rubbing clumsily at tired eyes. "But I'm glad it's all right. If it wasn't there to pull me out—oh, shit. Yui!"

The mortar fire. The incoming rounds. The Nogami dolls, stolen away from all walks of life, dying around her. Yui's expression, an image of abject horror.

"Hey—hey, River. Stay with me," Kasu instructed, taking River's hand in both of her own. "Yui-san wa mada igidennossha. Anzugodo negasu." ⟨*Yui-san's still alive. Ain't nothin' to worry about.*⟩

River frowned. She did not like the look in her Wielder's eyes.

"Define *alive*, ma'am," she said, trying and failing to sit up. "That doesn't . . . the . . . the way you said that doesn't instill me with the greatest confidence."

"She's stable, but it's going to be a little while until she's on her feet again. Her chassis is going to need replacement." Kasu sighed, her eyes distant. Then quieter, she added, "The Yakumaru people took a lot from her."

"Kasu-*sama*, please, we can't let her suffer any more, we really need to—"

"Make a new chassis happen." The Wielder nodded. "Yes, that's already happening, and I'm dealing with the paperwork so Tomoka-*san* doesn't have to. They're back in Sendai already. Yui's been transferred to Yōkendō University Hospital, so she's with some of the best specialists there are and only a ten-minute drive from home."

"We . . . we have to do what we can for her business. Hell, the others too! They had families, people—shit, she must've been gone—wait, shit, how long have *I* been gone?"

"It's late June, darling," Kasu replied gently.

Late June. It had been early May when they left Sendai on that trip-of-the-damned to Tokyo! Just shy of two months, but it felt like longer.

"Useless." River groaned. "For all I can supposedly do, I was just so fucking useless, wasn't I?"

"River, listen to me. You hung on long enough that you were able to come back. You didn't give up. That's not useless," Kasu insisted. "There's going to be a lot to do to make things right. Debriefing, testifying, listening, repairs and building, and a lot more beyond that. It's going to take a long time. You don't have to worry about it all, not right now. Let's focus on getting you better and doing what we can, as we can, when we can, as a team—just like always. *Isshin dōtai.*"

The battle-scarred doll's voice was small, as she repeated the words—a balm to her tired heart.

"Yes, ma'am. One heart together."

After a quiet that brought little comfort to Wielder and blade alike, River asked hesitantly, "How many of the Nogami dolls did we manage to save, ma'am? All told."

"Rescued alive? The landing parties brought back four hundred twelve Nogami-type dolls from the island, most of them in isolation pods in bays around the Yakumaru facility. Some are ambulatory; most are going to need a new chassis like Yui. They'd been getting slowly taken apart while plugged into the system. There may have been other places not on the island—we don't know yet, but the SDF and PSIA are looking for them. They're looking for Yakumaru-*san*'s spectator guests, too, though I'm not sure they'll find too many of them. What's the expression, 'low friends in high places'?"

"Something like that."

"Either way: Shura is done."

The words lingered in the air like incense smoke, a comfort to River's aching soul.

"Say it again, ma'am."

"Shura is done," the Wielder repeated. "And we're going to make damn sure it stays that way."

"Promise me, Kasu-*sama*," the doll demanded. "Promise me we're going to make this right, no matter how much it costs. Please."

"As right as we can for everyone we saved and the rest

of the Nogami-type population. I promise." Kasu squeezed River's fingers. "Like I said, we're going to have a lot to do. Miyakozawa-*san*'s people are already working with Aneha and the staff at Urato to set up for this. We handed off the Shirakami to the SDF while you were gone, so we've got even more room to spin up production for the Nogami population. And I intend to see this project through, one way or another. Because I made a promise and because it's the right thing to do."

River nodded slowly.

"I . . . I'm kinda scared to ask. How many did we lose, all told? Did anyone else from Yui's squad make it?"

Kojirō リ-217. Matsu ま-119. Aoi さ-217. Toki う-12. Shunsuke け-21. Yūichi さ-90. Nao せ-102. The names were still burned into her memory.

"I'm sorry, darling. Yui was the only one from her squad who survived long enough for the Coast Guard to rescue. The rest had been in the system too long. And between dolls of all types on the island, those who died when the artificial-reality system crashed and then in the uprising and the firefight that followed?" Kasu shook her head sadly. "I'll show you the numbers later, when we have final confirmation and when the military finishes its investigation on the island. But one way or the other? Too many."

Too many. Two words that carried all the death and suffering to which River had borne witness.

Yesterday, they stood at Osaka Barrier, a hundred thousand horsemen strong. Today, they cast off mooring lines in the western sea, barely seven thousand. The cloudy sea was silent. Even the clear sky was growing dark.

For all the pain, for all the waiting, for all who had fallen, for all the uncertainty and long, long odds—at long last, River wept.

Her own way home was clear, and there would be some justice done for those beside whom she had suffered, both the living and the dead. This much was welcome—this much, she knew, was a victory.

However, as war and its aftermath had taught her all too well—victory had once again come at a terrible price.

TWENTY-TWO

Path of the Straw Thief

Kinkasan Island
December 2022

The forest path descended ahead, down to the waters below—and in the predawn dark, the silence was comforting.

With the Wielder leading, River and Kasu walked at an unhurried but steady pace, a rhythm between their breaths as they cast subtle halos of fog in the still-chilly air. They had come the day before, stayed the night, and arisen ass-early to continue their pilgrimage around the island's little shrines on the cusp of dawn. First, they visited the shrine at the summit, and now, they made their way to the shore, trying to make their best time ahead of the sunrise. Through the tree line that had withstood tsunami and earthquake alike, the first glimmers of dawn grew in the east.

Sparrows and warblers chirped within the brush, greeting the coming dawn. Distantly, wheeling seabirds called, and as if in response, corvids cawed.

Kinkasan Island was not too far from home. Administratively, it was just another part of Ishinomaki City, but it was remote, up a back road and over a ferry ride. Even an heir of the august Isawa clan and her loyal blade doll had no choice but to tough out the trek if they wanted to be there. To the Wielder and her doll it was worth it, every time, to have that special kind of peace and quiet.

The surf was a steady undertone to the dirt-muffled crunch of the two sets of boot steps through the forested path. All of it, together, was part of the same all-encompassing tapestry.

Even on newly overhauled and upgraded joints, River found the hike to be a bit of a challenge. Recovery from her wounds had been a long process, slow and steady, but putting her joints to work was another part of honing herself, another part of tending to her sharpness. She had wanted to take the risk and come out for it: her body, the earth beneath her feet, the wind in her hair, the sound of waves, and her Wielder's outline silhouetted against the predawn light just ahead of her. After all, this, too, was service.

In the margins of her HUD, River noted the temperature: Warm for December, but still brisk, just shy of 13°C. Nice and cool, good to move in.

Then pain caught up with the unsuspecting doll.

"No, no, no . . ."

First one knee, then the other, then her feet. She halted, planted her feet firmly, and waited in vain for the HUD alert about chassis status.

"Shit!"

River did not notice Kasu double back, but then she saw her within arm's reach. The Wielder tugged down the shawl she had wrapped around herself for warmth, and the doll resolved the curve of her chin and the line of her lips.

"Omesan, dējōbu daiga?" *⟨Darlin', you all right?⟩*

River was tempted to feign everything being okay. All she wanted was peace and quiet with her Wielder—her bright light and guiding star—in the predawn shadows. But inasmuch as Kasu was her lover, she was also her Wielder. As her wife, her retainer, and her weapon all at once, the doll knew she owed the Wielder candor.

"The phantom pains are back," River reported, taking Kasu's proffered hand to steady herself. "My diagnostic tools aren't catching anything."

"Anzugodo dabe." *⟨Well now, that's worryin'.⟩*

"Konna itami wa mō nakunatta hazu nanoni—" *⟨I thought I was done with this kind of pain, but—⟩*

"Breathe," her Wielder gently instructed.

Kasu laid one hand on her doll's shoulder, the other gently alighting to cup River's cheek. The doll's breath hitched. She was in good hands. She was safe.

"Good. You're okay," the Wielder hummed and sent the doll's vision swimming. The pain was still there but distant now, washed out in the face of endorphins.

"O-oh . . ."

"There we go. Good. Now, can you breathe for me? Nice and easy?" She tilted River's chin up just enough to peer down at her, sending the doll's cheeks into an even-redder blush.

"Y-yes. Yes, ma'am." *Inhale, exhale. Inhale. Exhale.* Slow and steady. The doll registered her pounding heart and buzzing circuitry starting to settle. "Yes, ma'am."

"Good doll," Kasu murmured, hand still steady on River's cheek. "You're okay. You're fine. All right, now ping your internal diagnostic tool for me? Let's get a picture of what's going on in there."

River nodded. "Yes, ma'am."

The diagnostic subroutines booted up and began their sweep. As they progressed, the doll felt herself relax a bit more.

"Fuck." River sighed, eyelids fluttering. She tried to focus on their points of connection, her Wielder's gaze and hand on her cheek. "I . . . I'm sorry, ma'am. I thought we'd put these phantom pains to rest. I fucking hate this."

"You're more important than this hike," Kasu declared matter-of-factly. "Do we need to stop and double back, or do you feel up to keeping on with the hike?"

River thought it over. It would be nice to go back, to lie down again and just be held for a while. But that was too easy.

"I think I can keep going. Yeah, I think I'm good to keep going." She nodded, taking a deep, steadying breath. "So maybe let's go nice and easy, ma'am? At least until I get the diagnostic report?"

"Of course, darling." She nodded in return. "Hold my hand?"

River took Kasu's hand in hers.

"Always."

They walked on into the mist, the blade doll and her Wielder. In the shadow of the mighty cryptomerias, their breathing settled into a steady rhythm anew.

Six months. Six long months since she had come home, but it also felt to River like an eyeblink. Debriefs, testimonies to the Japanese government, cataloging and analysis of the Kikai site, River's own refits and partial reconstruction—as well as spinning up the Nogami Project to full capacity, under Santaku auspices—and its delivery to the Nogami population through collaboration with the Yōkendō University Hospital System.

There was so very much to do in the aftermath of her abduction and the uprising that had ended Shura and Yakumaru Sakae's control of the Nogami dolls. It was a victory, of course—but even victory came at a price, and success was not an overnight, one-and-done matter.

Justice was being done, little by little.

It would take awhile, River knew, to get through the immediate aftermath. It was all worth the effort, of course, because it was the right thing to do. But it took a toll all the same.

More than anything, these days, River felt tired, and strangely guilty that she was tired. Even if she knew that her exhaustion was nothing to be ashamed of, after all she had endured, she still felt guilty.

I should have done more, she kept thinking. *I should have saved more of them.*

"Ma'am?" she asked her Wielder.

"Nandabe, kokesu yo?" ‹*What is it, doll o' mine?*›

"Thank you for choosing me every damn day." River squeezed Kasu's hand. "Scars and all."

They descended the forest path, and the trees gave way to shrubbery and a constellation of rocks, big and small, worn smooth by wind and waves. From this point, the mark of the 2011 tsunami was clearly visible. The forest stopped higher than it once had, with only broken fossil stumps marking its onetime extent. Far below, the deep, wine-dark embrace of the Pacific washed against mighty boulders with their feet in the tide.

The Wielder and her doll were still hand in hand, and in the minimized projection of her HUD, River could still see the cycling through of her diagnostic tool. When she saw the rocks, the blade doll gave the Wielder's hand a squeeze. Taking the doll's meaning, Kasu paused.

Kasu peered down at her through the dim predawn light. "Najosuta, omesan?" *‹What's up, darlin'?›*

River could not help but gasp, gesturing with her free hand at the tide and the rocks as the wind whipped around loose wisps of her hair. She was breathless, awed at the sight of it.

"Wow . . . it's incredible, ma'am."

"I'd have to agree," said her Wielder. Only when the doll caught a glimpse in her peripheral vision did she realize her Wielder was not looking at the tide.

The doll blushed and bit her lip.

"Kasu-*sama* . . ."

Kasu chuckled, squeezing her doll's fingers. "How's that pain? Are you still up for the descent?"

River nodded. "Still got half the diagnostic cycle to complete, but I'm doing better. Pain's mostly gone."

Kasu gestured to where the path ended on the shore. "C'mon. Let's get a seat before the sun's up. You ready?"

River glanced at her HUD, reviewing the diagnostic cycle's progress and the projected elevation change ahead. "I think I can do it, ma'am." She nodded. "I got this."

From dirt to rocks to the beach's rocky, wet sand, they descended until they were nearly in the surf. The beach was called Senjōjiki; the boulders cast staggered ranks of dark, weathered silhouettes against the gradually brightening sky.

"You good to climb, River?"

"Yes, ma'am!" the doll replied. "But let me get a hand?"

With her Wielder offering a bracing hand, the blade doll managed to make the first long pounce up to the nearest handhold on their chosen boulder, pulling herself up before turning back to return the favor. Little by little, they worked their way up. At long last, they arrived at the boulder's apex and arranged themselves as comfortably as they could. It would not be long before sunrise.

For a long time, they sat in silence together, fingers intertwined, skin to synthskin. Above, the cry of seabirds. Below, the crash of the waves. There, atop the boulder, a doll and Wielder, being themselves in the here and now—all they needed to be.

The sun rose in triumph over the broad Pacific horizon.

"After all the darkness, all the pain, and everything, dawn still comes," River murmured. "Even now."

Over the interlink, River felt the familiar twinge of Kasu's anxiety.

"Are you sure you're all right, darlin'? We've still got to hike the whole way back uphill."

River squeezed at her Wielder's hand. "Yes, Kasu-*sama*." She nodded, "I think I'm okay. Not feeling any pain right now, and besides, I have the honor of the two finest views on the island. This is always worth it."

The Wielder blushed and gently shook her head.

"My, as charming as ever, sweet doll. But if you say you're all right, then that's a relief."

The blade doll smoothly unslung her bag, handing the Wielder a rubber-banded cedar bento box, and she set two cans of coffee between them.

"The *anpan* in there should still be a little warm from the toaster from before we left the guesthouse." River gestured. "A modest breakfast, I know, but I figure we can go have something a little more proper when we make it to the shops along the pier."

"Nanuka dattennoya, kokesu yo." Kasu shook her head with a smile. ⟨*Nonsense, doll o' mine.*⟩

Then in English, "I wouldn't have it any other way."

All was well.

That night, back home in Ōmori, River awoke with a start, yanking free of her diagnostic cable, stumbling out of bed and into the dim living room.

Six months since she had come home, the nightmares still plagued her, kept her waking up far too many nights. They were real, as the illusion had been, and if she were brutally honest, some days, they fooled her.

All was *not* well.

She hurried through the corridor and into the living room, as if on autopilot. The shadows were loud. The flooring was loud. Her footsteps were loud. Everything hurt.

One foot, then another, she staggered through the house, wobbling step after step until she reached the windows, where she could brace herself against the wall and pull the blind aside and try, somehow, to catch her breath.

The curve of the main hall's eaves was lit by the few nighttime lights that shone in the Santaku complex's court-yard. The arches of the greenhouses and bounding fence sat silhouetted against them.

Santaku Headquarters and Ōmori district were per-fectly still—but to River, that was no comfort.

Standing silent sentinel, outlined by the starry sky, she could just make out Mount Jōbon, the line of cypress and cryptomeria at the foot of the mountain that enfolded

Santaku Headquarters, and the Ōmori district—darker forms against a dark night.

River was there, and she was not there.

The smell of spent rounds. The jagged edges of shattered concrete and broken rebar. Humid, sweltering air. The way the wind would shift and carry the scent of gas and shit.

The faces of the Nogami and Agatsuma dolls she could not save, looking at her as if wanting to ask, *Why not us?*

Broken earth beneath broken tread. Boots pounding asphalt.

Distantly, a familiar voice. "Omesan, dējōbu daiga?" ⟨*Darlin', you all right?*⟩

The roar of tank engines coming to life. Aching fingers fumbling as they worked to switch mags.

Her Wielder was calling for her. "River! River, hey. Hey, hey, I'm here. Breathe. You're okay. You're okay."

Tumbling, tumbling, back down to earth, back down to the here and now. Back to Ishinomaki, to the night, to the stars outside the window. To the worry in Kasu's eyes. To the interlink's emotional undertow pulling her back to the here and the now.

To Kasu's hands, pulling her close. Arms enfolding.

Once a soldier. Now a blade doll. Broken and reforged, broken and reforged again.

Home now.

"I'm sorry. I'm sorry. I'm sorry. It hurts, it hurts."

Home now.

Doll now.

Safe now.

Safe.

Kasu's arms, holding her close, held her brokenness together—bringing her back across the years, across the miles.

Wielder and blade doll sat together in the dark.

Breath settling. Heart rate settling.

After an eternity, River felt herself exhale.

"I'm here," her Wielder replied, her embrace still steady. "I'm not going anywhere. It's all right, darling. It's going to be all right. I've got you."

"Why do you put up with my shit, ma'am?" the doll chuckled, voice still choked by her tears. "I'm not much use to anyone like this."

"Because I have always loved you, scars and all, as a human and as a doll." The Wielder petted at her doll's disheveled blue hair. "Because you don't have to be of use for me to love you. Because you put up with *my* shit for reasons that are sometimes beyond me. And because you are the blade and I am the Wielder, and I swore an oath to stand with you."

River exhaled and allowed herself a tired smile. It was going to be okay. "One heart together?"

Kasu nodded. "One heart together."

They lay together in silence, letting the current of their emotions settle to a gentle, warm tide. Eventually, River sat up, stretched, and did her best to drop the tension from her shoulders with slow, steady rolls as she arched her back.

"Well, now that I'm up, I could use an herbal tea, ma'am. How about you?"

"Mm, yes. That might be nice."

Kasu rose first and offered a hand for River to take. Her hand in her Wielder's own, the doll rolled to her feet. Echoes of the nightmare lingered in River's ears, but her fingers never once faltered in their grip around Kasu's hand.

River put the kettle on, gathered up mugs and tea bags, falling back into the familiar rhythms of the mundane.

They sat facing each other across the kitchen table,

holding hands as the tea steeped. River was grateful for the silence.

It was enough.

"It's silly, ma'am," River said quietly, "but I . . . I feel like I'm back to square one, that day on Mount Hiyori, wishing I could be whole again."

"Nonsense, River—"

"I know." The doll sighed, pinching the bridge of her nose and peering down into the rising steam from her tea mug. Her HUD, minimized for nighttime, marked the heat source. "At least intellectually, I get it. Deep down, it's . . . it's hard to internalize." She paused, squeezing her Wielder's fingers. "So, it's a good thing I've got someone to remind me how different things are now."

"For both of us," Kasu replied with a tired smile. "Neither of us is quite who we used to be, but I think that's a good thing, even if life has come at us fast sometimes. I'd like to think we've grown together. Unbroken the world just a little."

The aftermath of the Nogami crisis was ongoing, even six months later, but Santaku had taken the forefront in rising to the challenge, albeit years later than it should have, as Kasu was first to admit. Far too many dolls had suffered before this response began in earnest. However, already Santaku was now the industry leader in a government program offering any Nogami-type doll a new Santaku-made chassis, and it had dramatically improved the options for maintenance and adaptation.

It was imperfect. But it was a beginning.

"I wish I could've saved them all, ma'am—back on the island, I mean." River shook her head. "Too many of those Nogami and Agatsuma folks died that day."

"What is it that 065 always says?" her Wielder asked.

"'Remember that you can't save everyone,' is what it always says. And it's right, but I just wish that wasn't the case."

"Me too, love." Kasu sighed. "Me too."

The two of them sat in the late-night silence and finished their tea. The weight of the past six months seemed to linger in the air.

"Ma'am?" the doll asked, eyes averted, looking into the darkness at the bottom of her tea mug.

"Hm?"

River frowned. "How the hell am I going to be a mom at this rate? Like, whenever we manage to have things settle down enough to pull the trigger on IVF. I'm mostly intact in body, but inside, I dunno. How can I in good conscience think about being responsible for more than me and you?"

"Kanpeki na oya wa nen da, kokesu yo." Kasu shook her head. *⟨There ain't any such thing as a perfect parent, doll o' mine.⟩* In English, she added, "But you're working at putting yourself back together, just like I am, and I think that's the most important thing here. To put it all together into something new, and wear it, scars and all, as proudly as we can. The world is cold and hard as it is, and it tends to break humans and dolls alike, so what could be a better or more important example to a child than that?"

"I guess so. And I'll be with you every step of the way, love," River pledged. "Ever and always, even if I have to drag my broken, sorry ass the whole way."

"Ever and always." Kasu smiled, squeezing her loyal blade's fingertips. "One heart together."

There was much still to do, to set the world right, even after they had come through the immediate aftermath of the past year. Some things would linger for a long while yet. But River felt a stirring of new determination to keep going, to keep doing what needed to be done, in putting herself back together and helping everyone she could. She might not have been able to save everyone, but she could try her best to help herself, stay present beside her Wielder, and pray to be made equal to the challenges ahead.

That much was enough. That much, she knew, was a beginning.

And even if the view out the kitchen windows was to the south, River knew—high above and to the north, amid the course of the Straw Thief's Path that had guided her home—was Polaris, unbowed and free.

EPILOGUE

A River of Stars

Sendai, Miyagi Prefecture
December 2024

*C*old air. The lively hubbub of a festival crowd. Coffee from Green Leaf Café, in well-worn mugs. After the storm, after so many long, hard fights to claw forth a way, Kasu and River were on Jōzenji Avenue again, under zelkova trees strung with points of light, mingling with the festival crowd. For the moment, the storms and worries of life were at bay.

Against all odds, all was well.

The Starlight Festival was one of Sendai's year-end rituals, gathering locals under winter-bare zelkova trees brimming with light. Kōtōdai Park had concerts, and the art galleries in nearby Ichibanchō district boasted open houses. Even historic sites like Bansuisōdō, the house museum down on Bansui Avenue to which it had given its name, were decked out festively in lights ahead of the new year.

Center stage amid it all was that broad boulevard of zelkovas, swathed in light. The trees of Jōzenji Avenue were planted in the late 1940s as an act of faith by the city, after the Second World War reduced downtown Sendai to ash. In the nearly eight decades since, the trees had grown giant, spanning both directions of traffic in a verdant canopy in spring and summer, and they formed a mighty archway on which the festival's lights were strung each December.

The festival was a beautiful, defiant stand against the deepest, darkest, coldest nights of the year. It was a reminder that despite everything that the city and region might face, it could come back from the ashes. The light would return. That dawn would come.

Kasu took the fore as they ambled slowly under the warm glow. She had grown more protective since River had returned from captivity. Once, River might have felt uneasy about her Wielder taking the lead; it was her job to protect Kasu, especially now that she had gone from heading just Santaku Dynamics to also being assistant director of Santaku Group as a whole. Kasu had reminded River: whatever their working or personal titles, this was a two-way dynamic, and from the start, they had always been a team.

Besides, darling, she had added, *nobody can expect either of us to do everything and be everywhere all at once.*

In all honesty, River loved it when her Wielder would take the lead, walking just ahead and close enough so that her body language said: *This doll is mine. Make way for her.*

"Hamono-san! Kasu-san! Kocchi, kocchi!" ⟨*Miss Blade! Kasu-san! Here, over here!*⟩

River bounced excitedly and waved back. "Yui-san! Tomoka-san! Oban degansu!" ⟨*Yui! Tomoka! Good evenin'!*⟩

The two couples met there in the cold under the river of stars.

Over the past two years, with a lot of steady work, Yui had adapted well to her new Santaku-made chassis. She was still the same soft-spoken, lavender-haired giant of a bakery doll, even if the invisible scars lingered under the surface of a new, more reliably performing body. True to her word, even amid her own recovery, River made sure Yui had what she needed to acclimate and keep her business going.

The shared experience had brought them close.

They exchanged greetings. Then Yui turned to River. "Can I hug you?" she asked, as she always did.

River nodded. Yui hugged her tight, until the blade's feet left the ground.

River laughed as Yui released her. "Glad to see you doing so well! Junbi ii?" *‹You ready?›*

"Un!" *‹Yup!›*

Tomoka nodded. "Yes. Let's get going; don't want to be too late. You know how the subway at night."

Kasu rolled her eyes and laughed. Over the past two years, work had meant much more time on this side of the bay. "Oh, all too well."

From Aoba-dōri Ichibanchō Station, they took the subway west, over the Hirose River and out to Kawauchi Station. After a few minutes through dark residential streets, they passed through the parking lot and under the lower torii of River's home shrine. The weeping cherry's broad branches and scaffolding were bare from winter but likewise strung with lights. This was not as crowded as the shrine would be shortly for the New Year's holiday, but the grounds were modestly lively as the community gathered for its part of the Starlight Festival.

The two couples ascended the long stone steps, among the little stalls of *yakisoba* and *amazake*. *Gagaku* music played from the shrine's sanctum. They washed in the purification basin, and then in the shadow of the inner torii, they joined the line for the shrine's offertory.

"Rainen no Seieisai ni naru to kora to issho da ne," Yui remarked. *‹By next year's Starlight Festival, it'll be with our kids in tow.›*

It was not just recovery and physical therapy they had bonded over. More recently, both River and Yui had each finally succeeded in their second attempt and were at last in the early weeks of pregnancy. It would be awhile before either was ready for an announcement to the rest of the world. For now, both were grateful for the understanding that only someone with whom they had been to hell and back with could have.

"With any luck, yeah." River nodded with a smile. "Happy and healthy and all together, the six of us."

She hoped, with all she was, that it really would be a peaceful, healing year ahead. After everything, she appreciated the mundane, quiet days all the more.

They each made a generous offering of coin at the offertory, and then pulled sharply on the braided cords of the sacred bells. Beyond the offering box and the main hall's veranda the middle sanctum was brightly lit, with offerings of sake and food freshly laid out.

Great kami Hachiman, guardian of my heart and hearth, River silently prayed, *thank you for strengthening my hand and aim in my lady's service in this past year. Watch over my sorry ass in the year ahead and help me be a good mother when the time comes.*

Afterward, they chatted idly by the stands of votive plaques, watching the festival crowd pass by.

"De, Hamono-san," Yui said, "saikin mou hitotsu no ii shirase ga kitasō yo ne, tashika ni?" *‹Oh hey, Miss Blade, you said the other day, you got some more good news recently, didn't you?›*

"Ah, yeah, I did, yup." River nodded. "I got the acceptance letter last Friday! As of January 10, I'm going back to school at Yōkendō U as a remote-learning grad student in their Faculty of Letters. Just got word back from Terashima-*sensei*, and she's agreed to be my advisor, so I'm all officially official! Going to finish the doctorate in history I started while I was still in the army."

Yui beamed. "Congratulations!"

"Thanks. Maybe I'll audit some other courses in stuff that's idly got my interest too," River added. "We'll see. It's just that after everything I've been through, I figure grad school isn't as intimidating as it was the first time. And besides, if I'm looking at taking time off from ground-pounding and range maneuvers over the coming year as I get closer to my due date, I might as well make the most of it, set a good example for my kid, and see one more thing through."

Yui grinned. "Jaa, sore nara sugu uchi 'Hamono-hakase,' ka na?" *‹So it'll be 'Dr. Blade' soon, huh?›*

The blade blushed and shook her head with a laugh. "Maa, maa, ippozutsu susumimashou." *‹Now, now, let's take it one step at a time.›*

"I could do with some *amazake*," Tomoka remarked, turning to squint in the direction of the line for the stall. "That line, though . . . Yui-chan, daijōbu?" *‹Yui-chan, you gonna be all right?›*

"Hey, you two have a seat. We'll get some for you both. Muri shinakute ii." River gestured to the low wall under the tree line where others had already staked out perches. *‹No need to overdo it.›*

Wielder and blade wove their way into the crowd toward the line for the *amazake* stand. The hubbub, the music, the river of starlight: all was well.

Out of the corner of her eye, River caught sight of a familiar vulpine tail.

"Wait, isn't that . . . ?"

Across the shrine grounds, atop the stone steps and lingering in the shadow of the inner torii, Miyakozawa Akiko and her vulpine doll, Zee, met River's eyes. They were both in formal kimonos for the occasion, albeit a bit less dazzling than how they had first met the Wielder and blade doll. Since the events of two years earlier, they had become regular colleagues of Kasu and River in the long-term work for the Nogami-type population—although, that still did not stop them from having an eerie sense of timing.

They dipped their heads in greeting. Hand in hand, Kasu and River bowed back as one.

It was a little strange finding them there, once again, never too far away—but they were in the business of knowing things, after all. Ever since that day that Zee caught her as she fell ass-first out of Shura, River felt strangely comforted by its presence. It was good to have friends watching her back from half a step within the shadows.

With little more than a nod, Akiko disappeared into the festival crowd with Zee close beside her. River could swear she saw just a hint of a fang-baring smirk from both Witch and vulpine doll as they took their leave.

"Yabai hito da naa, Miyakozawa-san wa." The blade doll nodded in quiet admiration. "Demo mikata de nanka anshin da." *‹She's not to be underestimated, Miyakozawa-san is. But I'm glad she's an ally; somehow, it sets my heart at ease.›*

"That's true. And she expects a great deal from us both. So I guess we'd better keep getting our shit together." Kasu chuckled, shaking her head. "Sou denēnoga, kokesu yo?" *‹Ain't that right, doll o' mine?›*

"With you all the way, ma'am." River nodded, squeezing her Wielder's fingertips—a point of warmth, a guiding star in the dark. "One heart together."

HISTORICAL ESSAY

North Star Forever

Confluence is a cyberpunk story. Even so, the local history of the Tohoku region that underlies this story is real. It was a significant part of what I studied as a graduate student, and it continues to interest me as both a topic of historical research and as fodder for fiction. However, both the people of Tohoku themselves, as well as those like me who study that region, often come under fire for being parochial—in other words, for being unimportant.

That being the case, I'd like to say a few words here on the topic, in the interest of better rounding out your appreciation of these things. If I'm really lucky, and I hope I am, then you, the reader may choose to go and learn more on your own. So, let's talk about northern Honshu, its semiautonomy and history of technological innovation in the late Edo period, and those who laid claim to being its stewards.

Northern Honshu and Its Semiautonomy

Northern Honshu, today known as the Tohoku region, was not part of Japan from the start. The Yamato state, the political entity overseen by what today is the Japanese imperial family, was not able to exert any control over it in the seventh century. That state's northernmost frontier was Shirakawa Barrier, an outpost in the southern part of modern Fukushima Prefecture, which the state and the average Yamato courtier and subject alike considered a barrier between the civilized and uncivilized worlds. It was viewed as being so far from central Japan that the term *Shirakawa Barrier* endured throughout history, showing up in later poetry as a means of evoking physical or personal distance. Beyond the barrier lived the people that the Yamato state collectively called "Emishi," regardless of whether or not they were all one people. It is unclear as to what the people or peoples called themselves, at this time, but we can assume they did not call themselves "Emishi"; we might render the word into English as *barbarian*.

The Emishi people, north and east of Yamato control, stubbornly refused to submit to the Yamato aegis, no matter what the Yamato tried to do. There is some debate as to whether the Emishi had a state like the Yamato, but from Yamato's perspective, it was foreign land regardless. The state steadily expanded its regional control through force: armed colonization, combat, and a line of fortress settlements that over the years, pushed ever northward on the island's sides, bordered by the Pacific and the Sea of Japan. After the discovery of gold in the region, the pace of colonization picked up. By the late eighth century, the northern provinces were governed from Fort Taga (the modern city of Tagajō, Miyagi Prefecture), a government outpost and military installation just east of modern-day Sendai. Notably, the Emishi-led stubborn defense of local autonomy set a precedent that continues into the modern era.

As the Yamato government strengthened and solidified its control over the North, it divided the Emishi into two groups: *fushū* and *emishi*. The *fushū* were "surrendered barbarians" or "captives." They were Emishi who submitted to the court's authority and assimilated at least some of Yamato culture but did not necessarily submit altogether. It was from among the *fushū* that the Northern Fujiwara family emerged.

The Northern Fujiwara, who claimed both Japanese and *fushū* ancestry, ruled the Tohoku region as a semiautonomous kingdom. Their capital, Hiraizumi, was not only in the *fushū* heartland, but also astride the Interior Great Road, much of which later became the Ōshū Highway. By looking at the amount of material wealth available for the Northern Fujiwara's patronage of religion and the arts, one can also assume that the Northern Fujiwara, and not the Yamato state, were the North's principal revenue collector. Hiraizumi was also halfway between the North's two major geographic edges: Shirakawa Barrier to the south and Honshu at its northernmost tip. Thanks to its Emishi roots, the Northern Fujiwara family was able to maintain lines of communication along this route, and even had some measure of actual control much farther north than the Yamato state could manage. Thus, Hiraizumi's central location was one befitting of a capital that rivaled Kyoto in size and regional prominence. Clearly, the Emishi thread survived, albeit spun into new, part-Yamato cloth.

However, the Northern Fujiwara did not last. Several centuries later, it was the ruins of the Northern Fujiwara capital of which poet Matsuo Basho, pioneer of the modern haiku, said, "Summer grass/all that remains/of warriors' dreams." Minamoto no Yoritomo, who made himself the first shogun of the Kamakura military government in the late twelfth century, sent an expedition that subdued the

Northern Fujiwara and installed a Kamakura-backed steward to oversee the North on Yoritomo's behalf. This was the real Isawa Iekage, whose grave in Rifu, Miyagi Prefecture, was the setting for part of the eighth chapter of *Confluence*, "Steward of the North." Iekage was a trusted bureaucrat with an established reputation, whom Yoritomo posted to Tagajō, and to whom he granted the title of Steward of the North (*Ōshū Rusushoku*).

The office of steward was hereditary; the Isawa were ordered to thereafter oversee northeastern Japan on Kamakura's behalf. Despite the name, both this office and the concurrent office of Mutsu Chief Commissioner (*Mutsu Sōbugyō*) held authority also extending to neighboring Dewa, the other historic province that comprises what is now the Tohoku region. Although the Isawa family owed allegiance to Kamakura, it continued the tradition of semiautonomous northern governance in the wake of the Northern Fujiwara's destruction, as they still had charge of administration for a frontier province, despite any regular contact with Kamakura. The Isawa also openly claimed inheritance of the Northern Fujiwara mantle: what we might call "northern kingship." In time, the office of Steward of the North ceased to have any practical authority, but the office of steward—*Rusushoku*—became the source of the Isawa family's new name. Now called the Rusu, it was absorbed into the house of Date of Sendai by marriage, becoming the cadet branch that today is called the Date of Mizusawa, owing to its castle town of Mizusawa, which is now part of Ōshū, Iwate Prefecture.

House Date of Sendai Domain was not originally from the territory it would come to rule from 1600 to 1868. It originated in nearby Date County, from which it took its name and which is now part of Fukushima Prefecture. At

625,000 *koku* in agricultural production—using the system of rating a territory's agricultural production by bales of rice (which was how a feudal domain's size was measured)— Sendai Domain was one of Japan's largest domains during the Edo period. One *koku* was enough rice to feed an adult for a year. Sendai Domain was third in wealth after the Maeda clan's Kanazawa Domain bordering the Sea of Japan, and the Shimazu clan's Satsuma Domain in southern Kyushu. The real Kikai Island, setting of the story's latter half, used to be part of Satsuma Domain.

Like the Isawa, the Date family would in turn claim the mantle of northern kingship, ultimately becoming the region's center of gravity through the Boshin War of 1868. During the war, it rallied the Northern Alliance, the regional coalition that stood against the imperial army during the war's northern phase in the spring to early winter of 1868. Its battle flag, an interwoven five-pointed star representing the North Star and the five phases of traditional East Asian elements, inspired part of the Santaku Group crest in *Confluence,* which appears in the illustrations. It was also used as the symbol of the 1906 Kokeshi Uprising, from which River draws inspiration and renewed strength in making her stand against Yakumaru Sakae.

In rallying the alliance, House Date of Sendai laid claim to being the North's center of gravity and argued that because of where it was located—in the old Isawa and Northern Fujiwara heartland—it was the inheritor of those predecessors, and thus the entire North owed obedience to its command. This was not just something it claimed under duress, and it extended to more than abstract political claims. From the domain's beginnings, the Date clan also took great care to preserve the historic sites associated with the Northern Fujiwara and document their stories.

It is thanks to Date intervention that the Northern Fujiwara family temples of Chūson-ji and Mōtsū-ji survived the Edo period. Both temples, now in the town of Hiraizumi in southern Iwate Prefecture, have become UNESCO World Heritage Sites.

Education, Innovation, and Shipbuilding

A domain school (*hankō* in Japanese) is the institution that trained a feudal domain's vassals in scholarly, military, and sometimes practical arts. This was where a domain would train up its next generations—not only scholars, but also administrators, and in the late Edo period, its military leaders. Some domains would send these schools' exceptional graduates to pursue further postgraduate work at the Shoheizaka Academy, the Shogunate's preeminent educational institution.

As we learn in *Confluence*, Santaku Group was founded in the wake of the Boshin War by Kasu's ancestor, a Date retainer and engineer named Isawa Jinsai. Jinsai was inspired by real Sendai retainers, many of them alumni of Yōkendō, the Sendai Domain's school for the Date clan's retainers. While many of the real Date retainers who worked on such projects were unable to do so following the Boshin War, Jinsai continued his prewar research as a private business, and he turned his old country estate into the headquarters of what became Santaku. He also turned the old Date clan naval station and shipyard at Sabusawa Island into a test facility. This facility is what we see in *Confluence* as the Urato Research Center in chapter four, "Mist on the Bay."

Established in 1736 as the Gakumonjo, Yōkendō moved to what is now Kōtōdai Park, the site of both the Miyagi Prefectural Assembly and Sendai City Hall, in 1761. It received its best-known name, Meirin Yōkendō, or

Yōkendō for short, in 1772. Yōkendō was one of the major domain schools in Edo-period Japan, albeit not as famous as places like Mito Domain's Kōdōkan Academy, Sakura Domain's Juntendō Academy, or Aizu Domain's Nisshin-kan Academy. Yōkendō alumni drove Sendai Domain's involvement in a wide range of research in the closing decades of the Edo period. The people of the Ōtsuki family, a long line of distinguished linguists, physicians, and scholars, are perhaps the most famous to the scholars of nineteenth-century Japan. Yōkendō was overseen by members of the scholarly Ōtsuki family for fifty-six years and three successive holders of the office of rector, including Ōtsuki Heisen, Ōtsuki Jukusai, and Ōtsuki Bankei.

These three generations of rectors shaped the school's priorities and curriculum with an eye toward improving the domain's ability to contribute to Japan's collective defense. Their tenure saw the first institution of Russian studies in Japan in light of Date forces' frequent encounters with Imperial Russian expeditions during coast guard duty in Ezochi (now Hokkaido, the Kuriles, and southern Sakhalin). Just prior to the Boshin War, Yōkendō also offered English-language classes. Yōkendō leadership, and Sendai Domain in general, understood the importance of at least understanding a potential adversary rather than simply and categorically keeping the outside world at arm's length.

In modern Japan, possibly the single most famous Yōkendō alumnus was Ōtsuki Fumihiko (1847–1928), son of one of the school's rectors. After a course of study at Yōkendō, which included English-language study, he saw service as a staff officer during the Boshin War. Later, he went on to earn a PhD, becoming one of the first Japanese people to earn a Western-style doctorate. In an act that helped revolutionize the development of modern Japanese,

Ōtsuki Fumihiko compiled one of the first modern-Japanese dictionaries—*Genkai* 言海, or *Sea of Words*—in 1891. He followed this up with *Daigenkai*, or *Great Sea of Words*, which was published posthumously in multiple volumes from 1932 to 1937. He was also involved in the editing of *Sendai Sōsho*, a multivolume compendium of major primary source material, legal records, and genealogical information pertaining to the old Sendai Domain. The sources in *Sendai Sōsho* made my doctoral dissertation possible, and they served as the source of much of the real-world history that went into the backdrop of *Confluence.*

Among Yōkendō's alumni was also Takano Chōei (1804–1850). He was a physician and scholar of Dutch studies in the early to mid-nineteenth century. He was born into a family serving one of the Date daimyo's senior vassals, the Date family of Mizusawa—as noted earlier, the descendants of the real Isawa family. After getting his start at Yōkendō, Chōei went on to study in Nagasaki under the Prussian doctor Philipp Franz von Siebold, where among his classmates was scholar and painter Watanabe Kazan (1793–1841).

The research these people and others like them undertook sought to harmonize Japanese and Western techniques in everything. They and their scholarly connections were responsible for driving some of Yōkendō's particularly pioneering work in engineering, cannon casting, medicine, foreign studies, and shipbuilding.

These efforts culminated in Sendai Domain's building of a hybrid Japanese-Western schooner, the six-gun sail warship *Kaiseimaru*, at the Yamazaki shipyard on Sabusawa Island. *Kaiseimaru*'s construction was a joint project involving Sendai Domain retainers led by Confucian scholar Onodera Hōkoku; Yōkendō rector Ōtsuki Jukusai; local labor; and Shogunate-affiliated naval engineers summoned from Edo, led by Miura Kenya. In *Confluence*, this shipyard becomes the Santaku Dynamics Urato Research Center.

Kaiseimaru was launched in 1857, tested at short distances in Sendai Bay, and had one long-range cruise delivering rice to Shogunate officials in Edo. It was meant as what we might today call a proof of concept. It was meant to test out new shipbuilding techniques, train a new wave of sailors, and prepare the way for future larger, heavily armed, steam-powered vessels. Sabusawa Island had long been a transshipment point and was conveniently placed for coast defense as well as for mercantile purposes. However, forces beyond even the best of the Date retainers' best intentions prevented those efforts from coming to fruition.

Boshin War

Despite this curiosity and interest in hybridization, experimentation, and innovation, Sendai Domain could not escape the impact of economic forces. Northern Japan, especially Sendai Domain's territory, was hammered by decades of natural disaster and crop failure, which in turn impacted its population and tax base. The famine was so terrible that in one part of the Tohoku region—Morioka Domain, now central and northern Iwate Prefecture—a contemporary observer reported that even music stopped. This meant that even under the best of circumstances otherwise, Sendai Domain started the Boshin War of 1868–69 at a disadvantage. Armies need people to staff them and money to be fielded, after all. All its best intentions could not save Sendai Domain, given this starting point. In the 1860s, in an effort to rebuild its broken finances, the domain leadership slashed its budget to one-sixth of usual amount.

Regardless, as noted above, Sendai Domain, together with its near-peer neighbor Yonezawa Domain, rallied the Northern Alliance to arms during the Boshin War. This was a regional coalition of thirty-one domains that pulled together the Tohoku region's fiefdoms with an eye toward common defense against aggression by the nascent imperial government, which threatened longstanding regional semi-autonomy. Sendai Domain was the alliance's lynchpin, and the Date clan argued for its primacy in leading this alliance. It did this by positioning itself as heir to the mantle of leadership over the North, which began with the Emishi and continued through with the Northern Fujiwara and the Isawa family. However, starting the war with the financial difficulties and lack of personnel, along with a command structure that was decentralized rather than unified, all the while plagued with lines of competing feudal sub-loyalties, doomed the alliance's efforts, practically from the start. By contrast, the southwestern coalition, which formed the victorious army, benefited from a unity of command and purpose, and the unbeatable source of clout that was imperial sanction. This was the origin of the modern Japanese Empire and its military. With its surrender to the imperial troops in the late autumn, the alliance ceased to exist.

Miyagi, Its Dialect, and Its Dolls

After the alliance's defeat in the Boshin War, the victors—who built modern, imperial Japan—cast Tohoku locals as backward, traitorous barbarians. The North's material wealth and people were both co-opted by the empire during its expansion in the late nineteenth century, especially its colonization northward into the lands of the Ainu people. Having lost everything in the Boshin War, many northern samurai were grateful for the chance to go to what is now

Hokkaido—to them, it was the closest thing to a chance at redemption and survival. The cities of Sapporo and Date were two Hokkaido cities founded by those exiled Date samurai.

To this day, a common use of any of the northern dialects in popular media is shorthand for "idiot hick." While this has, in past decades, been cause for some Tohoku locals to feel embarrassed and depressed in other parts of Japan, it has also been an impetus for stubborn pride in the face of discrimination, in others. This is why, in *Confluence*, despite Kasu being a cosmopolitan person who speaks standard Japanese and English just fine, and having pursued higher education in Tokyo and Nagoya, she chooses to speak in Sendai dialect, especially with River.

Thankfully, the negative portrayal of northern Japan as a backwater and home of uncultured idiots has begun to change in recent decades. Even your humble author has benefited from glossaries and social media accounts which focus on revitalizing Northern dialects and preserving local stories. Those histories in danger of vanishing entirely have been preserved, thanks in no small part to determined local folklorists like Mihara Ryōkichi, to whom this book is dedicated. He was the inspiration for the Mihara-*sensei* in *Confluence*—Kasu's tutor—who always exhorted her to be humble despite her power and family wealth, reminding her that "the rice stalk that bears the most, bows the lowest."

Confluence posits a broader use for the term *kokeshi* than in real life; it is applied to all cybernetic beings, be they all-artificial or transhuman, who are referred to as "dolls" in English. The real *kokeshi* is a type of traditional handcraft, a cylindrical wooden doll often painted with floral patterns and a reassuring smile. Mihara Ryōkichi; woodblock artist Kumagami Kōnen; sake vendor and entrepreneur Amae

Tomiya; and other local Miyagi colleagues in the early twentieth century were responsible for preserving and popularizing the real *kokeshi,* the style of wooden dolls that originate in the prefecture. Because Santaku originated in Miyagi, it seemed logical that a Miyagi doll term would become broadly popularized in the world of *Confluence,* given Santaku's influence and reach in the development of artificial intelligence and humans' cyberization. Although artisans in neighboring prefectures in the real Tohoku region have developed other variant styles of this dollmaking tradition, *kokeshi* remain one of Miyagi Prefecture's most recognizable symbols to this day.

Although the real-world *kokeshi* are stationary, other historic dolls moved. *Karakuri ningyo,* a kind of clockwork automata, had their heyday in the late Edo period. They could carry tea, write calligraphy, dance, even shoot arrows, via programming that was handled through clockwork gears. While readers might not have seen a *karakuri ningyo* specifically, they probably have heard of the company whose earlier form was founded by Tanaka Hisashige, the preeminent builder of *karakuri ningyo.* Founded in Tokyo's Shibaura area, it later merged with Tokyo Electric. With the "To" from Tokyo Electric and the "Shiba" from Shibaura, it became what is known today as Toshiba.

Conclusion

As you, the reader, can see, the Tohoku region's past is multifaceted and complex, and it has always been a diverse place with a rich history and culture. Yet, it is also all too often misunderstood and even belittled as unimportant by dint of being off the beaten path of Japan's better-known metropolises. Rather than try to paper over the Tohoku region's complexity, I believe we should embrace it, explore it, and try our best to understand it.

If there is one thing I would have you take away from all this, it is that this region is worthy of our attention, our appreciation, and our respect. You do not have to have a doctorate in history; look around on the Internet or in your local library and see what you can find! Do not let the Boshin War's victors dictate what you value. Do not keep your perspective in Kyoto or in Tokyo and let the Shirakawa Barrier be the limit of your world. Ask yourself too: What are the stories closer to home that are likewise complex but worth trying to understand?

The answer might surprise you.

North Star Forever.

—NAB
11 October 2022

Illustrations

Long before I wrote any of the story, River and Kasu were characters I drew, starting in the autumn of 2020. They've come a long way since then, and I'm glad there's finally a story to go with the pictures.

The following pieces are just a small fraction of the art and bonus content I've created, thanks to the support of my patrons on Patreon. If you've enjoyed this work, consider joining them at patreon.com/riversidewings.

sidearm
key
phone
Shiogama Shrine omamori
lapel button
mace can
hand cramp, bagged
money clip knife, 1000 yen notes

Isawa Kasu, Ph.D. | 伊沢滓
b. 30 July 1974 | Ishinomaki, Miyagi Pref. | blood type B Pos.

Former heir apparent to house Isawa of
Ishinomaki, which owns Santaku Group.
CEO of combat doll-focused subsidiary, Santaku Dynamics.
Driven, capable, hands-on leader hiding a current of anxiety
under practiced poise. Bad at delegating.

Wife and Wielder to River.

BS in cybernetic engineering from Shoheizaka U. (Tokyo)
M.S., Ph.D. in cybernetic engineering from Atsuta U. (Nagoya)

"The rice stalk that bears the most,
bows the lowest."

pistol
brush pen, ballpoint
stylus
phone
safe childbirth amulet
tablet
hand stamp, bagged
River Victoria M59A1
b. 11 July 1982 | Philadelphia, Pennsylvania | blood type O neg
born to Armenian diasporan parents in the US,
raised in Beirut, had an ill-fated career as a US Army officer.
Became a combat doll out of a desire
for new wholeness and service to her wife and community.
Now works for Santaku Dynamics.
Wife and blade to Kazu.
BA in Japanese literature, Callowhill College (Philadelphia)
MA in history, Moyamensing University (Philadelphia)
"Here and now, before you and my gods,
I swear service..."

The Santaku Group monogram depicts the five-pointed Seimei bellflower—a representation of the North Star—containing the kanji for the *sawa* of *Isawa*. It sits beneath a mountain (*san*). This is an example of a Japanese rebus monogram, a long-established style of business logo dating back to the Edo period (1600–1868).

The Isawa crest depicts three straight blades (*tsurugi*) radiating from the center of a doubled cherry blossom (*yaezakura*). The doubled blossom is associated with the city of Shiogama; when they were Stewards of the North, Kasu's ancestors cared for Shiogama Shrine.

The Urato facility's crest depicts a *tsurugi* superimposed over the outline of Sabusawa Island in gold, which makes the *tsurugi* look aflame. The characters flanking it in seal script read *kaibutsu seimu*: "Advancing Knowledge, Seeing Things Through."

This is Kasu's very first design from the autumn of 2020. Back then, she didn't have a name yet, so I called her The Engineer. The freckle-like dots are what became the four birthmark-like sensor nodes on her face in her current design.

It's hard to believe it all started with this sketch of River back in the autumn of 2020. Soft and pretty in her kimono and *hakama*, she's probably dressed for a fancy occasion. She's carrying a folded-up utility knife. I'm kind of amazed just how much of her design survived unaltered.

Kasu and River dressed for work on Sabusawa Island, posing together.

One of the running jokes in the Empty Spaces scene where *Confluence* originated was dolls' wonder at partners who wear The Big Hat. Kasu has a few Big Hats, one of them being a sun hat she wears on more relaxed outings with her wife.

A pencil sketch of River in a leather jacket. Still a little intense.

The moment after River and Kasu swore their oaths to each other at Kamiwarisaki.

Glossary

ARSR: Air Route Surveillance Radar. A military radar system set up to monitor and control airspace, especially within and around national borders.

Corpsman: A navy medic.

HUD: Heads-up display.

IVF: In-vitro fertilization.

JASDF: Japan Air Self-Defense Force. Japanese air force.

JCG: Japan Coast Guard.

JGSDF: Japan Ground Self-Defense Force. Japanese army.

JMSDF: Japan Maritime Self-Defense Force. Japanese navy.

Katsu: A shout in Japanese Buddhist practice meant to induce initial enlightenment.

Kokeshi: The local Tohoku term for both transhuman and all-synthetic dolls in the world of *Confluence*. In the real world, *kokeshi* are historic wooden dolls first made in Miyagi Prefecture.

Kokesu: *Kokeshi* in Sendai dialect.

MDC: Machias Droneworks Corporation. An American combat-doll maker.

MFA: Ministry of Foreign Affairs.

MOD: Japanese Ministry of Defense. Headquartered in Ichigaya, a neighborhood of Shibuya City, Tokyo Metropolis.

MPD: Short for Metropolitan Police Department. The police of Tokyo Metropolis.

Nue: A creature from Japanese folklore, reminiscent of a chimera.

PSIA: Public Service Intelligence Agency. Japan's domestic intelligence agency, comparable to the FBI.

RHIB: Rigid-Hull Inflatable Boat. A small inflatable boat used for boarding parties by the American and Japanese navies.

-*sama*: Honorific suffix after a person's name.

SBR: Short-barreled rifle.

SBU: Special Boarding Unit. JMSDF unit trained to board ships and counter smuggling and terrorism. The Japanese version of a VBSS team.

SDF: Self-Defense Forces. Japan's military, comprising the Air, Ground, and Maritime SDF.

"Seigaiha": "Blue Ocean Waves." A song in the *gagaku* repertoire of Shinto ritual music.

Six Roads: In Japanese Buddhism, the six realms into which beings are reincarnated. One of them is Ashura, also known in Japanese as Shura, the "hell" of battle.

VA: The US government's Department of Veterans Affairs.

VBSS: Visit, Board, Search, and Seize. US Navy teams trained to board ships and counter smuggling and terrorism. The American version of the SBU.

References

Bakkalian, Nyri A. "The Sparrow's Dream: The Meiji Revolution and Local Self-Assertion in Northern Japan." PhD diss., University of Pittsburgh, 2017.

Batten, Bruce L. *To the Ends of Japan.* Honolulu: University of Hawai'i Press, 2003. 84.

Bird, Winnifred. *Eating Wild Japan.* Berkeley: Stone Bridge Press, 2021. 85–88.

Farris, William Wayne. *Population, Disease, and Land in Early Japan, 645–900.* Cambridge: Harvard University Press, 1985. 78–79.

Hoshi Ryōichi. *Ōuetsu Reppandōmei: Higashinihon Seifu Juritsu no Yume.* Tokyo: Chūōkōron, 1995. 34.

Hosoi Kazuyu. *Nanbu to Ōshū Dōchū.* Tokyo: Yoshikawa Kōbunkan, 2002. 150.

Hudson, Mark J. "Ainu Ethnogenesis and the Northern Fujiwara." *Arctic Anthropology* 36, no. 1/2 (1999): 73–83. 76–78.

Ishii Takashi. *Ishin no Nairan.* Tokyo: Shiseidō, 1977. 282.

"Japan–US Security Treaty." Japan Ministry of Defense. Accessed September 30, 2022. https://www.mod.go.jp/en/j-us-alliance/joint-declaration/treaty/index.html.

Kaufman, Laura S. "Nature, Courtly Imagery, and Sacred Meaning in the Ippen Hijiri-e." In *Flowing Traces: Buddhism in the Literary and Visual Arts of Japan,* edited by James H. Sanford et al., 47–75. Princeton: Princeton University Press, 2014. 57.

Keene, Donald. *Frog in the Well*. New York: Columbia University Press, 2006. 90–91.

Kikuta Sadasato. *Sendai Jinmei Daijisho*. Sendai: Sendai Jinmei Daijisho Kankōkai, 1933. 1120.

Kobayashi Seiji. *Date Masamune*. Tokyo: Yoshikawa Kōbunkan, 1966. 164–6.

————. *Sengoku Daimyō Date-shi no Kenkyū*. Tokyo: Koshi Shoin, 2008. 3–65.

Kokeshi Wiki. "Mihara Ryōkichi." Kokeshi Wiki: Gendai ni Ikiru 'Kokeshi Jiten' e no Chōsen. Updated August 15, 2020. https://kokeshiwiki.com/?p=23911.

"Kufu shi tsuzuketa 'Toyo no Hatsumeio' Karakuri Giemon." Accessed October 6, 2022. https://web.archive .org/web/20140517152719/http://www.chiiki-duku ri-hyakka.or.jp/1_all/jirei/100furusato/html/furusato 085.htm.

Kurihara Shin'ichirō. "Ōuetsu' Reppandōmei no Keisei Katei ni kansuru Kenkyū." PhD diss., Tohoku University, 2007. 71.

Mihara Ryōkichi. *Kyōdoshi Sendai Mimibukuro*. Sendai: Hōbundō, 1983.

"Miyagi-ken Chosha no Oitachi." Accessed September 14, 2022. https://www.pref.miyagi.jp/site/profile/oitati .html.

Miyagi-ken shi vol. 2. Sendai: Miyagi Kenshi Kankōkai, 1987. 674, 690.

Mizusawa-shi shi vol. 3. Mizusawa: Mizusawa Shi-shi Kankōkai, 1976. 407–83.

Nihonshi B Yōgoshū. Tokyo: Yamakawa Shuppansha, 2000. 92.

Ogawa Kyōichi, ed. *Edo Bakuhan Daimyōke Jiten*. Tokyo: Hara Shobō, 1992. 395, 804.

Ōishi Naomasa, and Nanba Nobuo. *Hiraizumi to Ōshū Dōchū*. Tokyo: Yoshikawa Kōbunkan, 2003. 62–63.

"Ōshū Amarume-kiroku." *Sendai Sōsho* vol. 8: 17–40. Sendai: Hōbundō, 1972. 19–20.

Oskow, Noah. "Yabai! The Most Versatile Word in the Japanese Language?" *Unseen Japan* (14 May 2022). https://unseenjapan.com/yabai-the-most-versatile-word-in-the-japanese-language.

———. "Zuzu-ben: How Japan's Northern Dialects Became Shorthand for 'Hick.'" *Unseen Japan* (June 10, 2021). https://unseenjapan.com/zuzu-ben-japan-northern-dialects.

Otokozawa Chisato, Itō Sukemasa, Yano Michisato, and Imamura Moriyuki. "Boshin Shimatsu." *Sendai Sōsho* 12: 41–325. Sendai: Hōbundō, 1974. 161–2.

Ōtsuki Gentaku. "Ōtsukike Kyūzō Ōbun Reiyōshu." *Kotenseki Sōgō Deetabeesu*, early 19th cent. http://www.wul.waseda.ac.jp/kotenseki/html/bunko08/bunko08_a0262/index.html.

Rakuzan-kō Ryakureki. *Sendai Sōsho* 12: 1–40. Sendai: Hōbundō, 1974. 28, 30, 31.

Sappinai Yoshinori. "Mizusawa-yōgai." *Sendaijō to Sendairyō no Shiro, Yōgai*, edited by Kobayashi Seiji, 341–53. Tokyo: Meichō Shuppan, 1982.

Satō Nobuaki. *Hōnai Meiseki-shi. Sendai Sōsho* 8, 189–379. Sendai: Hōbundō, 1972. 360–2.

"Sendai Fugaku Yōkendō." Accessed September 14, 2022. https://www.library.pref.miyagi.jp/about/publication/kotobanoumi/kotoba-7/kotoba-7.html.

Suzuki Takuya. *Emishi to Tōhoku Sensō*. Tokyo: Yoshikawa Kōbunkan, 2008. 113.

References

Takahashi Tomio. *Hiraizumi: Ōshū Fujiwara-shi Yondai.* Tokyo: Kyōi-kusha, 1978. 268.

———. *Miyagi-ken no Rekishi.* Tokyo: Kyōikusha, 1978. 92, 93.

———. "The Classical Polity and Its Frontier." Introduced and translated by Karl Friday. *Capital and Countryside in Japan, 300–1180*, edited by Joan Piggott, 128–45. Cornell: Cornell University Press, 2006.

Takegahara Kosuke. "Genji gannen ni okeru Sendaihan no dōkō: Hanshu Date Yoshikuni to Ichimon Date Rokurō wo chūshin ni." *Yonezawa Shigaku* (October 2014): 27–40.

"Tanaka Hisashige monogatari." Archived at Toshiba Science Museum. Accessed October 6, 2022. https:// toshiba-mirai-kagakukan.jp/learn/history/toshiba_history/roots/hisashige/index_j.htm.

Tanaka Kitami. "Morioka-han," 173-212 of *Shinpen Monogatari Hanshi* Vol. 1 (Tokyo: Shin Jinbutsu Ōraisha, 1975), 201.

Totman, Conrad. *Early Modern Japan.* Berkeley: University of California Press, 1993. 240–2.

Tsukahira, Toshio G. *Feudal Control in Tokugawa Japan.* Cambridge: Harvard East Asian Monographs, 1966. 25, 39.

Yamakawa Kikue. *Women of the Mito Domain.* Translated by Kate Wildman Nakai. Stanford: Stanford University Press, 2001. 44.

Yamashita Fumio. *Shōwa Tōhoku Daikyōsaku.* Akita: Mumyōsha Shuppan, 2001. 28.

Yiengpruksawan, Mimi Hall. "Hakusan at Hiraizumi." *Japanese Journal of Religious Studies* (1998): 25 3/4, 261ff.

"Yōkendō no Zōsho to Shuppan." Accessed May 7, 2021. https://www.library.pref.miyagi.jp/about/publication/kotobanoumi/kotoba-22/kotoba-22.html.

"Yōkendō to sono Zōsho," pt. 1 A, B. Accessed May 7, 2021. https://www.library.pref.miyagi.jp/about/publication/kotobanoumi/kotoba-22/kotoba-22.html.

Zielonka, Ryan, Daniel Taninecz Miller, and Jonathan Walton. "Timeline of Operation Tomodachi." The National Bureau of Asian Research. Accessed September 24, 2022. https://www.nbr.org/publication/timeline-of-operation-tomodachi.

Works Cited

Elishe the Chronicler. *Srpo Hor'n Mero Yeghisheyi Vartabedi.* Venice: San-Lazarro Monastery, 1838. 12.

"Masamune-kyō Shikashū." *Sendai Sōsho* 1, 47–86. Sendai: Sendai Sōsho Kankōkai, 1922. 84.

Heike Monogatari: Nagatobon. Tokyo: Kokusho Kankōkai, 1906. 1, 501.

Movses Khorenatsi. *Movsisi Khorenatsvo Badmutiun Hayots.* Tbilisi: Arakadib Mnatsagan Mardirosian, 1913. 85–86.

Adom Yarjanian. *Siamanto: Complete poems, Volume 1.* Boston: Hairenik Press, 1910. 85.

About the Author

Dr. Nyri A. Bakkalian is an author, journalist, historian, and accomplished raconteur. She is a staff writer for *Unseen Japan* and the author of *Grey Dawn: A Tale of Abolition and Union* (Balance of Seven, 2020). She hosts the podcast *Friday Night History* and cohosts the podcast *Cleyera: Conversations on Shinto*. The secret to her success is Arabic coffee. She misses Sendai daily. You can support her work by subscribing at patreon.com/riversidewings.